CONRAD SULZER REGIONAL LIBRARY
4455 N. LINCOLN AVE.
CHICAGO, ILLINOIS 60625

JUV/
FIC
SHEARER

SULZER

Chicago Public Library

W9-BKU-128

regs

THE CHICAGO PUBLIC LIBRARY

CON DISCARD

CHICAGO, ILLINOIS 60625

sea Legs

sea legs

Alex Shearer

SIMON & SCHUSTER BOOKS FOR YOUNG READERS
new york   london   toronto   sydney

SIMON & SCHUSTER BOOKS FOR YOUNG READERS
An imprint of Simon & Schuster Children's Publishing Division
1230 Avenue of the Americas, New York, New York 10020

This book is a work of fiction. Any references to historical events, real people, or real locales are used fictitiously. Other names, characters, places, and incidents are products of the author's imagination, and any resemblance to actual events or locales or persons, living or dead, is entirely coincidental.
Copyright © 2003 by Alex Shearer

First published in Great Britain in 2003 by Hodder Children's Books,
a division of Hodder Headline Limited
First U.S. edition 2005

All rights reserved, including the right of reproduction in whole or in part in any form.
SIMON & SCHUSTER BOOKS FOR YOUNG READERS is a trademark of Simon & Schuster, Inc.

Book design by Mark Siegel
The text for this book is set in Garamond.
Manufactured in the United States of America
10 9 8 7 6 5 4 3 2 1
Library of Congress Cataloging-in-Publication Data
Shearer, Alex.
Sea legs / Alex Shearer.— 1st ed.
p. cm.
Summary: Twin brothers Eric and Clive are ready for adventure on the high seas, so instead of staying with their grandparents yet again, they stow away on the cruise ship on which their father serves as Senior Steward.
ISBN 0-689-87143-0 (hardcover)
[1. Stowaways—Fiction. 2. Cruise ships—Fiction. 3. Twins—Fiction. 4. Brothers—Fiction. 5. Single-parent families—Fiction. 6. Adventure and adventurers—Fiction.]
I. Title.
PZ7.S5377Se 2005
[Fic]—dc22   2003026522

CONRAD SULZER REGIONAL LIBRARY
4455 N. LINCOLN AVE.
CHICAGO, ILLINOIS 60625

R0404229993

sea Legs

one

Five Minutes

THE FIRST THING you need to know is that my brother Clive is a nutcase and the second thing you need to know is that I sometimes help him out when he's busy and when he can't manage all the nutcasing on his own, which isn't often.

I'm the oldest, but only by five minutes. Clive has always said that he wanted to be born first but I wouldn't let him and I got him with my elbow and pushed him out of the way.

I don't see how he can know that. I don't see how he can remember that far back. I can't. I don't know anyone who remembers about being born, but Clive says I pushed in. He says he should have been first and he was standing there waiting to leave when I came up behind him and elbowed him out the way. But I don't think that's true, and even if it is, there weren't any witnesses and it wouldn't stand up in court.

Clive says he's going to take me to court one day and sue me for being the eldest. But I don't see how he can, and anyway, I told him that if he took me to court for being the eldest, I'd take him to court for being the youngest. And if that didn't work, I'd punch him.

It works both ways as far as I can see, and maybe I would rather have been the youngest and then I could have done all the mucking about and he would have to be the one who always takes the blame.

Although Clive and me are twins, we aren't identical, I'm glad to say. I'm what you might describe as the good-looking one in the family while Clive has a face like a cowpat. When I say he has a face like a cowpat, what I really mean is that he has a face like a cowpat that a pig has just sat on. So he's really the ugly one, but I don't suppose he can help it unless he buys a bag.

Clive has got big ears too, and when it's windy, we have to lock him up and not let him out in case he blows away. In fact, if you tied a long string around him he would make a pretty good kite, even if something of a fat one. He also has a big nose which I think is due to the fact that he is always sticking his finger up it, and if he hadn't done so much of that it might be a great deal smaller.

Clive has also got flat feet. I told him it was because he'd spent too much time standing on

ALEX SHEARER

them. He said what else would he stand on, but I thought that was just a stupid attitude. So he said, what was he *supposed* to do, stand on somebody else's feet? So I showed him my feet, which are pretty good feet and not flat at all. And I said, "See Clive, that's the difference between you and me, I've looked after my feet and you haven't."

"Why should I look after your feet when I've got my own to look after?" he said.

"But that's just it. You haven't looked after them, have you?" I pointed out. "You've neglected your feet and let them go to seed."

Anyway, shortly after that Clive started to put sausages in his shoes and when Dad noticed the smell and all the bits of meat in his socks he asked him why he was doing it and Clive said it was to support his feet. So Dad asked Clive why he thought he needed to support his feet with sausages. So Clive explained it was because I'd told him his feet were flat as pancakes.

Anyway, Dad said then that I was wrong saying Clive had flat feet as he didn't have flat feet at all, although he does as far as I'm concerned. He said there was nothing wrong with Clive's feet and I said you can't have smelled them then and Dad said not to be cheeky but I was only saying.

Dad told Clive he had to stop putting sausages in his shoes as we couldn't afford it and if he did it again he'd make him eat his sneakers. I don't think Dad meant it but Clive started to cry and he said it wasn't his fault about the sausages in his socks and it would never have happened if he'd been born first only I pushed in and elbowed him out of the way which isn't true, as I've said.

Anyway, I didn't mention the flat feet again so as to keep the peace, but I did point out to Clive that he had ingrown toenails and if he wasn't careful they'd go on growing all the way up through his body and eventually come out through the top of his head—or possibly even through his eyeballs, which wouldn't be very nice.

Clive started to scream then and Dad came up the stairs and said if there was any more trouble there would be trouble. I would have thought that was obvious, but I didn't say anything, as I didn't think Dad was in the mood to appreciate it.

When Dad had gone back downstairs, I told Clive that I was afraid he also had bad breath and that the only cure for it was to brush his teeth with red-hot chili-pepper paste—a tube of which we luckily had in the kitchen—and that he should have a bucket of water handy for gargling with.

Unfortunately Dad caught Clive squeezing a big dollop of extra-strong red-hot chili-pepper paste onto his toothbrush, and I don't really remember very much about the rest of that night although I don't think there were bedtime stories or any cocoa.

Anyway, the way things stand, there's me, there's Clive, and there's Dad. Mum died when Clive and me were very young. We were too young to even be sad about it because we didn't really know— though maybe in some ways we did. And even

ALEX SHEARER

though we never knew Mum very well, we still miss her.

You miss not having a mum, but as Dad says, we just have to do the best we can and that is what we do, and that is why I try to be so helpful toward Clive about his personal problems.

People think sometimes that as we are three blokes all living together then it must be a pigsty. But it isn't. Except in the area of Clive's bed, of course, but then Clive is the sort of person who could make a pigsty anywhere. There's a saying our teacher said once that you can't make a pigsty out of a sow's ear or something like that. But Clive could. Clive could make a pigsty out of anything. You could give Clive fifty-thousand pounds and he'd turn it into a pigsty in a matter of minutes.

Sometimes ladies come round who want to marry Dad or at least get engaged to him, but then they get a look at Clive and change their minds more or less instantly. Not always, but most of the time. There was one lady with bad eyesight who wanted to marry Dad in spite of Clive, but I didn't like her very much and so I had to take her to one side when we were in the kitchen and ask in confidence if Dad had told her yet about Clive's problems: his sudden fits when he foamed at the mouth. And did she know that he suffered from leprosy— not that it was anything to worry about as it was curable, but if she did find one of his toes in the bathtub, she wasn't to make a fuss about it and just leave it to dry out on the radiator.

She never did come back. I think Dad was a bit baffled and wondered if it had been something he had said, but I didn't think so.

Anyway, when ladies come around, they expect our house to be a mess because we are all blokes living together (apart from Clive, of course, who is half bloke, half pig and half nutcase). But our dad keeps everything shipshape and Bristol fashion. At least that's what he says. I don't quite understand what keeping things Bristol fashion means, but when I asked Dad he said it meant always tidying your room up and doing your homework on time and putting your dirty pants in the washing machine. So I suppose that they must do a lot of that in Bristol, putting their pants in the washing machine. It does seem an odd thing to be famous for, though: putting your pants in the washing machine. It doesn't seem that special to me.

Now, the reason we are all so shipshape and Bristol fashion is because Dad is a sailor and you may well ask how Dad can be a sailor when he has us to look after and that's where it starts getting complicated.

When Dad is away, we go and live with Grandma, who is nice, and Granddad who is a bit hard of hearing, and also a bit hard of brain. They are very kind to me and Clive but they can be so boring sometimes and Granddad's idea of a good night out is to stay in. This is all right in the winter when it's cold as we can have cozy nights sitting in front of the TV. But in the summer, especially during the long summer holidays when Dad works hardest and longest of all, me and Clive wish that we could be with him, enjoying the life on the ocean wave.

Clive says that I would need a sick bag to go on to the ocean wave and I wouldn't be a very good sailor. But I tell him that I've lived with him all these years and I've survived that without needing a sick bag, so the ocean wave would be nothing.

We're always bugging Dad to take us to sea with him, but he says he can't. He says he wants to give it up and he's always looking for a job on dry land so he can be with us full-time. But jobs on land aren't so easy to find for someone who's always been at sea. And I feel that a part of Dad too would be sorry to leave the sea, as he's seen too many sunrises and too many sunsets on too many oceans, and I think they sort of become part of you, and you don't ever really want to leave them, and you'd be sad if you couldn't see them any more.

So every time it gets near to Dad going back to sea, we go on at him and say, "Take us with you, Dad, can't you take us with you?" And he gets a bit short-tempered, but I think it's only in self-defense, and he says not to be silly, as we have to go to school. But in the summer when we don't have to go to school, he can't say that and he just says, "I'm sorry, it's just not possible. I wish I could take you with me, I really could. But I can't. I'm sorry, kids, I'm sorry."

And we all feel sorry for a while then, and then

we have to pack up our things and go to Grandma's.

Once when Dad had one of the ladies around who wanted to marry him, I sneaked out of bed and pushed the door open a little way to hear what they were saying to each other down in the living room, and the lady said that it must be difficult bringing me and Clive up on his own but I didn't see why particularly. I mean, Clive, maybe. But me, I was no trouble at all.

Dad was quite loyal and wouldn't say a bad word about us and just said it was difficult sometimes but we were all right really. And then the lady said a funny thing. She said, "But who is there to be a mother to them, John? Who is a mother to them?"

And Dad thought for a moment and sort of shrugged and said, "I am, I suppose."

I thought about that a lot when I went back to bed. It made me smile, but it made me think too, that Dad wasn't just our dad; he was our mum as well.

It seemed like quite a lot, really, for one person to do on their own. And on top of that he had to give us pocket money.

I have to say in all fairness that not all these ladies did want to marry Dad, but quite a few of them seemed to stay the night anyway. Dad said that this was because they lived a long way away and it had got too late and they had got too tired to go home. So I suppose that was quite kind of him really, putting them up for the evening.

Anyway, you might be wondering what sort of

ALEX SHEARER

a sailor our dad was and whether he was a pirate with an earring and tattoos and a parrot, or whether he had a lot of gold braid around his arms and drove the ship and parked it in the docks when it came home.

Well, first off, Dad never had a parrot. To be honest, I've never seen a sailor with a parrot. I think they might have had them in the old days but now most sailors have a Discman instead. I think that basically that was what a parrot was—it was like an old-fashioned Discman and it was something to listen to when you got bored. Mind you, to have parrots in stereo, you'd have needed two parrots, one for each shoulder and for each ear and the squawking would have been terrible, not to mention the mess down the back of your coat.

Dad didn't have any tattoos either, though a friend of his, Kenny, had a walrus on his arm which he had had done in Shanghai. I asked him if there were walruses in Shanghai. But he said no, just tattoos of them.

Dad used to have an earring, just one in his right ear, but then he stopped wearing it. Clive said that he fancied an earring but Dad wouldn't let him get his ear pierced, as he was too young. Clive was disappointed and got a bit upset about this, so from the kindness of my heart I offered to put a hole in his ear for him with a fork. Clive was most grateful about this and I had just persuaded him to lie down on the kitchen table and given him a packet of tissues to bite on for the pain and had got the fork out, when Dad came into the kitchen to make a cup of tea and asked what we were doing.

I didn't want to mention the earring, as he had already forbidden it, so I just said that I was giving Clive acupuncture, which is a Chinese word for sticking forks in people. They do it to relieve people's aches and pains and you get a lot of people in China who have had forks stuck in them and they are all a lot better for it. I told Dad that Clive was stressed out about his homework and to relieve his mind I was going to give him acupuncture in the bum with the old fork. Two or three stabs in the bum with a fork would be just what the doctor ordered—well, an acupuncture doctor anyway.

But Dad got a bit annoyed then and he said I wasn't to do it and I wasn't properly qualified to practice medicine at my age and what possible good could a fork in the bum do for anyone. I didn't want to argue with him but me and Clive were both very disappointed about that. I was sure I could have done a good job on Clive's ear lobes with the fork and he could have had enough holes for three earrings, never mind one.

So no, Dad didn't really go in for parrots and tattoos or even earrings that much. Sailing has moved on a long way since those days. Dad's friend Kenny did have a parrot once though, which he bought from Pets Universe out at the shopping center. It cost him a lot of money—over three hundred pounds—but it died shortly afterward when Kenny left the window open and a cat came in.

ALEX SHEARER

"Three hundred pounds down the drain," he said. But it wasn't really down the drain, it was three hundred pounds inside the cat.

Anyway, Dad wasn't one of those old-fashioned pirate kinds of sailors, nor was he the captain who parked the ship and made sure it was going in straight lines when it had to. He did have a smart uniform though, a very smart one, and it had some gold braid on it too, around the sleeves and a bit on the shoulders and when Dad put his uniform on, he looked dead smart. Almost as smart as I look when I am wearing my football uniform. Clive doesn't look smart in his football uniform though, as he likes to wear his shorts inside out so that you can see the pockets. He thinks it is cool and he says he is the Amazing Inside-out Boy and that he is a member of the League of Super Heroes and is dedicated to the fighting of crime and the vanquishing of evil—I think he got that idea out of a comic.

When Clive puts his shorts on inside out he runs about the house and says things like "Inside-out Boy to the rescue!" even when nobody is in trouble or has any problems. Far from being a member of the League of Super Heroes, he looks like a member of the League of Stupid Nerdoes. No, the only one in our house with problems that I can tell is Clive— and they're mostly to do with his personality. Though I don't ever tell him that, as he is inclined to be sensitive.

Anyway, getting back to Dad, he is the sort of sailor who is called a Steward—well, a Senior

Steward in Dad's case—and that means that he works on great big luxurious cruise ships like the *QE2* and the *Titanic*—although that sank. Dad tries not to go onto ships that are going to sink, though you can't always tell in advance.

Dad's job as Senior Steward is to look after all the passengers and to make sure that they're comfortable and that they're all enjoying themselves and having a good time. As Dad says, it may be a holiday for them, but it's no holiday for him. His job is to see that they enjoy their holiday, and possibly even will want to come back again. He doesn't have to enjoy himself just as long as they do. But although it is hard work, I think that he does enjoy himself just the same.

Dad doesn't get enormous wages for this—even though he is a Senior Steward—but he does get what are known as Big Tips. This is when, at the end of every voyage, the passengers give you an envelope with money in it to thank you for helping them to enjoy their cruise. Of course, if you haven't helped them enjoy their cruise, or if the weather has been bad and they have been seasick, you don't get very much, if anything. But if the weather has been glorious and everything has gone well, they usually give you a Big Tip. On a good cruise Dad can get lots of envelopes with Big Tips in them, and we can always tell if it's been a good trip or not from the look on his face when he comes to Granddad and Grandma's to pick us up and take us home. If he's all smiles, it's Big Tips all around. If he's all scowls, then me and Clive know better than to ask. But when it's Big Tips, Dad always buys us something, so we're all quite keen on Big Tips round at our house.

Dad always brings us a little something back from every voyage, whether it's Big Tips or whether it isn't. It's usually something from one of the ports that they have stopped at on the way. Something from Spain, or Africa, or Brazil or even Alaska sometimes, as he's sailed all the way up there too. He's been all around the world really, several times, front ways and backward and from side to side as well.

It's hard work being a Senior Steward though, as I have said. You might be on call all through the night. People get into a party mood when they go on a cruise and they might decide that they want a bottle of champagne at two in the morning, or a packet of crisps at midnight, and you have to be there to bring it. And if you get a difficult customer who is rude and demanding and is nothing but trouble, well, you don't let it make any difference and you just go on being polite and cheerful no matter how unpleasant they are to you.

You need a lot of patience to be a Senior Steward, Dad says. It's no good if you've got a short fuse and are inclined to fly off the handle, you wouldn't last five minutes, so I don't think Clive would ever make it, as he's always having tantrums over absolutely nothing. He even had a tantrum when I locked him in the closet to help cure him of his claustrophobia, which only goes to show how highly strung and out of control he is, as he was only in there for half an hour, at the most. And I only did it because he wanted me to. He'd said he wondered what it would be like to be in a submarine, so I showed him.

Yes, Clive has such a short fuse he basically has no fuse at all.

WELL, WHEN IT CAME to Dad going away to work, I have to admit that we gave him no end of misery those last few days before he actually went. Especially when it was the summer holidays and we didn't have any school to go to.

"Can't you take us with you, Dad?"

"There must be room for two small ones, Dad—well, one medium-sized one and one fat one like Clive."

"We could share your cabin, Dad!"

"No," he said. "I don't have a cabin to myself. I have to share one with three other stewards."

"We could share your hammock then, Dad!"

"Clive, how many times do I have to tell you that I don't have a hammock."

"How about if we brought a hammock with us?"

"No. We haven't got a hammock to bring."

"Is it right that sailors used to do knitting, Dad?"

"In the old days, yes."

"Do you do knitting, Dad?"

"No."

"If you learned how to do knitting, Dad, you could knit us a hammock."

"Clive, I am not knitting you a hammock. And I'm trying to watch football here. Can we finish this conversation?"

"How about the crow's nest, Dad? Have you ever been up in the crow's nest?"

"Yes. Years ago. When I first went to sea."

"How about we sleep in the crow's nest then?"

"I'm starting to lose patience here—"

"How about if we slept in one of the lifeboats, Dad?"

"No."

"How many pockets do you have in your life jacket, Dad?"

"I'm not even listening to you two any more."

And it was usually around about then that bedtime would come early. It was funny how bedtime would come early whenever we brought up the subject of going on one of Dad's cruises and keeping him company.

Once, bedtime came so early we hadn't even had breakfast. Dad did relent after a little while and let us get up, but only on condition that we didn't go on about going on the cruise with him.

Dad took us on board one of the cruise ships once for a look around. It was huge, like a floating town. It had everything you could think of: swimming pools, restaurants, a gym, squash courts, a bowling alley, a nightclub, two cinemas, a hairdresser's, shops, a laundry, a doctor's office, even an operating theater, in case you needed to have your appendix taken out. There was even a casino where you could gamble all your money away or win a big fortune.

It had looked great to me and Clive, and we'd wanted to stay. But we were only allowed to look around, as it was open day for all the people who worked on board and their families. I could just see myself on a lounger by the swimming pool, cruising around somewhere nice and warm, with an ice-cold drink in my hand and the sun beating down and miles and miles of blue water as far as the eye could see. It seemed a whole lot better than being taken down to Granddad's house to watch him get the weeds out of his potato patch. Clive and me used to discuss whether his bottom was getting any bigger. Clive thought it wasn't but I thought it was. When Granddad bent over to pull the weeds up you could see his great big corduroy bottom just sort of staring at you, like it was waiting for you to paint circles on it and to fetch a bow and arrow. But to be honest, I think that if most people were given the choice between going on a cruise and having to look at my Granddad's bottom as he pulled the weeds up, they'd take the cruise any day.

Anyway, it wasn't an option for us and so we just had to live with it. Dad could see that we were disappointed that he was off again, so he said that he would try to make this season his last, and then he would try to get a job on land and give up the sea forever. We were sad for him having to give up the sea, but it wasn't much of a life for us, so we had mixed feelings too.

"So this might be Dad's last summer at sea, Clive," I told him. I usually had to explain these things to Clive like that in big simple words with underlinings, otherwise he wouldn't know what was going on.

"Yes," Clive said. "It's a pity, really."

"Yes," I said. Then I thought about it and said, "What's a pity?"

Clive said, "It means we'll never get to go now. We'll never get to go with Dad on one of his cruises to faraway and exotic parts and lie by the swimming pool with big drinks in the sunshine and be waited on hand and foot, and knee and leg as well."

And I could see that was a pity.

"We could just go anyway," Clive said.

And I want you to remember that it was Clive who said that, because that makes it his idea and everything that happened afterward is basically all his fault.

"How do you mean—'just go anyway,' Clive?" I asked.

"I mean we could just sort of sneak on board," Clive said, "when no one is looking. And then sort of find ourselves an empty cabin somewhere and just sort of settle down for the trip. I mean, let's face it, it has to be better than looking at that big corduroy patch on the bottom of Granddad's trousers."

(Clive and me do agree on some things sometimes.)

I was quiet for a while and then I said—though I was only making conversation really, and didn't mean anything by it, "Yes, but what about Grandma and Granddad, Clive? They'd wonder where we'd gone."

"Not if they thought we'd gone with Dad they wouldn't," Clive said. He is very devious, is Clive, and he is not above telling fibs sometimes even when he knows they aren't true.

"But why would they think we were going with Dad when we never go with Dad?" I said.

"Because we would tell them there had been a last-minute change of plan," Clive said.

"Oh," I said—as that kind of thing is lies and deception and they don't come easily to me. "But how would we get on board?" I said. "We don't have any tickets."

"Easy," Clive said. "By sneaking."

And the way he said it, it sounded as if he had quite a lot of sneaking experience. Only I hadn't known that, and thought he must have been doing sneaking that I wasn't aware of, and that was a bit worrying, to think of Clive doing sneaking and me not knowing about it.

"Sneaking?"

"Sneaking on board," Clive said. "We've been on ships for a look around. We know the layout. If anyone can do any sneaking, it's us."

"But what about Dad?" I said.

"We just avoid him," Clive said, "and stay out of his way. It's a huge ship, isn't it?"

ALEX SHEARER

"But what if we can't avoid him and he sees us anyway?"

"Then it'll be a nice surprise for him," Clive said.

But I couldn't see it that way somehow. I didn't think Dad would be surprised to see us on board his ship as nonpaying passengers. I thought he'd be more likely to go ballistic. I could see bedtime coming very early that day—very early indeed. In fact, I could see a whole lifetime of not getting up again stretching in front of me after that. But then again, as it would have all been Clive's idea; I wouldn't really be to blame.

So, "Tell me more, Clive," I said, "about this idea of yours. Tell me more, oh brother of mine."

And he did.

TWO

Packing

NOW BEING AS our dad was a sailor, we lived quite near to the docks. We didn't have to, but we did, as it was handy for Dad getting to work. Clive said that he would rather that we lived on a farm, because then we could have had some cows and a few chickens. But I pointed out that living on a farm wasn't so convenient for sailing. Clive said he didn't see why you couldn't have a boat on a farm, so I said Where would you sail it and he said In the duck pond.

But I said that was stupid. I said for one thing you'd never fit the *QE2* into a duck pond and then, for a second thing, I said who would want to go on a two-week cruise around a duck pond anyway. But Clive never thinks of things like that, which is why he was born second. He was just too dumb to be born first and he doesn't like to be reminded of it as it makes him feel inferior—which he is.

Anyway, us being so near to the docks would help me and Clive in the plot we were planning, and the plan we were plotting was how to smuggle ourselves on board the cruise ship *Mona Lisa,* which was her name.

Clive said that he didn't agree with ships usually having girls' names so much and he said that there ought to be a ship called *Clive.* But I said who'd get on a ship called *Clive?* You'd know it was doomed to start with, with a name like that. I'd only get on a ship called *Clive* if I could spend the whole voyage sitting in a lifeboat.

Now Dad always had to be on board ship a good while before they cast off (which is what they call it on ships when they get going; it's like taking the handbrake off when you're in a car). There was always a lot to do and to get ready. Sometimes he would be on board a few days before the ship sailed, checking that all the right supplies were there and that the glasses had been polished and that there were plenty of peanuts.

Clive asked me when the rats went on board, as he had heard that rats were fond of cruises too and that no ship or boat was complete without a few rats. I told him that was rubbish and pointed out that we'd gone off in a pedal boat at the seaside once and there were no rats in that. But Clive said there were as he had seen them swimming along behind. And then there was the time we went canoeing, and there were no rats in my canoe, I said. But Clive said that his canoe had been full of rats and they would have gone up his trousers only he had put rubber bands around the bottoms to keep them out. But I think he was making it up, as I know that rats aren't afraid of rubber bands and would chew through them in no time.

Now when Dad went on board the boat, we were packed off to Grandma's, even if it was still a few days before Dad sailed off. But she used to let us walk down to the harbor and we could see the big cruise boat in the out-of-bounds area, and sometimes we would see Dad on deck and we would wave to him and I would call to him about how Clive was being a right pain in the neck and had rubber bands around his trousers. And Clive would call to him, going on about how he should have been born first and it wasn't fair. And sometimes, when we did that, Dad would pretend that he didn't know who we were and he'd disappear from sight for five minutes until we stopped yelling.

When it was time to go to Grandma's, Dad always used to let me or Clive ring up and say that Dad was going away again. Normally I would do the talking, as whenever Clive tries to string more than three words together, he gets knots in them. Now our plan was to say to Gran (when Dad was out of earshot and eyeshot) that Dad was going away— only we would be going with him this time. And we would leave it until the very last minute and then hopefully we would be able to sneak off to the docks and on board the boat before anyone discovered what we were really up to—or at least that was the plan. If that didn't work and we ended up at Grandma's anyway, we would just have to sneak out of the house and leave her a note saying that we had run away to sea and we would ring her as soon as we got there so she would know that we were all right.

In the meantime, we had to make our preparations and decide what to take with us and what bags to pack.

Clive said we had to be really clever about it so as not to make anyone suspicious. He said we should wear our swimming trunks instead of pants and that way we could go for a swim on board the boat without anyone being any the wiser. That sounded a bit crazy to me, so I put my trunks in my bag. But Clive wore his trunks on top of his pants for a day to try it out. Then we went to the local swimming pool and he jumped in with his trunks and his pants on, which meant he had nothing dry to wear when he got out. Dad asked him why he had gone swimming with his pants on when we got home, but Clive said he wasn't allowed to reveal why, as it was top secret, and all he could say was that he was working for the government and doing research on underwater pants.

But nobody believed him, not even Clive, and it was him who had said it.

The first time we did an experimental pack-up, I got all my stuff and everything I needed into my backpack. But Clive ended up with six bags and a trunk, as he wanted to take all his War Hammer models and his Lego, and his mountain bike.

I had a bit of a go at him then, as I felt he was being stupid.

"How are you going to sneak on board a ship, Clive, with six bags and a trunk?" I asked him.

"I'm going to act casual," he said, "and sort of sidle up the gangplank so no one will notice."

"How can you sidle up a gangplank with six bags and a trunk?" I wanted to know.

"I haven't worked out the details yet," he said, "but I'll cross that bridge when I come to it. And not only will I cross that bridge when I come to it, I'll cross that gangplank when I come to it as well."

"Look, Clive," I said. "There's no way you can be a stowaway with six bags and a trunk. Stowaways usually have all their belongings wrapped up in a spotty handkerchief or a plastic bag from the super-market."

"Then I'll take everything out and put it in a handkerchief," Clive said. "I've probably got a snotty one."

"Spotty!" I said. "Not snotty. And you can't get the contents of six bags and a trunk into a hand-kerchief!"

"I can if it's a big handkerchief."

"If you had a handkerchief that big you'd be blowing your nose on a tent."

"I've only got tissues anyway."

In the end I persuaded Clive to leave his mountain bike and his Legos at home and he settled for some colored pencils. We got our luggage down to one backpack each, which was about what we normally took with us to Grandma's anyway.

And then all we had to do was to wait for the day to arrive.

Dad was due to sail off on the day after the start of our summer holiday. School broke up on Friday and Dad sailed on Saturday. Gran and Granddad knew he was going soon, and on the Friday Dad rang them up to say cheerio. He then ended his phone call in the usual way by saying, "I'll put the boys on now. I think they've got some special news for you."

Now this was like a ritual in a lot of ways. It was a big sort of pretense and a kind of false surprise. What happened then would be that Dad would leave us to talk to Gran and the big surprise was that we were coming to stay with her. And she made out it was a big surprise too. And we all pretended to be surprised that we were doing what we usually did and that was what the big surprise was. Only it wasn't a surprise at all really; in fact it was pretty boring.

Only this time it was different. As soon as Dad was out of the room I said, "Gran?"

"Yes, dear?"

"It's an extra-special surprise this time."

"Is it, dear?"

"Yes. Not only is Dad going away—we're going with him!"

There was a moment's silence then she said in a tone (which if I hadn't known better might have sounded like a tone of relief), "You're going with your Dad, dear?"

"Yes, Gran. Tomorrow."

"Both of you? Clive, too?"

"Yes, Gran."

"So you won't be coming to stay with us?"

"No, Gran."

And do you know—I mean I'm sure I must have been mistaken—but I could have sworn that I heard someone who sounded like Granddad sort of cheering in the background. It was almost as if they were having a celebration. And the next thing I heard was this noise like somebody opening a bottle of beer. And then there was a sound like fireworks going off. But it must have been some interference on the line.

"Well, I'm sorry you won't be staying with us, dear," Gran said. "But I hope you have a nice time. Isn't it wonderful that your Dad managed to get permission to bring you along?"

"Wonderful," I agreed. "Almost a miracle, in fact."

"You have a great time and send us a postcard and we'll see you when you get back."

"Okay, Gran. See you then. Would you like to speak to Clive?"

I don't think she wanted to but she had to say yes, so I put him on.

"Hello Gran," Clive said. "It's me, Clive. I should have been born first, you know, only fate conspired against me."

He sort of ran out of conversation after that. It was the same at school when we all had to stand up in class and talk about ourselves for two minutes. Other people talked about their families and their interests. But all Clive could say about himself was that his name was Clive. So he spent two minutes doing that. He spent two whole minutes saying that his name was Clive. That might not sound like a long time to you, but when you have to listen to it, it does your head in something chronic. I reckon that many people have been driven mad and ended up in the funny bin, the loony farm, and the bonkers hotel by other people saying to them "My name is Clive" over and over again.

Anyway, once he had run out of telling her that his name was Clive, he left Gran to do the talking. Maybe she spent two minutes saying "My name is Gran" over and over.

Finally he managed to put the phone down.

"Well?" I said.

"Not so bad," Clive said.

"No," I said, feeling that I had to explain absolutely everything to him and that was my punishment for having been born first, "I don't mean are you well, Clive, as in the opposite of ill. I mean, well, did she believe it?"

"She seemed to," Clive said. "I gave her the old one-two."

"And what exactly is the old one-two?"

"I don't know," Clive said. "It's a bit like the old three-four, only sort of divided in half."

ALEX SHEARER

But then Clive was never all that good at math, not even during English.

"Did you convince her that we were telling the truth or not? Did you pull the wool over her eyes?"

"Why would I want to pull wool over anyone's eyes?" Clive said. "Wouldn't you be better off with sunglasses?"

"Clive," I said, "did she suspect anything?"

"No," he said, "I don't think so."

"Good," I said. "That's all I wanted to know. Then the plan goes ahead."

Clive gave me one of his vacant looks.

"What plan is that?" he said.

"The stowaway plan," I reminded him. "Remember, us sneaking on board the ship. Is it on or isn't it?"

"Yes," he said. "I reckon it is."

And I reckoned it was too. And so next day, we put the plan into action.

THREE

PLAN A

CLIVE SAID THAT if Plan A didn't work we could always use Plan B.

But I pointed out that we didn't have a Plan B.

So Clive said that we had better use Plan A then, and as we didn't have a Plan B, then if Plan A didn't work, we would have to use Plan C.

I pointed out to Clive that we didn't have a Plan C either.

Clive said that we should use Plan D then.

I pointed out to Clive that we didn't have a Plan D, we only had Plan A.

Clive said that we should have a Plan E then. If we didn't have a Plan B, C, or D, we should make a Plan E.

I asked Clive what Plan E should be.

Clive said Plan E should be that if Plan A

didn't work, we would go on to Plan F.

I pointed out to Clive that we didn't have a Plan F.

Clive said in that case we should stick to Plan E.

I pointed out to Clive that Plan E was to use Plan F, only we didn't have a Plan F, so what use was Plan E?

Clive said that perhaps a Plan G might be better.

I asked Clive what Plan G was.

Clive said he didn't know.

I said, in that case, how about Plan H?

Clive asked what Plan H was.

I explained that Plan H was where I opened the window, Clive put his head on the windowsill, and then I closed the window very hard and very fast on Clive's head.

Clive said he felt it might be best to stick to Plan A and that if Plan A didn't work, we'd better just give up.

So we went with Plan A.

NOW, PLAN A was to somehow make us late. Dad was going to drop us off at Grandma's in the morning before he went to get on board the boat. Normally that would have meant him driving us around, helping us with our backpacks, walking up the path, banging on the doorbell, going inside, having a cup of tea, having a chat, saying good-bye, all the usual stuff.

So we had to make him late so that he wouldn't have time for any of that.

Gran now believed (though Dad didn't know what we had told her) that we were going on board the ship with Dad, so she would have been rather surprised to see us turning up at her house in the morning and we would have got into big trouble. (Though Clive says that big trouble is really the only sort of trouble there is, and that small trouble is not really trouble at all.)

So what we had to do was to make Dad so late in the morning that he wouldn't be able to take us to the door of Gran's house. We wanted to make him so late that he would be forced to boot us out of the car at the corner of Gran's street and say something like, "There you are boys. I'm sorry but I can't wait to come in with you. I should have been on the boat half an hour ago. Just grab your stuff and go on into Gran's and I'll see you when I get back."

And then we would get out of the car and say good-bye through the window and then Dad would drive off, and he would look into the mirror as he went to see us walking to Gran's house. And then as soon as he was around the corner and out of sight, we would run as fast as we could—before Gran or Granddad came out of the house for the milk bottles and spotted us there and wondered what we were up to.

So that was Plan A. It was also known as the Master Plan. There had been another plan at one time, but that was known as the Half-wit Plan, as Clive had thought of it. Clive's idea had been for us to make two big cardboard cut-out copies of me and him and to leave them in the car for Dad to take to Gran's while the real us hid under the bed.

But I didn't think there was much chance of it working and said so.

Anyway, the plan was to make everything late the next morning, and we did this by getting up early. We set our alarms for five o'clock in the morning, got up, sneaked into Dad's room and turned his clock back an hour so that he would get up an hour later but still think that he was getting up in time.

Then we went back to bed.

Now, you might think that what we did was a bit sneaky and not very nice, but what you have to remember is that me and Clive only wanted to be with Dad really and to go off with him and for us all to be together. And that isn't such a bad thing, I don't think. We knew that if he saw us he would go ballistic several times over. But just the same we would be able to keep an eye on him and see that he was all right, and we would also be on hand to save him from all those ladies who wanted to marry him.

Clive and me were not against Dad marrying ladies in principle, so please don't think that. In fact we would have been quite happy for Dad to have married as many ladies as he wanted. But we didn't want Dad to go marrying any ladies without first getting our approval.

The thing about Dad is that he is a bit of a soft touch. He is always putting his money into charity collecting boxes, even when it isn't necessary. Dad is the sort of person who would give you the shirt off his back. This is as opposed to Clive, who is more the sort of person to give you the socks off his feet. Only the chances are that you wouldn't want them, not unless you were thinking of making a cheese omelette.

Personally I don't think it's a good idea to give too many of your shirts away, as you won't have any left, and then if you had to go to an interview, all you would have to wear would be your vest and your jacket, and you wouldn't get the job.

What really worried me and Clive was that Dad would go off to sea one day on one of his cruises, and he would meet a lady on board, who might be a bit rich, and he would get sea fever or something and they would ask the captain to marry them—as ship captains are allowed to do that sort of thing.

So Clive and me used to worry a lot that Dad would come home from one of his voyages with a lady he had married in a moment of madness and he would say, "Here you are boys, meet your new mum!"

Only what if we didn't like her? Or she didn't like us? And when Dad was out and not there to protect us, would she hit us with the cheese grater and lock us in the shed and not give us anything to eat until teatime?

The other dangerous thing was that people will do strange things when they are at sea and when they are on their holidays. Dad had told us many times about people going a bit bonkers on their holidays and doing things that they would later regret. So we were worried that Dad might marry somebody who looked all right on a ship, but when you got her on to dry land, you might think she was a big mistake. Someone like a mermaid, who we would have to keep in the washbasin.

Clive and me had very strict views on getting a new mum and who Dad should remarry, if anyone.

We decided that first she would have to be good and kind and very fond of children and also that she would be very generous too, and in favor of big helpings of pocket money.

We also saw her as being the sort of lady who would not stint on the ice cream and who would be fond of outings to Disneyland.

I also decided that it would help if she was pretty, as then she would be nice to look at, because when you have to live with somebody like Clive, it is a nice change to have someone pretty to rest your eyes on every now and again.

In fact, when things get too much for me, and I feel I can't stand the sight of Clive a moment longer, I go upstairs and lock myself in the bathroom and I sit on the floor and contemplate the toilet bowl. I usually find that this helps to restore my spirits, and it is nice to have a well-designed and attractively laid-out toilet bowl to look at after seeing something like Clive.

If I can't get into the bathroom, as Dad is in there, I generally go and look at the watering can instead. It is not as good looking as the toilet bowl, but it is still better looking than Clive.

Not that Clive is all bad, mind you. He is quite nice in lots of ways and has many good qualities. It is just that for the moment I forget what they are.

But the point is, what I'm trying to say is, that although what we did might seem wicked and misguided to some people and not very nice, we did it all with the best of intentions and only because we love Dad and wanted to be with him and for him to be happy and for us to be happy too and we didn't want him to go marrying anyone who might be cheesy and to stop him giving all his shirts away. And that was all, really. And I don't think that's so bad. Not when you consider all the other things that go on in the world, for which you can be heavily fined or even sent to prison—which is probably where Clive will end up. Or maybe he will end up working on a pig farm.

WHEN DAD'S SEVEN o'clock alarm went off at eight, and when he put the radio on and found out what the time really was, he went ballistic. I have never seen anyone move so fast, not even Clive when he saw that they were giving away free cookie samples at the supermarket and he leaped over three shopping carts at once to get there before they ran out.

Dad charged into our bedroom and started yanking our duvets off and saying, "We're late, boys! We're late! I'm going to be late for the boat. Come on, quick, get dressed. I've got to take you around to Grandma's—now!"

Well, this was just what we had been lying in bed waiting for, so we got dressed as slowly as we could to make things even later, and Clive made out that he had lost his socks.

Dad was going frantic down in the kitchen, getting a quick breakfast ready and trying to pack his bag.

"Breakfast!" he called. "Come on!"

"Have I time to wash my face?" Clive shouted.

"Not a face as dirty as yours," I told him. "It'd take you two years with a scrubbing brush to clean that."

"Be quick!" Dad called back.

"Have I time to brush my teeth?"

"Before breakfast? Clean them at Grandma's! Come on!"

"What about putting a second coat of varnish on my model airplanes?"

"Clive! Get down here now!"

So we had to at least make a show of hurrying up; otherwise he would have got suspicious. We got our things ready after breakfast and Dad checked everything and put on the burglar alarm and bundled us into the car, and then we drove off toward Gran's at breakneck speed.

We got stuck in a bit of traffic though and Dad started to look at his watch until finally he said, "Look, lads, it's no good, I'm not going to be able to come in with you. I'll just have to drop you on the corner and you walk the rest of the way to Gran's— Okay? It's only a few meters."

"Ah, but Dad—" we moaned (not trying to seem too keen straightaway or he might have got suspicious about that too).

"I'm sorry, boys," he said. "But I've got to get to the boat or I'm in trouble."

We turned off the main road then and came to the corner of Gran's street.

"There you go," Dad said. "I'll see you in a few weeks. Have a good holiday. Love you both!"

And a quick hug, a quick kiss, a quick good-bye, and there we were, standing there on the pavement with our backpacks at our feet, waving forlornly to Dad as he drove off into the traffic and on toward the docks.

Suddenly none of it seemed like such a good idea any more. We felt a bit small and lonely and at the mercy of everything in sight.

Clive tried to hold my hand, but I wouldn't let him—at least, not for long.

"I don't want to go now," Clive wailed. "I don't want to be a stowaway. I don't want to go and hide on a ship. I want to go to Gran's. It's nice and boring at Gran's and you know where you stand. The food might be awful but at least it's there."

To be honest, I felt the same, and it was on the tip of my tongue to say, "All right, come on, let's go to Gran's then. We'll think of something to tell her."

And I could have blamed it all on Clive too. He'd have been the chicken, the one who had backed out and lost his nerve, and I could have never let him forget it for the rest of his life.

So I was just about to say, "Have it your way then, Clive. I always knew you were a big baby. I always knew you were a quitter. If it was left to me I'd spend my whole life as a stowaway. But now, once again, you've held me back, Clive. Once again you've prevented me from reaching my full potential and having adventures. But there we are. That's how it is. You've always been a burden to me, Clive, and let me down at every turn."

But just at that moment a bus came along. It was the 284, the one that goes to the docks. And I don't know if it was the sight of the bus, or maybe the 284 was some kind of magic number as far as Clive was concerned, but he suddenly changed his mind.

"It's a bus!" he said. "*The* bus! It'll take us to the dockside. Come on!"

And he grabbed his backpack and started to run. So what else could I do but run after him? I couldn't leave Clive to be a stowaway on his own, could I? Not when he was five minutes younger than I was and I was the eldest and had to be responsible and look after him.

He flagged the bus down and it stopped and the doors opened and Clive hopped on board.

"He'll pay," he said to the driver, and he went and sat down across the aisle from a woman with a shopping bag and started to make disgusting faces at her, which he does deliberately to put people off.

So I had to pay the bus fares out of my own hard-earned pocket money.

"Two to the docks," I said.

"Singles?" the driver asked. "Or returns?"

I hesitated a moment. Singles or returns? A return ticket was usually only valid for a day. A week at the most in some cases.

Singles or returns?

Well, we wouldn't be coming back today, would we? I thought. And we'd be away for longer than a week. In fact who knew if or when we would be coming back at all? We might decide not to ever come back. We might decide to be stowaways for ever and ever. Or to get off the boat at some foreign port, or to start a new life in Australia.

"Well?" the driver said impatiently. "Singles or returns? What do you want? Are you coming back or aren't you?"

"Singles," I said. "We're not coming back. I don't think we'll be back for a long time."

Then the bus lurched as it moved off and I went to sit next to Clive.

"Stop making those disgusting faces, Clive," I said.

He looked at me, a bit surprised.

"I'm not making any disgusting faces," he said indignantly.

And then I realized he was right. It was just his natural expression.

swanker

NOW, BEFORE I GO telling you about how we got on board the boat and how we almost got arrested and killed and had several narrow escapes—some of which were so narrow that they should have been in *The Guinness Book of Narrow Escapes*—before we even got up the gangplank, I first ought to tell you a bit about Swanker Watson.

Swanker Watson was in our class at school and he was called Swanker for reasons to do with being swank. If it hadn't been for the swanking reasons, we wouldn't have called him Swanker; we would probably have called him something else, like Dog Breath or Gorilla Armpits or Kangaroo Face or something like that.

Swanker was in the same class as me and Clive. I had tried to get Clive put into a different class when we first went to school on the grounds that as he was five minutes younger than me he would be better off in the nursery group where he could be with the younger children who were nearer his own age and brain size.

I was worried that as he was so much younger, Clive would find things like arithmetic and sums (which are very similar) rather difficult and he would fall behind.

I was very surprised therefore when Clive came second from top in the math test and I came third from bottom. I can only think that the math teacher wasn't very good at math and she had added up my marks wrong.

Anyway, Swanker Watson was in our class from the outset and he introduced himself to me and Clive by saying, "Good morning to you, my name is Angus Watson, and who might you be?"

Clive gave him a look and said, "Agnes? That's a bit of a funny name for a boy."

"Angus!" Swanker said. "Not Agnes. And where do you live?"

We told him and then we felt that we'd better ask him where he lived as it was probably why he'd asked us where we lived so as we'd ask him where he lived and so as he could tell us.

"We live," he said—and I worked out from the way he said it that there was more than one of him and he wasn't there on his own—"We live," he said, "in the Old Manor."

We must have looked a bit blank because then

he said, "You have heard of the Manors?"

Clive brightened up a spot then.

"Of course we've heard of manners," he said. "Do you mean good manners or bad manners?"

"Not that kind of manners," Swanker said, "I mean manors—as in manor houses. There are two of them in the Greville estate, the New Manor and the Old Manor and we live in the Old Manor."

"Oh dear," Clive said. "I'm sorry to hear that, Agnes. I'm sorry to hear that you only have an old house to live in. But not to worry, maybe your luck will change and you'll be able to afford a new one like ours. We've got three bedrooms in our house. How many have you got in your house?"

"Twelve," Swanker said.

Clive gave him a look.

"Is it a big house then?"

"Enormous," Swanker said.

"How can you afford that then?" Clive said.

"We're rich," Swanker told him.

"How's that then?" Clive said. "Are you crooks?"

"Not at all," Swanker said indignantly. "We certainly are not. We are very honest. We just happen to be rich."

Clive looked at him suspiciously and poked him with his finger. Swanker didn't like this as his shirt—unlike Clive's finger—was very clean and fresh that morning. Clive's finger was not clean, nor was it fresh on that morning. Clive and his finger had been together since the beginning, and even though he is my brother and I ought not to say it, Clive and his finger are as dirty as each other. And if you had to give a prize for who was dirtiest—Clive or his finger—you'd be hard pushed to know who to give it to.

"If you're so rich," Clive said, "what are you doing at our school? Why aren't you off at rich school with all the rich kids, doing lessons in being rich and learning your rich times table or whatever it is you have to do?"

"Because," Swanker explained, "my parents believe in state education."

"Are you trying to say that our school's in a bit of a state?" Clive demanded, looking a bit angry. "It's a good school this school is, even if the toilets are cracked—that could happen anywhere. And just because the roof leaks a bit in the hall and we have to have umbrellas for assembly, it doesn't mean we're not proud to be here."

"No, no," Swanker said, backpedaling a bit, as he could see that he had got Clive's dander up. (And you don't want to mess with Clive when his dander is up. I don't know what a dander is exactly, all I know is that when he's got it up, you don't want to mess with him.)

"No, no," Swanker said again. (At least I think he said it again. He might have only said it once.) "I think this is a very nice school. My parents sent me here because they thought that if they sent me to a rich school I would only meet the children of rich people and I would have a very narrow circle of friends and a very narrow view of life as a result and become spoiled. But by coming to a school like this one, where not only are there rich people but poor people and medium people and scruffbags as well, I will get a better education and be all the richer—in terms of life experience—for it."

Clive gave him another of his looks.

"What was that you said about scruffbags?" he asked.

"I said," Swanker said, "that coming here meant that I would be able to broaden my horizons and rub shoulders with scruffbags."

Clive thought this over a moment.

"Do you like scruffbags then?" he asked.

"Well, I'm talking to you two, aren't I?" Swanker replied.

So anyway, that was Swanker Watson and he was always going off with his family on expensive holidays. They went on safari in Africa to photograph elephants, but Swanker got ill and spent most of his holiday in the toilet, and the only elephant-type things he saw were elephant-sized poos. Then they went to India to see the Taj Mahal, but Swanker got ill again, and spent most of his holiday in the toilet there too.

So although Swanker had been to some fantastic places, his holiday photos weren't all that interesting as they tended to be mostly of the insides of toilets.

In fairness I have to say that Swanker was quite a decent bloke on the whole and didn't really do a lot of swanking at all. We just called him Swanker as a sort of warning to let him know that if he did do any swanking, then we would nickname him Swanker and he wouldn't like it.

And that was why we called him Swanker.

So that's all I have to say about Swanker for now, but the important thing to remember about him in case he crops up again (and I'm not saying that he will, only that he might) is that Swanker and his family were always going off on expensive holidays.

Expensive holidays, that is.

Like safaris.

And cruises.

That kind of thing.

ANYWAY, THERE WE were. Clive and me were sitting on the bus heading for the docks and our whole lives were ahead of us.

"Have you ever run away to sea before, Clive?" I asked —just to keep the conversation going, as something of a moody silence had settled over Clive and I didn't want him brooding. I was worried that he might change his mind again and want to get off the bus and go to Gran's after all.

"Have I ever run away to see *what* before?" he said.

"No, Clive," I explained, "I mean sea—as in the wet stuff—not see—as in looking at."

"Of course I haven't run away to sea before," Clive snapped. "How could I, with the amount of homework I get? And anyway, if I had, you'd have noticed, wouldn't you?"

"I suppose so," I agreed.

"You ever run away to sea?" he asked in his turn.

"No," I said. "Never."

"No, nor have I." Clive said. "Although I did have a bath once."

"Is that right, Clive?" I said. "I didn't know that. I thought you were more of a shower man."

"Showers are better," Clive said. "They're more hygienic and they don't have to last as long as baths. And they get you cleaner." (Though they certainly didn't get *him* any cleaner.) "In fact, did you know," Clive said, "that if you do a handstand in the shower, it's a good way to clean your bottom."

"Oh," I said. "Have you stopped using the sandpaper then?"

It was a joke, but he didn't get it. I didn't have time to explain it though, for by then we were approaching the docks and it was our stop.

We got off the bus and headed for the boat terminal. There were hundreds of people milling about everywhere, and the scene looked like one of those biblical sorts of things when people pack up their belongings and set off for the promised land. Or maybe it was a bit like Noah's Ark, only without the animals, and instead of going on board in an orderly way, two by two, everybody was trying to charge up the ramp and all get on at once.

Fortunately, there were sailors in uniform lining

the way, trying to help people get up the gangplank and to keep order. They seemed quite good humored and looked as if they had done all this a hundred times before—which they probably had.

Now Clive and me had one big problem about getting on board the cruise liner. I don't suppose you'll have guessed what it is, as it is a pretty difficult and complicated problem, and to be honest I don't think that many people would have thought of this in advance.

You see, there was something we didn't have. We had our luggage, yes; we had our swimming trunks, yes. We had a change of pants each, yes. But there was one thing we didn't have.

We didn't have any tickets.

Now, although I am not what you would call grown up yet, if there is one thing that I have learned in life, it is that you must have your tickets. You can't do much without tickets in this world. If you want to get into the cinema, you need a ticket, if you want to get on the bus, you need a ticket, if you want to see your favorite pop band at the local concert hall, you won't get in without your ticket. However, there is one sort of ticket that costs nothing to get and yet nobody wants it—and that, of course, is a parking ticket.

For most tickets, you pay first and get the ticket after. With parking tickets you get the ticket first and then you have to pay.

Now, as Clive and me milled about in the great, huge departure terminal, we realized that our lack of tickets for the boat could easily be our undoing if we weren't careful.

It was quite a scene on the dockside that day. There was Dad's boat, the *Mona Lisa* (named after a famous painting of the same name) parked directly outside the terminal (in the water, that is, not on the actual docks) and all along the dockside were other big boats, waiting to unload their cargoes or to get underway.

"Do you think we'll need a magazine for the trip?" Clive asked as we passed a newsagent's kiosk in the terminal.

"Get a comic," I said. "That should last us two weeks."

"Okay," Clive said.

And he went to buy one.

While he did, I looked around and sized up the situation.

The boat terminal was like an airline terminal in a lot of ways. People were checking in their big luggage, just like you do on an airplane. I sidled nearby to listen to what was going on. The procedure was that people showed their tickets and were given their cabin number and then they loaded their big cases onto the conveyor belt and they were whisked away.

"Your cases will be brought to your cabin for you, madam," the lady behind the desk explained to an anxious passenger, who seemed worried about her big hat box. "Here's your boarding card—oh, and if I could, may I see your passport?"

Passport!

I felt in my pocket. No, it was all right. There they were. I had them both, mine and Clive's. You might think that we were young to have our own passports, but Dad had sorted them out for us for a school trip we went on. They sent us off to France. Clive and me had quite a nice time there. The teacher wanted us to speak French, but Clive and me thought it would be better if instead of learning French we tried to teach them English. So we tried that, but they didn't seem very good at learning.

The passenger at the desk showed the lady behind it her passport. The lady nodded and returned it and handed the passenger her boarding card.

"There you are, madam. Enjoy your trip."

"Thank you."

"Next, please."

She spotted me.

"Are you next?"

"N-no," I stuttered. "Just waiting for someone."

"Then could you stand to one side, please. You're blocking the aisle."

I got out of the way and waited for Clive to come back with his comic. He was gone a long time. When he finally did turn up, his face was covered in chocolate.

"Have you been eating chocolate?" I said.

"No," he said.

I noticed that he had a Mars Bar wrapper stuck to his coat.

"Did you get any for me?" I said.

"I never had any," he said.

I was sure that he was lying but I didn't have any witnesses to prove it, so what could I do?

"Well be sure to let me have a read of your comic," I said.

"All right, but no staring at it," Clive said. "You stared at the last one so hard you read a hole in it."

"I never read a hole in it."

"You did," he said. "You stared a hole right through it."

I noticed then that he also had a bag of malted milk balls stuck to his trousers. I just hoped that he wouldn't regret all this chocolate once the boat got going.

Assuming we ever got on it, of course.

"Okay, listen Clive," I said. "We've got a problem about getting on to this boat."

"What's that?" he said.

"No tickets."

"No tickets? Why haven't we got any tickets?"

I started to get a bit impatient then.

"Because we're stowaways, of course."

"Well can't we just check in at the stowaways' desk then?" he said. "I'm sure that if we ask somebody they'll tell us where it is."

"Clive," I said, "there is no such thing as the stowaways' desk. That would be like going round to Swanker Watson's house to rob it and asking if someone could please direct you to the burglars' entrance."

Clive looked a bit stunned then.

"You mean," he said, "there's no such thing as a burglars' entrance either? You're joking?"

"Look, Clive," I said. "If we're going to get on board the ship, there's only one way we're going to do it."

"How?"

"Confusion."

Clive looked blank again.

"Confusion? How do you mean?"

"You know—confusion."

"No, sorry," he said. "I'm a bit confused."

"It's simple, Clive. What's there to be confused about?"

"Well, the confusion. That's what's confusing me."

"How can you be confused about the confusion?"

"I'm not sure."

"Why not?"

"I'm confused."

"Look, Clive," I said. "I've been watching the procedure here, and there are three—no, four—gates for us to get through. Look."

I pointed them out to him.

"First there's the passport control."

"We've got passports."

"Yes. Then there's the security control."

"What will they be looking for?"

"Knives, guns, and bombs. Have you got any of those?"

Clive seemed a bit shifty and he wouldn't look me in the eye.

"Clive," I said. "Clive—I want the truth now. Did you bring your bombs with you?"

"No," he said.

"Are you sure?"

"Positive. And anyway, they were only pretend bombs that I made for my grenade launcher. They never exploded."

"They hurt when they landed on my foot though. Have you got any guns then?"

"No."

"So what have you got?"

"My Swiss army knife."

Dad had brought us back one each from his last trip, only I had lost mine.

"That'll be all right," I said. "Just tell them you've got it. Don't try to hide it, that's all. And Clive—"

"What?"

"Don't go threatening anyone with the can-opener attachment."

"As if I would."

"Okay. Now, we should get through passport control and security control all right. That'll take us outside onto the dockside. That's where it gets difficult. See."

I took him to the window so that he could see the ramp that led up and onto the ship. There were two checks, one at the bottom of the ramp, where people were showing a uniformed sailor in a flat hat their boarding cards, and a second check at the top of the ramp where—I guessed—another sailor was checking their cards again and presumably directing them to their cabins.

"See that, Clive. That's where our problem lies."

"I've got an idea," Clive said. "Instead of going up the gangplank, why don't we just swing onto the boat on ropes. Like Tarzan, you know. We can just grab hold of some vines and swing onto the deck when no one's looking."

"Clive," I said, "what vines?"

He was quiet for a while, as it was plain to see that there weren't any vines to swing onto the boat by.

"Didn't you bring any vines then?" he said, in an accusing sort of way.

"Of course I didn't bring any vines! How would I have room in my backpack for vines! Where would I get vines from anyway, Clive! Where exactly can you buy vines around where we live?"

"I don't know," he shrugged. "The vine shop?"

"What vine shop? Vines Are Us? Or Kentucky Fried Vines? Is that who you're thinking of, Clive? Eh?"

"No need to be nasty," Clive said. "If we haven't got any vines maybe we could swing on board on the crane then."

I looked out at the boat. He had an idea there. Cranes were loading supplies onto the deck. For a second I thought I got a glimpse of Dad, walking across the deck with a clipboard in his hand, looking smart in his navy blue uniform. He had a white uniform too, but he only wore that one when it got hot and when the ship had sailed into the tropics.

But before I could tell Clive, Dad was gone.

"Look, Clive," I said. "What we have to do is to latch onto a big party of people and go through with them, so that the guards will think we're with them. We get in front of them at the bottom of the gangplank and tell the man there that the people behind us have got our boarding cards. When we get to the top of the gangplank, we tell the man at the top the same thing. We say that the people just coming up behind us have them. Then, while he's waiting for them, we disappear. Hopefully, if it's a big party, there'll be so many people and so much paperwork, the men checking the boarding cards will get confused and we'll be away and out of sight before anyone knows what's happened."

"Okay," Clive said. "I suppose."

"Well, do you have any better ideas?"

"We could get snorkels," Clive said, "and swim to the boat and then climb up the side with rubber suckers on our feet then—no, maybe not."

"Come on then," I said. "Let's do it."

So we shouldered our backpacks, held onto our passports, and headed for checkpoint number one.

"Passports!"

I handed the man our passports. I had to look after Clive's as well as my own, as Clive couldn't be trusted with documents. Clive was so useless with anything made out of paper that every time he went into the bathroom he lost the toilet roll.

"You boys on your own?" the man said.

"Er, no," I said. "No. That's our mum and dad, just over there."

I waved toward a man and a lady in the middle of a crowd of people just ahead of us.

"Well, you go and catch them up," the man said. "And don't go getting lost, eh? And tell them to keep a better watch on you."

Then he made the mistake of looking at the photo in Clive's passport.

"What's this?" he said.

"It's Clive," I explained.

"It looks barely human," he said.

Well, I didn't feel it was up to me to argue with him.

"You look like you were sitting on a cactus," the man said. "I'd get that photograph changed as soon as possible, if I were you."

He handed the passports back and waved us on our way.

"Next!" he said.

And we were past hurdle number one.

Hurdle number two was the security check. You had to put your bag into an X-ray machine and put anything metallic in your pockets into a tray while you walked through a scanner.

Clive emptied his pockets out and put his stuff into the small dish that the security lady was holding. There are things in Clive's pockets that you don't really want to know about, and exhibiting them in public like that was giving her quite a nasty turn.

"Why have you got a dead termite?" the lady asked, as Clive dropped it into the tray.

"It's a pet," Clive explained. Then he put his penknife onto the dish and walked through the scanner. Silence. I followed him, we got our things back from the dish, picked our backpacks up, and we were through.

Over the second hurdle. Now it started to get more difficult: hurdles three and four. Or more precisely, hurdle three, bottom of the gangplank, hurdle four, top of the gangplank, and, finally, on board.

We hung around for a little while by the doorway which led to the dockside, pretending to be sorting out the things in our luggage. There the boat was, right outside. It looked absolutely enormous, towering up almost like a great skyscraper. The liner was so huge, you could have landed an airplane on the deck. And as you looked up, you could see rows and rows of portholes, all looking back down at you, and the white painted hull glared in the sunshine, and you wished you'd brought your sunglasses. (Well, we *had* brought our sunglasses, as a matter of fact, but it didn't seem like a good time to wear them, not when we were trying to sneak on board a boat.)

What the liner really looked like was a great floating city, and considering the numbers of people who could fit on board, that is exactly what it was.

Clive and me loitered by the doorway, waiting for our chance. A few elderly couples walked by. There seemed to be quite a lot of old people getting on board. None of them liked the look of Clive very much. For some reason, he seemed to make them nervous. Clive has that effect on old people. Also on policemen. People in hospitals get very anxious when Clive is around too. Especially people who are attached to tubes and things.

When we went to visit Granddad in hospital, when he was having a new hip put in (Clive said he ought to have a new brain put in as well while he was there), all the other people in the ward got very agitated at the sight of Clive. They would ask the nurse to draw their curtains and hold on tightly to all their rubber tubes.

Anyway, at last our chance came. Approaching us through the departure lounge came a great bustling crowd of people. It was several generations of the same family, with grans and granddads and uncles and aunts and children and grandchildren and nephews and nieces, and maybe a few old friends as well, and they were bustling along in this great commotion, and all heading for the gangplank at once.

"Come on, Clive," I hissed. "Now!"

We joined them. We squeezed and elbowed our way in and walked along with them to the first boarding card check at the bottom of the gangplank.

"Boarding cards. Can I see your boarding cards, please?"

"Dad's got them," we said.

"Just wait, children, while your father sorts out the boarding cards."

We kept walking. So did some of the children with the family.

On we went, up the gangplank.

"Hang on, children. Not so fast."

The other children ignored them. We ignored them. On we went. Up the gangplank. Heads down, feet determined, on and up. This was it now. Make or break. Get past the next check, we were in. If not, we were out. And in something else—trouble.

"Hey, you two!"

"Dad's got the tickets."

The man looked down toward the bottom of the gangplank where the big, extended family were still rummaging in their pockets and sorting out their boarding cards.

"Okay. Just wait here till they come up. Stand to the side there, so you're not in the way."

We did as he said. Stood to the side, just by the top of the gangplank. And then we sidled. Little by little, inch by inch. A sidle here, a sidle there. Another sidle. A sidle again. And each time a little bit farther away. And then:

"Okay, Clive. Go!"

And we were gone.

⚓

FIVE

RaT CLaSS

NOW me anD Clive were not total strangers to the insides of a cruise ship, and though we had not been on the *Mona Lisa* before, we had a pretty good idea of how it would be laid out.

Dad used to take us along on open days to see the boats he was working on, like I said. And he would tell us all about them, and explain just how they worked.

The *Mona Lisa* hadn't had an open day yet, but we had been on what was known as its sister ship (that is a similar ship in the same fleet and with the same owner). This was a boat called the *Da Vinci*. Apparently Da Vinci was the man who had painted the *Mona Lisa,* which must have taken him a long time as it was a very big boat indeed. Clive said he must have got through several cans of paint and quite a lot of brushes. He said it was a big job for one bloke to paint a boat that size and his arms must have been aching by the time he'd finished.

Most big cruise liners are laid out in the same way, and the general rule to remember is this: luxury at the top, rubbish at the bottom.

It's exactly the same as a town, really. All the good stuff is above ground level; all the other things, like the sewers, the gas pipes, the electricity cables, and the drains are all hidden away out of sight.

On a cruise liner, the most interesting things are on the upper deck levels. Here are the swimming pools and the gyms and the cinemas and the ball-rooms and the restaurants and the bars and the game rooms and the casino and the shopping arcades and everything else. Here, as well, are the biggest and the most expensive cabins, the first-class luxury and premium ones, which can cost an absolute fortune, even just for two weeks.

Sometimes people can spend as much as ten or even twenty-thousand pounds on a single holiday, so Dad told us. Twenty-thousand pounds! It was hard to imagine. It was probably more money than Clive would earn in his entire lifetime—even if he worked Saturdays as well.

Now the luxury cabins really are just that— luxurious. They have lots of space and big double beds and bathrooms with sunken baths and big pic-ture windows with great views of the sea. Next down from that are the "superior" cabins, which have smaller beds and maybe a porthole instead of a big picture window. Then there are standard outside cabins, which are smaller still. They have showers instead of bathtubs, and maybe bunk beds instead of ordinary ones. But at least they still have a little porthole and some natural daylight coming in.

Then you start to go down, and you start to get that sinking feeling. And as you go deeper down into the ship, you come to the tiny, most inexpensive cabins, which are right inside the ship and which have no portholes at all.

Here, in the cheapest, tiniest cabins, way down in the insides of the ship, there isn't room to swing a lobster, and you wouldn't know if it was day or night, except by looking at the clock, as there's never any daylight in here at all, even at high noon, though up on the deck the sun could be blistering the paintwork.

The other thing about the cheapest cabins (and it's something they usually forget to mention in the brochure when you're planning your holiday) is the noise.

The farther and farther you go down into the ship, the nearer and nearer you get to the engine. And the nearer you get to the engine, the louder it becomes. Up on the promenade deck, the engine may be no more than a faraway drone and a faint vibration, as the ship sails gracefully along.

Down in the smallest cabins, however, you can hear the thud of the engine and feel the tremor of it through the metal floor and walls.

But even the smallest and cheapest of the tourist cabins is better than any of the ones the ship's crew have to sleep in. (With the exception of the captain and the senior ships' officers, of course.)

Dad told us that the stewards' cabins were sometimes right above the engine room, or even right next to it, and you could hear it chugging and pounding all through the night. He said that you got used to it, and didn't notice it after a day or two. It was only when you got home and into your own bed and your ears stopped ringing that you once again appreciated what silence was, and how noisy it had been. It was also four to a cabin too, and some of the other stewards were pretty big on snoring. And not just snoring either. Other noises as well.

Anyway, as Clive and me had a rough idea of the *Mona Lisa's* layout, we knew that it was no use us looking for an empty cabin up on the top. There was no way that we were going to find a luxury cabin with two big double beds in it and picture windows with splendid views standing empty on the upper deck, with the door hanging open, and a sign on it saying "Welcome Clive and his brother. Just walk in and help yourselves."

No.

No. Nor was there much hope that we were going to find a cabin anywhere else waiting for us. Each cabin had its own key, and you only got the key for it on production of your ticket and your boarding card. And as Clive and me had neither tickets nor boarding cards, we weren't going to get any keys.

Our only hope was to go down. And down. And down. To see what we could find.

And that was where we went.

Now, in defense of the cheap and nasty cabins, I have to say that in some ways it didn't matter how small and cramped they were. Because all you had to do was sleep in them. You didn't have to do anything else. The rest of your trip you could spend up on the other decks, enjoying exactly the same facilities as all the other passengers—apart from maybe some special privileges that were for first class only.

And that was what I said to Clive as we walked on down from one deck to the next, looking for a place to leave our stuff.

"It's only to sleep in, Clive," I said. "We just need a cubbyhole to leave our stuff in and crash out in. The rest of the time we'll be off enjoying ourselves, sitting around the pool having long, cool drinks, going for swims, sunbathing on our deckchairs, and all sorts of stuff like that."

"And eating," Clive said.

"Yes, and eating. And then going for jogs around the deck."

"And then eating some more," Clive said.

"Yes. And then maybe going for a game of quoits, or using the on-deck tennis court for a game of tennis."

"And eating," Clive said.

Clive was very keen on eating.

"And drinking as well," he said.

He was keen on drinking too.

"But we'll be doing some sports too," I reminded him. "We won't just be slobbing around and making pigs of ourselves. And we'll be able to maybe go to the kids' club"—(every big liner had a kids' club on board)—"and we'll be able to do painting and making things and we'll be able to take up hobbies—"

"Like eating," Clive said.

"Shh!" I told him. "Someone coming. Duck down here!"

People had been milling around everywhere. But this was different. This was someone in a steward's uniform. And this was my greatest fear, that even though it was a huge, immense ship, that sooner or later Dad would run into us, or we would run into him. And then all heck and quite a bit of heck that hadn't yet been constructed would break loose.

Of course, Clive and me had known this from the word go. Yet, although it was an ever-present danger, it wasn't quite the risk you might have thought.

Dad was quite an experienced Senior Steward. This meant that usually he was put to work on the first-class cabins to keep the first-class passengers happy. So as long as we avoided the first-class areas, our chances of being discovered by him were greatly reduced.

The other thing in our favor was that even if Dad did see us, he simply might not recognize us.

Now you might think that this would be impossible. He was our dad, we were his sons, how

ALEX SHEARER

could he possibly not know who we were?

Well, there are two answers to that. One is dark glasses, and the other is this: you often don't see what you don't expect to.

As far as Dad knew, we were at Gran's. And if he were to walk past the swimming pool on the promenade deck, with his tray in his hand, and see a couple of boys stretched out on their deckchairs in their swimming shorts and with their sunglasses on, so what? He'd think nothing of it. We'd just be two more kids by the pool, that was all. And yes, he'd see us, but in another sense, he wouldn't see us at all. It wouldn't register who we were. And why should it? Because we couldn't possibly be there. It couldn't be me and Clive. We were somewhere else. So we weren't there. Even when we were.

We hid around a corner until the steward had gone past. It wasn't Dad anyway. It was a short, tubby steward with a waddly walk. His shoes squeaked, as if they were brand new. We stayed hidden until the squeaking had gone, and then we moved on.

Nobody seemed very interested in us—not that we were complaining (although Clive is very fond of attention). There were great commotions going on everywhere, with people bustling and barging down narrow corridors, saying "Excuse me," and "Beg your pardon," and smiling nicely, even though what they probably really wanted to do was to scream "Get out of the flipping way before I flatten you with this suitcase!"

Stewards and porters were delivering passengers' big luggage to their cabin doors.

"When do we sail?" I heard someone ask. "Are we on time?"

"In just under an hour, I believe, madam," the porter said, and he carried a big red suitcase into a cabin. The lady gave him a tip on his way out.

"Thank you."

"Thank *you*, ma'am!"

And off he went.

Dad got his tips at the end of the cruise, as I said earlier, and he always did his best to see that all his passengers enjoyed themselves. He didn't just do it for the tips though, I don't think. He'd have done it even if there weren't any. He just likes people to be happy. And even if you were in one of the smallest cabins and didn't have any money to spare for tips, it wouldn't have mattered to Dad. He'd have treated you just the same as the poshest and richest first-class passenger.

If he'd thought it would have helped you enjoy your cruise, he'd probably have given *you* tips, if he'd had the money to spare.

Down we went, deeper and down. Big ships are amazing places, their insides seem to go down to the very depths of the ocean. You half expect to discover Neptune living there, holding his trident, or open a door to find a cabin with a couple of mermaids in it, sitting combing their hair with razor shells and weaving diving suits out of seaweed.

Down we went. Clive started to complain. It's

only ever a matter of time before Clive starts complaining. Clive and complaining are a bit like cows and cowpats—wherever one goes the other just seems to follow.

"Are we there yet?" he said.

"How do I know?" I told him. "How can we be there yet when we don't even know where we're going?"

"My shoulders are getting sore," Clive said. "The straps of my backpack are digging in."

"It'll make a man of you," I told him.

"I don't want to be a man yet," Clive said. "I want my share of being a boy first."

"Well you've certainly had your share of being a wimp," I said.

He muttered something then. I didn't quite hear what he said. I think it was something about somebody having a face like an octopus's bum. But I didn't catch who he was talking about.

Down again. Our feet rattled on the steps. We seemed to have left the cabin decks way behind now. There wasn't so much hustle and bustle, and there was a smell in the air of engine oil.

A man passed us. He was wearing blue overalls and had a greasy face.

"You lost, boys?"

"Em, I think so."

"Here you are, I'll show you the way."

He led us back up the steps we had just come down. When we got to the top, we thanked him, dawdled along till he had gone on his way, then went back down again.

We came to a sort of crossroads. A sign said "No Admittance Beyond This Point. Crew Only." We turned and looked down the next corridor. It seemed dark and dingy, but there was no "Crew Only" sign here. Instead it read "Storage and Services."

"Come on, Clive," I said. "We'll try down here."

We went on down the corridor and down even more steps. We were just above the engine-room level by now. You could feel the great engine idling away down under your feet. It was like being on top of a dragon's lair, you could feel all that massive power and strength half asleep beneath you, having a little snooze, but about to wake at any moment.

"This looks to me like rat class," Clive said as we went down the corridor.

And I didn't say as much, but I agreed with him. It did indeed look very much like rat class. We were now entering behind-the-scenes territory. No glamour and luxury here. Just rooms with old mops in them, and containers full of cleaning fluid, with brown cardboard boxes full of spare cutlery and plates. There were boxes of spare duvets, extra blankets, pillows still in their cellophane packaging.

We opened one cabin door and looked inside. The lights didn't work. Clive took his flashlight from the side pocket of his backpack and turned it on. Boxes again. But boxes with a difference.

They were covered in dust. That was a good sign. Covered in dust. It meant that people didn't come down here often, not if they didn't disturb the dust. It meant that down here were all the "just in case" things, all the spares and all the replacements.

We closed the door and went on down the corridor. It grew narrower, as if we were coming to one of the pointed ends of the ship. The front of the ship is called the bows and the back is called the stern, the left bit when you're facing forward toward the bows is called port, and the right bit is called starboard.

I don't know why sailors use these funny expressions. I don't know why they don't just say left and right and front and back, it would make things a whole lot easier. But they seem to like things as they are—difficult.

Anyway, judging from the way the corridor was narrowing and the way it was tapering, I thought we had to be at the pointed end, the front, and way down below the water line.

You wouldn't get any cabins with portholes down here. For a start there would be nothing to look at but fish. And if the glass broke, all the water would come in, and the ship would sink.

We came to the end of the corridor. There was nowhere else to go other than back. Only wait. There was one door left, one last door for us to try.

I pushed it open. Clive beamed his flashlight inside. I found a light switch and turned it on.

"Wow!"

We'd got lucky. The room was full up with exactly what we needed.

It was full of beds. Loads of them. It was a big storeroom, the size of three or four cabins knocked together, and it was full of spare beds and mattresses. There must have been dozens of them, all stacked one on top of the other and secured into place with webbing straps, presumably to stop them from sliding and crashing around if the weather got bad.

(*If?* Did I say *if* the weather got bad? I think what I really meant was *when*. But I'd maybe better tell you about that later.)

"Wow!"

"Well, what do you think?"

"Wow!" Clive said again. He seems to think that a lot. Most of Clive's thoughts seem to fit into one word.

"Wow!"

"It's perfect, Clive," I said. "It's got everything we need. We can set a couple of beds up. Then we can go back to that other cabin and get some sheets and pillows and blankets. It's perfect. We've got our own big roomy cabin, and no one will know we're here. By the look of it, no one hardly ever comes down to this part of the ship. What more could we ask for?"

Then Clive found something wrong with it.

"Where's the toilet?" he said.

"Toilet?"

"Where's the toilet?"

"You'll have to go upstairs," I said. "Before we come down for the night."

"What if I wake up and need to go?"

"You'll have to hold on."

"What if I can't hold on?"

"You'll just have to."

"But what if I can't?"

"You'll have to do it in the sea."

"How?"

"You'll have to do it out the window."

"There isn't a window. You said we were under the water line. You said if there was a window all the water would come in and we'd drown. You said you didn't fancy that."

"I don't much fancy all the water coming in because you're doing wees in here either, Clive."

"Maybe we could find a potty?"

"Yes, okay. We'll find something."

In the end we found an empty five-gallon drum standing in one of the other storage cabins.

"Only for emergencies," I said.

"Will it be big enough?" Clive asked. "I mean, it's a long trip."

I found a container of disinfectant.

"If you have to use it, pour this in afterward."

"Okay."

"But it's emergencies only, Clive. Got it?"

"Yes, all right."

And for the time being, it seemed to be the best I could do.

"Come on then," I said. "Let's get a couple of beds set up then. By the time we've done that, it'll almost be time to set sail. We'll want to be up on deck for that, for the big send-off, won't we?"

"Definitely," Clive said. "We won't want to miss that. That's one of the best bits."

And it was too, in my opinion. There was something really special about a great, big, beautiful ship just setting off on its voyage. The way it almost seemed at the mercy of the tugboats, as they pulled this seemingly helpless giant away from the harbor walls.

Then once it had cleared the harbor and the tugs cast it off, it came into its own. Now it had space and deep water. The great engines cleared their throats and then growled like lions for a moment and then settled back down to purr like cats.

And there all the people would be who had come to say good-bye, all lining the harbor wall. There they would all be, all waving their arms off, and calling good-bye. And even though it was just a cruise trip, and not a journey of no return, there would still be people crying, as if they might never see their loved ones again.

It was funny that. I'd felt the same, seeing Dad off sometimes. There was something about the ship sailing away and all the people on the deck all getting farther and farther away. It brought a lump to your throat somehow. It made you think of meetings and partings. It made you think of times gone by. It made you think of people you might never see again.

It made me think of Mum.

It made me think of how we'd never see her. As

ALEX SHEARER

if she'd sailed away on a ship of no return, and would sail the seas forever, along with all the other people who could never come home again.

I would always stop and watch the ships as they sailed away. They made me think of time going by. They made me think of growing up one day and getting old.

They would leave a white railroad on the blue water. And after a while, that would be gone too, and the ship would just be a speck on the horizon, and they were all off to have adventures, and you were left behind. And that gave you a pang too—of envy maybe, and sometimes, a sort of sadness that you were left behind and not going with them.

Only this time it was going to be different. This time Clive and me wouldn't be standing on the harbor wall, shouting our good-byes and waving our arms, as other people went off to have adventures and to see the world.

This time, we were going with them.

This time, we would be on board.

We finished setting the beds up, left our backpacks on them, and headed for the cabin door to go up on deck.

"You know what we are, Clive?" I said.

"Yes," he said. "We're brothers."

"That's right," I said. "But we're more than that too. You know what we are now, Clive? You know what else we are? The moment the ship leaves harbor, you know what we'll be?"

"What?"

"Stowaways, Clive," I said. "We'll be stow-aways."

"Wow," Clive said. "In fact, double wow."

And for once, I just had to agree with him.

SIX

SAIL AWAY

UP ON DECK there were people everywhere, milling around, leaning on the rail, peering at the other people on the dock wall who were waiting to see them off.

We didn't have too much trouble getting back up through the warren of corridors and turnings which led to our rat-class cabin down at the bottom of the ship. There was so much to-ing and fro-ing and coming and going that what difference did a couple of children on their own make? We might have been with anyone. We might have been let out on the loose by our parents for a little while.

I told Clive that if any of the crew looked at us suspiciously, we ought to pretend that we were with someone, and follow behind them closely, with a sort of sullen and resentful air, as if we had big grudges against them and there were things we could never forgive them for. That way they would think the people we were following were our parents. But we had to be consistent, I said. It was no use us following different people every five minutes, as that would raise suspicion. So we had to latch on to people who might be our parents and stick with them for a time.

We had a good look around when we got up on deck, to see who we might like to have as parents for a while. To be honest, none of the grown-ups there looked particularly suitable, not even the ones who had children with them. But after a while we spotted a pleasant-looking couple who looked about the right age and who didn't seem to have any children. (At least not with them, maybe they had left them at home. A lot of grown-ups like to leave their children at home when they go off on holiday. There is a boy at our school called Donald Davis and his parents left him at home when they went on holiday. They went off to Australia for six months and somehow forgot to tell him they were going, as it must somehow have slipped their minds.)

Anyway, we found this couple and we went and stood behind them as the sailors down on the dockside undid the ropes that were tying the boat up and we got underway.

Getting underway is a nautical term—that is to say, it has to do with boats and the sea. When a plane gets going, it takes off. But when a boat gets going, it gets underway.

ALEX SHEARER

And so that was what we did, we got underway. Two tugboats pulled the cruise liner out of the docks. There were people waving and music playing and someone let off a few fireworks as well. And then the captain gave a great big toot on the funnel—well, it was more of a blast than a toot really. It sent the shudders up your legs and the shivers down your spine. Then he gave another toot, and it was just like the ship's funnel was a great big nose and the captain was giving it a great big blow on this enormous but invisible hankie.

On the second toot, the tow ropes attaching us to the two tugboats were cast off, and then we were on our way, sailing under our own power, and the captain turned the front of the boat around and we headed for the wide, open sea. It was terrific. It was even better than ice cream.

The captain's voice came over the loudspeaker then. It was a bit crackly and distorted, but we could still make out what he was saying. He welcomed us aboard and hoped we'd be comfortable, then he told us about the weather forecast and how fast we'd be sailing and where we were heading (we were supposed to know that already, of course, only Clive and me didn't) and how long it would be until our first port of call. (That means places where you stop for a while so that you can go on land.)

He also said something about there being a safety drill some time, and then he wished us a happy trip and said he would be talking to us again soon, and then he signed off and concentrated on driving the boat.

Another voice came over the loudspeaker then. It was a lady this time, who said she was the Cruise Manager and Activities Director and that there was lots to do from the word go and that we were to visit her at her desk on the upper deck at any time and she would be pleased to give us all the help and information we needed.

Then other people came on to the loudspeaker and there was even more chat. But Clive and me were fed up with it by then and decided to go exploring.

We had a good old wander about all over everywhere then. Any bit of the ship that we were allowed to go into, we went into it. It was massive. There was something new around every corner. We looked into the gym and the shops and everywhere. We peered into a couple of the restaurants too. You couldn't go in yet, as they weren't serving anything, but there was the smell of cooking getting under-way, and there were great big silver tureens sitting on white-clothed tables, just waiting to be filled up with chips.

"I feel hungry," Clive said.

But then Clive always felt hungry, so there was nothing new in that.

Up on the sundeck we found the swimming pools. There were two of them, both as blue as a summer sky. Only there wasn't much sun about just then, in fact the sky was gray and cloudy, there was a slight chill in the air and the promise of rain.

It was too cold for outdoor swimming pools.

"It'll probably warm up in a day or two, Clive," I said. "Once we get farther south."

"I hope so," Clive said. "I'd hate to think I'd brought my swimming trunks for nothing."

We sat down on a couple of deck chairs then, and watched the trail of silver foam that the ship's propeller left behind in the sea. We watched as the coastline got farther away, and suddenly, for a moment there, I felt cold and a bit lonely, and I wished I hadn't stowed away and that I'd stayed at home.

And I think Clive maybe felt the same, because he said, "I wonder what Gran's doing?"

I looked at my watch. It was late afternoon. It was hours since we had left home with Dad and pretended to go to Gran's and had got on the bus instead. I couldn't think what had happened to lunchtime. We somehow must have missed it. Clive wasn't the only one who was hungry, I was getting pretty peckish too.

"I suppose Gran will be making a pot of tea, and Granddad will be out in the garden, pottering."

He did a lot of pottering, Granddad did. He spent most of the day pottering. He was a sort of pottering expert.

But anyway, as we sat there on our deck chairs, me and Clive together, it suddenly seemed as though we had a long, long day ahead of us to fill, and many more, long days after that.

What made it so bad was that, although we were on the cruise, we weren't really part of it. We weren't part of a big group, we didn't have any friends, we didn't have anyone apart from Dad—and we couldn't let him see us, or he'd have gone bananas.

Funny that. We'd sneaked on board to be with Dad, and now we didn't dare let him see us.

"You know," Clive said, "I wish—I wish . . ."

Then he trailed off and never finished what he was saying.

"You wish what, Clive?" I said. "Wish what?"

"Oh nothing," he said. "I just wish—well, you know—just wish, that's all."

And I sort of knew what he meant, or I thought I did. Because I kind of wished it too.

Then, "Look!" Clive said, pulling me by the sleeve and pointing with his finger. "Look! There!"

I thought that maybe he'd seen dolphins. But no, it was Dad. He was down on the deck below us, walking along toward the first-class cabins, carrying a silver tray in his hand. Sitting on the tray was a bottle of champagne in an ice bucket, and next to it were two glasses. And next to the two glasses was a single red rose in a little vase.

"Look," Clive said. "It's him."

We got out of the deck chairs and crawled to the rail and laid flat out so that we could look down on Dad without being seen by him, not even if he looked up.

He looked incredibly professional. His trousers were black and his jacket was white and he wore a shirt with a turned-up collar and a red bow tie.

"It must be someone's honeymoon," Clive said.

And I thought, from the look of the champagne bottle and the rose, that he was probably right. Dad came to a cabin door, checked the number against a little piece of paper on the tray, tapped on the door, and then vanished from sight.

While he was delivering the champagne, a tiny old lady, all covered in jewels, emerged from another of the first-class cabins. She was so old and frail that she needed a walking stick to get about. I think what made it even harder for her to walk was the weight of all the jewelry.

She tottered along toward the deck rail.

"She's decided to end it all," Clive whispered. "She's decided it's not worth it any more and she's too old and life's not worth living as it's simply not worth it getting up in the mornings and it's too much trouble."

"How do you know, Clive?" I said.

"I've seen it a hundred times before," he said. But I couldn't quite see how he worked that out. Clive had never seen as much as one rich old lady before, never mind a hundred.

"Yes," he went on, "she'll be chucking herself off over the side any moment now, I should think. It's why she's got all her jewelry on, so that she'll sink faster. Oh yes. Old ladies are always going on cruises and chucking themselves overboard. It's always happening. It happens so often it's not even news anymore."

Well, the old lady didn't seem to have any intention of chucking herself off anywhere, no matter what Clive might say. She just leaned on the rail and admired the view, and she smiled a nice old smile, the kind old ladies have when they stare off into the middle distance and think about when they were girls.

Dad came out of the cabin then. His tray was empty and he had it tucked under his arm. The cabin door clicked shut behind him. The old lady turned around at the sound.

"John!"

(That was our dad's name.)

"Mrs. Dominics. How nice to see you again."

"Oh, I'd never miss a trip on the *Mona Lisa*."

"Well, so how are you? Can I get you anything?"

"No, no. Not at the moment. I'm all right for now."

We lay there and watched and listened as Dad and old Mrs. Dominics had a bit of a chat.

It's funny to watch someone you know, when they don't know you're there. Because you know them, you can tell when they're putting it on, when they're false, and when they're pretending. You can tell when they're just doing it for the sake of appearances, when they're saying things they wouldn't normally say and talking to people they wouldn't normally talk to and putting on false voices or pretending to laugh at things that aren't really funny.

Only it wasn't like that. Dad and Mrs.

Dominics just stood there and chatted away quite ordinarily. And it wasn't like Dad was young and she was old, like she was rich and Dad wasn't, like she was the passenger and he was the steward. It was like they were just two people who sort of liked each other and who were having a chat because they were interested in each other and the things around them.

I felt sort of proud then. I felt sort of proud of Dad. I felt that he was a nice person.

"Well, I'd better get on then," he said, after a few minutes.

"Yes, I mustn't keep you."

"Ring if you need anything, Mrs. Dominics."

"Thank you, John. I will."

Then Dad suddenly looked up toward us—

No. It wasn't us. It was the sky.

"Might rain later, I'm afraid. But we'll have the good weather in a day or two. Right. Must press on."

And off he went.

Mrs. Dominics stayed by the deck rail a while longer, looking down at the sea as it slapped against the side of the boat.

"She'll do it now," Clive whispered. "Just you wait. She'll climb up on to the top of the rail—a quick flash of big, baggy bloomers, and she'll be gone."

But I couldn't see it. I didn't think Mrs. Dominics could have climbed to the top of the deck rail even if she'd had a ladder. I don't think she could even have managed it with a stair lift.

Clive seemed a bit disappointed.

"Maybe she's going to have dinner first," he said. "Then when she's had one good last meal, she'll jump off when it's dark. In fact—"

And his face screwed up with one of his thoughtful, helpful sort of expressions.

"In fact—do you think she might like a push? Because I could always go down there and give her a bit of help. You know—the old heave-ho. Just grab her legs and tip her over. It wouldn't be any trouble."

"Clive," I said. "If people want to jump off ships with all their jewelry on, that's up to them. But don't you go helping them. Not even if they ask. Don't you ever go grabbing them by the ankles and tipping them over, not even if they plead with you to do it and offer you money. Promise?"

"Oh, all right then," Clive said. "I suppose."

Then there was this loud rumbling sound, like the captain had given another blast on the foghorn. But I realized the noise wasn't coming from the foghorn at all. It was Clive's stomach.

"I'm starving," he said. "When's dinner, do you think?"

"Come on," I said. "Let's find out."

NOW, IF THere'S one thing you have to know about cruises and cruise ships, it's that there's a lot of eating involved. An awful lot of eating. In fact, some people don't go for the cruising at all. They are only there for the eating and that is all they do. In fact, some people bring special pairs of trousers with them. Or at least several pairs in different sizes. There is the before pair and there is the after pair, and what separates the before pair from the after pair is the eating. The before pair are always much, much smaller than the after pair. It is never the other way around. Nobody ever gets smaller on cruise ships, they just get bigger—especially around the middle.

As well as the eating, there is drinking too. And the great thing about all this eating and drinking is that it is all free, or rather, it has all been paid for in advance. It is all included in your ticket. So once you have paid for your cruise ticket, you can eat and drink to your heart's content, and to your stomach's content (or even your stomach's discontent) as well.

Now, there is not so much eating on the first day of the voyage, but once you are properly out on the high seas, it is full steam eating ahead.

Eating starts with breakfast, which can go on for hours. Breakfast might start at eight and go on till eleven, so you can have one breakfast at say, half-past eight, go for a stroll around the deck, work up a bit more of an appetite and come back for another breakfast.

In fact, on a good day, when Clive put his mind to it, he could even eat three breakfasts before ten o'clock and still have room for another one. His record for breakfasts was six. But even Clive had to admit that this was three breakfasts too many. He had to make up for it by easing off on his lunches that day and by only having two dinners.

Now after breakfast there was mid-morning coffee, if you wanted it, along with biscuits and cake. Then at twelve noon, lo and behold, it was lunchtime, and this went on until half-past two.

About an hour after lunch, once the plates had been cleared away and fresh tablecloths put on the tables, there was afternoon tea with scones, jam and cream, along with more cakes and shortbread.

Things took a turn for the worse then, and I know you will find this hard to believe, but once afternoon tea was over, *there was a full hour and a half with nothing to eat!*

Yes, I know. You are doubtless wondering how we survived and how we managed to struggle on through these times of deprivation and hardship. Well, to be honest, it wasn't strictly true that there was nothing to eat. If you were still hungry, you could always get a snack at the poolside bar, or order a sandwich to be brought to your cabin (or to your sun lounger) by one of the stewards.

Anyway, round about half past six in the evening, first sittings for dinner started. If first sittings didn't fill you up, you could go back at eight o'clock and be there for second sittings.

Although there were not officially any third sittings, as there were several restaurants on board, all you had to do was to go from one to the other and you could end up having so many sittings that you could hardly stand up.

After dinner there was quite often music and

entertainment and dancing. (Not that me and Clive did any dancing as he doesn't know how, and anyway, I wouldn't have wanted to dance with Clive as he is not a girl, and even if he had been a girl, I still wouldn't have wanted to dance with him, as Clive would not have made a very nice girl in my opinion and would probably have been the kind of girl who did handstands in a skirt without first checking that she had put her knickers on.)

Anyway, after you had been entertained and done some dancing, and had no doubt burned loads of calories off, if you were still feeling peckish, you could pop into the Galley for a bite of supper and a light snack.

Clive was always fond of a light snack. His particular favorite was a loaf of French bread, cut in half, with lashings of peanut butter, jam, a banana and chocolate and hazelnut spread. He often had one before we went to our cabin for the night as he said it helped him sleep. It didn't help me sleep though, as I had to listen to his stomach. I thought at first that it was the sounds of digestion, but then I realized that his stomach was crying for help.

I also said to Clive that if what he had for supper was a light snack, then what did a heavy snack look like?

He said I didn't want to know as I would have nightmares about it.

But the really odd thing about Clive was that he never got any fatter. After eight days of all this eating, he was just as skinny as ever (apart from his bum, of course). Other people were already on to wearing their special trousers, but Clive still looked like an undernourished beanpole, with ribs like xylophones.

"You must have worms, Clive," I told him.

"No, I haven't," he said. "I've never had worms. But if you'll tell me which of the restaurants has got them on the menu, I might give them a try tomorrow."

There's not much you can do with a brother like that.

Anyway, on that first day on board the boat, we realized as we sat on the sundeck, looking at the gray sky, that we ought to be getting ourselves down to the restaurant and getting something to eat.

"Do you think we'll have to get dressed up for dinner?" Clive said.

"I don't know," I said. "Come on. Let's find out."

So we left the sundeck and headed for the upper deck where the Cruise Activities Director had her desk and her office and where all the information was posted up.

While I stood there reading the information board, I noticed a group of people nearby standing in line, filling forms in and waiting their turns.

"Get your Cruise Card here," a notice announced.

"Oi!" Clive said. (He is not much good on politeness and manners. An elbow and "Oi" is generally the best Clive can do.) "Oi! What's a Cruise Card?"

I didn't know, but as luck would have it, it was explained on the information board in front of me. I read it out.

"On board the ship, Clive," I said, "we operate a cashless accounting system. This means that money is not used on board for purchases from the shops. Just apply for a Cruise Card, giving your name and cabin number. You may then use your Cruise Card as an ordinary credit card. Kindly settle up your account when presented with your bill at the end of your voyage."

And I thought no more about it. I just stood there reading about all the things there were to do on board, about all the organized activities and what have you and about the special things for children.

Apparently there were two children's clubs on board. The was the Little Pirates Club (for really small children) and then there was the Big Bosun's Club, which Clive and me could join.

I turned around to tell him about it.

"Here, Clive," I said. "Do you fancy being a Big Bosun? Shall we join up? I mean, it would make a nice change for you to be a Big Bosun. Your usual specialty is more along the lines of Big Bogies, isn't it, Clive—Clive?"

He wasn't there. I'd lost him. He'd disappeared. He'd maybe gone off and wandered back on deck, and fallen overboard, with all his jewelry.

And then I spotted him. He was at the front of the queue for Cruise Cards. I don't know how he'd got there so quickly; either he'd wriggled up to the front, or he'd been at it with the elbows again.

"I'd like a Cruise Card, please," I heard him saying. I wanted to stop him, but what could I do? I couldn't drag him away in full view of everyone. We were supposed to be keeping low profiles, not attracting major attention to ourselves.

The lady in charge of handing out Cruise Cards gave Clive a look.

"I can only give you a Cruise Card with the consent of your parents. Which class cabin do you have?"

"We're in rat class," Clive said.

The lady gave him another hard stare—extra hard.

"I beg your pardon?"

"That is—standard class," Clive said.

"Cabin number?"

"Don't have one."

She gave him even harder stares.

"You don't have one?"

"No. There was a number on the door, but when we slammed it, it fell off."

It was time to intervene. I barged up to the front of the desk and pretended to be breathless.

"Oh, there you are! Come along now. Dad sent me to find you. We have to get ready for dinner. Come along."

And I got him by the arm and dragged him away.

"What did you do that for?" Clive demanded

when we were safely out of earshot. "I nearly had a Cruise Card then. Think of the stuff we could have bought. We could have run up massive debts—absolutely enormous."

"Yes, Clive, and how would you have paid the bill at the end of the trip?"

"Oh," he said. "I never thought of that."

And that's Clive all over. That's why he was born five minutes after I was.

"Come on," I said. "We'll have to get back to the cabin. You have to look smart for dinner. It says that a certain standard of dress is required."

"I'm not wearing a dress," Clive said. "Not for anybody."

"They mean clothes. We'll need to put our good trousers on. Come on."

So back down we went to our cabin.

We almost didn't find it.

Once down inside the ship, it was an absolute maze. You half expected to see the Phantom of the Opera, or somebody like that, suddenly appearing out of nowhere in his cloak and mask.

Getting to and from the cabin was also the most dangerous part for us. It was when we were most likely to be caught or discovered. We were going into areas that were out of bounds for passengers, and although we could make excuses the first few times we were caught down there, saying we were lost and things like that, nobody was going to believe us more than twice. They were going to get suspicious and start asking questions.

"Listen, Clive," I said. "We're going to have to ration our comings and goings to and from the cabin. We'll have to try and keep the journeys down to two a day for the rest of the cruise if we can— morning and night—going there to sleep, then getting back up in the morning."

"Okay," he said. And then, "Someone coming!"

We could hear their footsteps clanking toward us from somewhere ahead. It had to be a member of the crew.

"Quick," I said. "In here."

I opened the nearest door and we ducked inside.

The footsteps got nearer, then they passed.

"Look," Clive said. "Look where we are."

We were in a small four-berth cabin. By the look of it all the berths were occupied. The cabin was small and cramped, airless and hot.

"Look," Clive said. "It's us."

And it was. It was Dad's bunk. And on the little table next to it, he had set up the photograph, the one in the frame, the one he always took with him, the one of me and Clive, back when we were small—me and Clive and Mum.

"I just want to sit on his bed," Clive said.

And he went and sat on Dad's bed. Which seemed a funny thing to do. I didn't sit on Dad's bed. But I did touch his pillow.

For luck, I suppose. Then we had to go.

We managed to get to our cabin down in rat class without meeting anyone else. We changed into the good clothes we had brought and then, after a little rest on our beds, we decided it was time to go up to the restaurant for dinner, as we were both starving by then.

We found another way back up by taking a left instead of a right this time when we came to the corridor crossroads. This way seemed much better, as we passed fewer cabins, so there was less chance of us running into somebody who might ask awkward questions.

"Do you think they'll wonder in the restaurant why we don't have a grown-up with us?" Clive said.

I'd been worrying about the same thing.

"They might," I said.

"So what'll we do?"

"Maybe we can find someone to sit with."

"Won't they wonder?"

"Maybe. We'll just have to tell them something."

"What?"

"We'll think of something. Come on. My stomach thinks my teeth have forgotten how to chew."

We decided to eat in the Promenade Restaurant as the information board said that in the Promenade Restaurant it was buffets every night.

Buffets were better for us than sit-down jobs where they bring it all to you, as Clive is not very good at sit-down jobs unless it is big jobs, which are the only kind of sit-down jobs that Clive has any talent for. Buffets were better because in buffets you help yourself and Clive was very good at helping himself and always had been.

The other problem with the sit-down, waiter and waitress service restaurants on board was that you had to book a table, and in doing so you had to give your name and cabin number. Well, we could hardly do that and tell them that we were in cabin number 1 down in rat class. And also, even if we did manage to get a table in sit-down jobs, the waiter would have thought it very odd that we were on our own, just two children with no grown-ups.

People are very suspicious of children with no grown-ups. I don't know why that should be. As nobody seems suspicious of grown-ups with no children.

The other danger of the sit-down jobs was that we might run into Dad.

So we headed for the buffet in the Promenade Restaurant where we could help ourselves. Clive is very good at helping himself and he headed straight for the puddings. I told him that this made us look suspicious and as if we were children on our own, as no grown-up would let their children start with puddings.

Clive saw the error of his ways and settled for a plate of starters. So we piled our plates of starters up and looked around for a table and for somebody to sit with.

And then we saw somebody—the old lady with all the jewelry, Mrs. Dominics, sitting all by herself.

I gave Clive a nudge.

ALEX SHEARER

"Best behavior," I said.

He gave me a look like he wasn't all that sure what best behavior was.

"Pretend it's like the vicar's come around," I said.

"You mean hide the beer?" Clive said.

"Shh!" I told him. "Now be polite, do what I do, and let me do the talking."

I led the way over to Mrs. Dominics's table and gave a small bow.

Clive gave a small bow too.

I think she might have wondered if we were Japanese.

"Good evening," I said. "I wonder if we might share your table."

I thought she was going to say no, but she didn't. She gave us a big smile and said, "That would be delightful, boys. I'd be very glad of your company. Please, do sit down."

"Thank you," I said. And we both bowed again and then sat down nicely.

"Pass the salt," Clive said.

I kicked him under the table.

"Pass the salt *please* would you be so kind?" he said, which was much better.

Mrs. Dominics passed him the salt. She had so much jewelry on she jangled when she moved.

"Are you boys here on your own?"

"Yes," Clive said.

"No," I corrected him. "That is, yes and no. We're here with someone—"

"Our dad," Clive said.

"Only—"

"He's feeling seasick," Clive said.

"That's right," I said. "And he doesn't feel like eating. He's down in the cabin at the moment, feeling rather ill—"

"With his head in a bucket," Clive added, for effect.

"Oh dear," Mrs. Dominics said. "That is a shame. I hope he feels better soon. It will ruin his holiday otherwise."

"Quite so," I said. "But he told us to come up and to get something to eat. So here we are."

"Eating," Clive explained.

"Yes," Mrs. Dominics nodded. "So I can see. Well, you dig in."

So there we were. Me and Clive and Mrs. Dominics, and soon we were getting on like a house on fire. She was quite a nice old lady really, even if she did jingle a bit with all the jewelry. Clive kindly offered to go and get her second course from the buffet for her, if she'd tell him what she wanted, as he could see that her legs were going and it was a bit of a walk.

She smiled and thanked him and sent him off with her order, and later on I went and got her pudding for her. She asked us lots of questions, but it was only to make conversation; she wasn't being nosy. And she told us that she went on cruises two or three times a year and she loved them more than anything and they stopped her feeling lonely—and sometimes they even stopped her feeling old too.

She asked us where our cabin was, and Clive went and told her we were traveling rat class before I could stop him. She said she hadn't heard of rat class before, and Clive said she didn't want to hear about it either. But I stepped in and said he was joking and it was just his sense of humor, and that we had a very nice cabin, quite a big one, with loads of beds in it.

And Mrs. Dominics said we must be very well off then to afford such a big cabin, and I said that we did all right with the little we had (which was sort of true) but I still reckoned she had more money than we did. (Though I kept that bit to myself.)

Anyway, after the puddings, Mrs. Dominics said it had been a long, tiring day and she thought she might turn in.

"Turn into what?" Clive said, so I had to kick him under the table again.

We helped Mrs. Dominics to her feet and got her aboard her walking stick and off she went in the direction of the first-class cabins.

One of the waiters came by to clear our table.

"Your gran gone off to bed?" he asked.

"Sorry?"

"The old lady with you? I assume it's your gran. She off to bed?"

"Oh, yes. Yes," I said. "She's a bit tired, yes."

And me and Clive sort of smiled at each other. We had our alibi. We had our reason for being on board. Everyone would think that Mrs. Dominics was our gran now, and that we were with her.

Well, if that was what they wanted to think, let them think it.

At least we had an identity now and a reason for being on board.

We were safe.

Sort of.

We thought.

AFTER DINNER IT was getting late, so we went and looked at the moon. It looked as big and bright as a huge silver button in the sky. We weren't the only ones looking at it either. There were other people, wrapped up against the chill of the night, all staring up at the sky. The wind was soft and the night was clear and there must have been a million stars. And there wasn't any land anywhere now, just acres and acres of sea. As far as you looked there was water, which had turned black in the night. And sometimes there were the distant twinkling lights of other ships, or the sound of a foghorn—though there wasn't any fog—booming in from far away.

It was nice to be on a cruise.

"Come on, Clive," I said. "Let's find a bathroom and brush our teeth and get to bed. It's a long day tomorrow, with lots to do. Maybe we can join the Bosun's Club. Do you want to be a Bosun's Boy, Clive?"

"I'm not sure," he said. "It sounds a bit dodgy to me. What do you have to do? There's no planks and hammocks involved, is there?"

"It's the children's activity club," I said. "Do you want to join?"

"Might do," he said. "I'll have to see."

We could hear music and singing coming from one of the decks below.

"It's the cabaret," Clive said. "Shall we go and have a look?"

"Tomorrow," I said. "I'm tired."

"Oh, all right. Tomorrow then."

I had brought our toothbrushes with us and a small tube of toothpaste. So we went and found a bathroom and had a brush and a spit and a bit of a wash—as best we could—and then we used the loo and then we headed for our cabin down in rat class.

The corridors were quiet and empty. It was a good time for us, as most of the crew were busy working.

We got to our cabin without any trouble and we got ready for bed.

"Tell me a story," Clive said.

But I didn't know any stories.

"Tell me a story you've read then," he said. "About the sea."

But the only story that I'd read about the sea that I could remember was *Treasure Island.* So I told him a bit about that, about Jim Hawkins and Long John Silver and the buried treasure and Blind Pugh and mad Ben Gunn and the pirates.

"Pirates," Clive said. "Do you think *we'll* meet any pirates?"

"Don't be stupid," I said. "You don't get

pirates. Not these days. Pirates are only from long ago. You don't get pirates with eye patches and parrots and wooden legs and skulls and crossbones and cutlasses and daggers and all that. Not these days. Pirates have all gone."

I said.

With every confidence.

But then what did I know?

And anyway, soon, I was fast asleep.

ALEX SHEARER

· seven ·

⚓

ALARM BELLS

WHEN I WOKE up again, I didn't know if it was morning or night. As we didn't have a porthole to let the light in, it seemed like nighttime all day long in our cabin.

Clive had said that we should get a big can opener and put our own porthole in the wall, but I reminded him that several gallons of salty water and a lot of large fish would come in through the hole along with the daylight, and that wouldn't be much fun.

I couldn't find the light switch and so I groped around on the floor for Clive's flashlight. Clive was snoring, as usual. Clive sometimes even snores when he's still awake, which can be very off-putting.

I found the flashlight and put it on so as to see my watch. It was getting on for nine o'clock, and we'd had quite a good long sleep. I thought I'd maybe better wake Clive up, knowing that he wouldn't want to miss his breakfast.

When it comes to breakfast, Clive likes to start the day right, usually with a couple of bowls of cereal and a loaf or two of toast with a jar of jam spread over them.

I went to give Clive a bit of a shake to wake him, thinking that if a bit of a shake didn't do it, I could maybe hit him over the head with my pillow a few times instead.

But then something saved me the trouble of trying to wake Clive up—all heck broke loose like a whole lot of ball bearings rolling everywhere.

Now that has always seemed like a funny expression to me—all heck breaking loose. It sounds like "all heck" is a creature in a prison somewhere, which suddenly breaks out and escapes. Well, judging from the noise, that is exactly what it had done.

Suddenly from somewhere bells were ringing and sirens were screaming and I could hear a voice shouting "Action stations! Action stations! All crew and passengers on deck. Repeat, all crew and passengers on deck!"

Now, you might wonder how we could hear this as we didn't have a loudspeaker in our room. It wasn't a proper cabin, after all, just a storage room for the spare beds, way down in rat class.

Well, it was funny but we could hear all sorts of things down in our little hidey-hole. Even whispers sometimes, from miles and miles away, way up on deck.

ALEX SHEARER

The sounds all seemed to travel down the ventilation pipe or the air duct, and sometimes people's voices would seem so close to you that you'd even turn round, thinking that someone was at your shoulder.

"Steward, may I have a cold drink, please," you might hear, just as if the person was right next to you.

Sometimes we could even hear people arguing. One night, when we were falling asleep, a voice came down the ventilation pipe saying, "I hate you. I wish I'd never come on this holiday with you. You're nothing but a pain in the neck and I'm never going on holiday with you ever again."

Clive thought it was me who had been speaking, and he sat up in bed and said, "Well I wish I'd never come on this holiday with you either. You're nothing but a big pain in the bum. And you stink as well."

But then he realized that it wasn't me at all, and we just had to sit there, listening to this man and this lady having a terrible row down the ventilation pipe. It was quite embarrassing really and not the sort of thing that Clive should have been listening to and I told him to put his fingers in his ears, but he wouldn't. This man and this lady were having a terrible row and it was like being forced to eavesdrop. You felt that you were spying on them.

Finally Clive went and shouted up the air pipe. "Can't you two be quiet! There's people down here in rat class trying to sleep."

Well, I don't know if they heard him or not, but the argument stopped shortly after that.

Other times we would hear spooky whisperings, like mice having conversations, or the murmurings of ghosts.

"This ship's haunted," Clive said one night.

"Ships don't get haunted," I told him. "It's houses that get haunted, not ships."

"It is," Clive insisted. "Listen. It's ghosts. You listen properly and you'll hear."

So we kept very quiet and listened as intently as we could to what the ghosts were saying, and we finally made out that one was saying to the other, "Did you remember to pack my seasickness tablets, dear?"

Which proved it couldn't be ghosts, to my mind. But Clive said it didn't prove anything and it could still be ghosts, as ghosts suffered from seasickness all the time and that was a well-known fact. Only if it was a well-known fact, it wasn't one that I knew anything about, so it couldn't have been as well-known as he thought.

Anyway, all heck broke loose, as I said. Clive woke instantly and sat up in his bed.

"What's that?" he said. "It's a siren, isn't it? It's the emergency siren! We're sinking! We're sinking!"

"No we're not!"

"Yes we are!" Clive said. And he leaped out of bed and pulled his clothes on. "We're sinking! We're going down with all hands—and all legs too," he added as an afterthought. "We must have struck an iceberg."

"How can we have struck an iceberg, Clive?" I said. "Icebergs are in the Arctic. We're nowhere near the Arctic!"

"It's a rogue iceberg," Clive said. "It's probably broken free from the pack and come down south to get us. It's an iceberg with our names on!"

"Don't be stupid," I said. "It's just the emergency drill. It said at the information desk that they had to have an emergency lifeboat drill within twenty-four hours of setting sail. It's just pretend, that's all. Like a fire drill at school."

We could hear footsteps running everywhere, with doors clanging and hatches banging.

"What if it's not a drill though?" Clive said. "What if it's for real? And we get stuck down here and—"

He had a point, I supposed. There was a faint possibility that it might have been for real. The noise outside had stopped now too. It was creepily silent, like we were the only people left on the boat.

"Oh, all right then. Come on," I said. "I suppose we'd better go out."

So I quickly got dressed too, and we made our way upstairs-ships, which is a sort of nautical expression for going up on deck.

We poked our heads around a door and looked out on to the promenade deck. There were people everywhere, hundreds of them, passengers and crew, all milling around in an orderly sort of chaos.

"Ah! Two more! Okay boys, what's your cabin number?"

A sailor with a clipboard had nabbed us as soon as we came out on deck.

"Ahh—well—"

"Can't remember, eh? Don't worry. It's only for ten minutes. You'll find your mum and dad later. Go and grab a life jacket and assemble by assembly station five."

He pointed us toward a big box of life jackets. We grabbed one each and put it on, and then joined a crowd of people who were standing around a steward who was by a part of the deck with a big number five on it, painted on a plate riveted to the wall.

"Okay," the steward said. "Remember now, in the event of an emergency, this is where you come to. This will be our meeting point, and this is the lifeboat we'll be taking, right here."

He indicated a big lifeboat, which was mounted next to us on a sort of crane, which would lower it into the water—which seemed a long, long way below.

"Any questions?" he asked.

"Yes," Clive said.

Typical. Clive would go and draw attention to himself.

"Yes, son?" the steward said.

"What if the lifeboat gets stuck halfway down?" Clive said. "We'll just be left dangling there."

"Don't worry, son," the steward said. "That won't happen."

ALEX SHEARER

"Yes, but what if it does?" Clive went on. "I wouldn't want to be left dangling."

"Shut up, Clive," I said.

Fortunately the captain came along then and the steward had to give him his attention.

"Everything in order, steward?"

"All present and correct, sir."

"Good. Carry on. We'll be finished in a moment."

And the captain moved on to inspect the other muster points, where other people were mustering.

I looked up to the first-class deck. I could just make Dad out. He was mustering too. He seemed to be in charge of a group of first-class passengers and he was helping Mrs. Dominics to put her life jacket on, as she didn't seem up to it on her own.

I almost shouted and waved to him.

But then I remembered.

The captain reappeared, just a short way from Dad. He went up to talk to him, nodded his head, and moved on.

I knew that his name was Captain Connerton, from the information board. And what made his surname so interesting was that it was the same as ours and not many people have it. But I didn't think we were related. He looked very much like a captain, too, in his dark uniform, white hat, and gold braid. He also had a bushy beard. In fact, it was so bushy that when Clive spotted it, he said we should have stowed away in the captain's beard instead. He said it looked like there was plenty of room in it for stowaways, in fact he probably had a few things living in there already.

When the captain was satisfied that the emergency drill had been done properly and that everyone knew what they were supposed to do in the event of a real emergency, he gave the order to go back to normal.

By that time, however, Clive had gone and blown his life jacket up. I'd thought that I'd heard some huffing and puffing, but I'd been too interested in other things to realize that it was Clive.

He had just got hold of the tube in the top of the life jacket and had gone on puffing until he had turned into the Abominable Fat Boy. He looked enormous. And as if that wasn't bad enough, as soon as the captain announced over the loudspeaker that the exercise was over, Clive must have forgotten he still had his life jacket on, and in his hurry to go inside and get to the restaurant for breakfast before anyone else, he went and got stuck in the door.

"Clive," I hissed. "What are you doing?"

"I'm stuck," he said.

"Let some air out," I told him.

"What?" he said. "Fart?"

"No, let some air out of your life jacket!"

A crowd of people was building up now behind Clive, all wanting to get inside and to get at the breakfast.

"What's the hold-up?"

"What's the delay?"

"What's going on?"

"I think there's some sort of fat boy stuck in the door."

Clive was wiggling and squirming by now, trying to either go forward or to go back, but the only effect it all had was to make him more stuck than ever.

"Come on, Clive," I said. "Deflate yourself."

"How?"

"I don't know. Pull one of those toggles!"

He did.

Big mistake.

He pulled the wrong toggle. Instead of letting the air out, there was a big whoosh as he released compressed air from the emergency inflation cartridge in the jacket.

He didn't just look like the Abominable Fat Boy any more, he looked like the Abominable Fat Boy and the Abominable Pizza Boy all rolled into one. And he was twice as stuck as before.

"What's happening here? I thought the drill was over! What's stopping us getting inside?"

"I've not had any breakfast yet, you know."

"No, neither have I."

"If we don't get in there soon, it'll all have gone."

Well, it wouldn't all have gone, but that didn't matter. All it needed was the *rumor* that it had all gone, and people started pushing and shoving more than ever.

"Excuse me," I yelled. "We've got a problem here. There are other doors, you know."

But they didn't want to know about other doors. They had their hearts set on this one. This was the nearest door and behind it lay the shortest route to the restaurant.

By now Clive was well and truly wedged into the door like a great big sponge cake. He sort of looked like a kind of massive beach ball, with a big fat middle, and little stick-like arms and legs poking out.

"Help!" he said. "What am I going to do? I can't spend the rest of the trip stuck in a door."

"Pull another toggle," I said. "One of them's got to deflate it."

"I can't reach them."

"Hold on."

I'd had an idea. I got my hand into Clive's trouser pocket.

"Oi!" he said. "What are you doing?"

"It's for your own good, Clive," I said.

"That's what you told me about the syrup of figs!" he protested. "I was on the toilet for weeks."

"It's all right! I've got it."

It was Clive's Swiss army knife. He'd always said it would come in useful one day, and now was its chance to prove its worth.

"Okay, Clive. Hold on. Have you out of this predicament any second."

"What are you doing? It won't hurt, will it?"

I pried the little attachment open. You know the one. The sort of short spiky one. I don't know what it's really supposed to be for, but I knew what it was for right then.

ALEX SHEARER

It was for putting holes in life jackets.

I drew back the knife and jabbed at Clive's middle.

Kerrrumpheeespewwthhhhjjjjhusssshhhhhsooooo!

It was a hard noise to describe really, and that is about the best I can do. It was that kind of noise you get when you let go of a balloon you have just blown up and it flies all round the room like a dying bluebottle and then comes to a stop, hanging from the lamp shade.

Which was more or less what happened to Clive.

The life jacket sort of exploded, and the blast sent him shooting down the corridor. He did a couple of somersaults and came to rest by a fire extinguisher and a bucket of sand.

I ran after him.

"Clive, Clive!" I said. "Are you all right?"

But he was fine. He just had to sit down for a moment in the bucket of sand while he dusted himself off and caught his breath, while I gathered up the bits of the life jacket and put them in the bin.

"I hope that doesn't leave them a life jacket short," Clive said.

"No, I shouldn't think so," I said. "I'm sure they'll have plenty of spares."

While Clive was catching his breath, a steward came over. We'd seen him a couple of times before and had christened him Lumpy, as he had a lumpy bald head. We'd both got the impression that he didn't like us very much.

"You two!" he said. "I want a word with you!"

"Us?" Clive said, all innocent. (Clive can be very good at all innocence when he wants to be. I think that this is true of a lot of criminals.)

"I saw what happened just then," Lumpy said. "And don't you two go thinking that just because you're here with your rich, posh granny that you can get away with misbehaving yourselves. Those life jackets aren't toys, you know."

"It was an accident," Clive said. "Sorry."

"Well it had better not happen again," Lumpy told him. "Or I'll be having a word with your gran. And if she's not able to keep you in order, I'll be having a word with the captain. And it might interest you to know that there's a brig on board this ship."

"A brig?"

"A little one-room prison, for keeping unruly passengers in, just in case they should decide to turn nasty. Now, you don't want to spend the rest of your cruise clapped in irons in the brig, do you?"

"I don't know," Clive said. "Is it better than rat class?"

"Rats!" Lumpy said. "Are you implying this boat has got rats?"

"I thought all ships had a few rats."

"Not this one," Lumpy said. "This ship is so clean it doesn't even have spiders! And just you remember it. And just you also remember that having a rich, posh gran cuts no ice with me. So you behave yourselves."

And off he went.

ALEX SHEARER

"Come on, Clive," I said. "Let's go and get some breakfast. You'll feel better when you've had a bucket of cereal and a couple of tubs of yogurt and a few dozen hard-boiled eggs."

"You're right," Clive said. "And I might have a biscuit as well."

"Why not," I said. "After all, we are on our holidays."

So we went off to the restaurant for breakfast, and very good it was too.

After breakfast we went for a stroll on the deck. We'd traveled quite a long way during the night. We were much farther south now, and already the weather was starting to get much warmer.

"I really think I'm getting my sea legs, Clive," I said.

"What are they?" Clive asked.

"You know," I explained. "When you get used to being on a boat and sort of get the feel for it."

"Ah, right. Then I'm getting my sea legs too," Clive said. "And my sea arms. And my sea elbows. And—"

But before he could say any more, a hand reached out from behind us, and it landed on my shoulder.

And I heard a voice say the words I had been dreading—the very words I had been dreading since the moment we had come on board the ship. They were the words which all stowaways must dread, which all stowaways must have dreaded throughout history, since stowing away first began.

"Hey! Just a minute!" the voice said. "What are you doing here? I know you, don't I?"

I would have run, but where was there to run to? For a second I even considered jumping overboard. First I could have pushed Clive over, and then I could have jumped in after him.

But it was a long, long way down. And even if we had survived the jump, the cold or the sharks or something nasty would probably have got us. Or, just as bad, the ship would have sailed on, leaving us alone in the water, to eventually die of exposure or to drown.

I slowly turned to face our accuser.

Was it over already? Our great adventure, our stowaway, our holiday? What would happen to us? Would we be clapped in irons? Put in the brig? And what would Dad say?

That was the worst bit.

What *would* Dad say? Would he believe us? Would he understand that we'd only done it to be with him and near him and not to be left behind all the time any more? Would he understand? Would he understand that we had good reasons? That it was hard for us to be left behind and not to have a mum? That all we wanted was to be with him really and for the three of us to be together? Would he understand?

Would he forgive us?

So I looked to see who the hand and the voice belonged to, to see who it was, who it was who would turn us over to the captain and to justice.

ALEX SHEARER

"Hello!" the voice said. "I thought it was you two. Well, well, well! Fancy meeting you here! Are you enjoying yourselves? I'm having a great time."

I was staring at the face of Swanker Watson.

⚓

An Invitation

AND HE WASN'T alone, either. Standing just behind him was his mother, Mrs. Swanker Watson, his dad, Mr. Swanker Watson, and next to them, the other little Swanker Watsons. All it needed to complete the picture was Fido Swanker Watson, Tiddles Swanker Watson, and Flopsy Swanker Watson, Swanker Watson's rabbit.

But fortunately he had left his pets at home.

"What a surprise," Swanker Watson said. (Though from where we were standing, it was more of a shock than a surprise.) "Fancy meeting you two here out on the ocean wave!"

"Who is it, Angus?" Mrs. Swanker Watson asked, peering at me and Clive over the tops of her sunglasses like we were unusual forms of marine life, and possibly distantly related to the prawn family or to clams.

"It's boys I go to school with," Swanker told her. "You know, they are ordinary boys, the kind of boys I am supposed to rub shoulders with to give me the common touch."

Clive and me shared a look of some surprise. Swanker Watson had never rubbed his shoulders with me as far as I could remember, nor Clive either. In fact, had he come up and suggested that we go off somewhere so as to rub our shoulders together, Clive would probably have clocked him.

"Oh, how frightfully nice," Mrs. Swanker Watson said. Then she put her hand out for us to shake. "So you're ordinary boys, are you?" she said. "How awfully nice to meet you."

So me and Clive had to wipe our hands on our sweatshirts and then give Mrs. Swanker Watson's hand a shake. It was all a bit like getting hold of a limp spring onion, or maybe a dandelion stalk.

"The pleasure's all ours," Clive said. (He had got that out of a film.)

"Not at all," Mrs. Swanker Watson said, though you could tell that really she agreed with him.

Now Clive and me knew that we had a big problem on our hands here with the sudden appearance of the Swanker Watsons, and the main problem was this.

Although Swanker Watson knew that our dad was a sailor, we had never truly told Swanker what our dad did.

Now, I don't want you thinking that we were

ashamed of Dad, because we weren't, not at all. Quite the contrary. Me and Clive were dead proud of Dad because he was popular and friendly and good at his job and he liked to help people and everyone liked him.

But that's not good enough for some people. For some people, that doesn't count for anything. All that matters to them is have you got a posh-sounding job title and do you make a lot of money.

Well, Dad didn't really have either of those things.

Now, while that didn't matter to us, at the same time we didn't want other people taking a dim view of our dad or swanking on about how important their dads were, and how rich they were, and that sort of thing.

We knew that Swanker Watson's dad was what is known as a captain of industry, which is a sort of rich and successful businessman. Swanker Watson knew that our dad was a sailor, and that he was away a lot on cruises, but he didn't know exactly what he did.

So one day, when he asked us what kind of a sailor Dad was exactly, Clive went and opened his big mouth and said, "He's the captain, actually, of the ship."

Swanker Watson had been pretty impressed by that, and it looked for a moment that Clive had outswanked him on all sides.

"Oh gosh," Swanker Watson said. (He said a lot of things like that. He must have got it from home. They must have all sat around the table in the evenings saying "Oh gosh!" and practicing other sorts of swanky expressions like that.

"Oh gosh, a captain! Of a great ocean-going cruise liner?"

"Yes, that's right," Clive had gone on, despite me frantically signaling him to shut up. "He started off paddling a canoe, and then he bought a rowing boat, and that was so successful, he got himself a pedal boat. After that our dad just went on to captain bigger and bigger boats. First it was a paddle steamer, then it was a cross-channel ferry, then it was an oil tanker, and now it's a cruise liner."

"Gosh," Swanker Watson had said. And I don't think he knew what else to say, as he had never been so completely outswanked before and he just didn't know what to do about it. "Well that must be great," he said. "Having a dad who's captain of a cruise liner. Do you ever get to go on trips with him?"

"Not yet," Clive had said, "but he's going to take us one day. And of course, being captain, he has a top-notch cabin, with hot and cold running water, and a big fridge with jars of Smarties in it."

"Gosh," Swanker Watson had said. "I wish my dad was a ship's captain. But he isn't. He's only rich, I'm afraid."

"Never mind," Clive had said. "No one can have everything."

And he'd given Swanker a comforting pat on the shoulder to make him feel better. It wasn't quite rubbing shoulders, but at least it was a step on the way.

ALEX SHEARER

And now we were on a boat where it so happened that the captain had the same surname as we did.

CLIVE FINISHED SHAKING Mrs. Swanker Watson's hand and gave it back to her.

"So what are you doing here?" Swanker said.

"Eh—what are *you* doing here?" I said by way of reply, needing time to think.

"We're on holiday," Swanker said. (Well, I didn't think he was there to paint the funnel.) "We've never been on a cruise before. We normally just stay at first-class and deluxe hotels in exotic and faraway places, but you get so bored with doing that every year, don't you?"

"Yes," Clive nodded. "You certainly do. Sometimes I think that if I see another coconut tree or another palm-fringed beach, I'll go mad."

Mrs. Swanker Watson looked at us over her sunglasses.

"You boys aren't here on your own, are you?"

"Oh no," I said. "Good heavens. My, no. They don't let children on to cruise ships on their own. Oh deary me no. That would be highly dangerous, wouldn't it, Clive?"

"Very," he said.

"Why, if we were here on our own," I said, "we might have accidents, and fall overboard—"

"Or eat too much and get stomachaches," Clive interrupted.

"Yes," I nodded. "And that would never do. The very idea!"

"So who are you here with?" Mrs. Swanker Watson persisted.

(And it struck me then that Mrs. Swanker Watson had a kind of steely resolve in her, that she wasn't a woman to be fobbed off, and that she would go on probing and asking questions until she got the answers she wanted. And maybe that was how she had got to be a Swanker in the first place.)

"We're here—" I began. "We're here—that is—we're here—"

"Yes, we're here," Clive nodded. "We're definitely here."

"And not only are we here, we're here with—"

"With—"

"With—"

"Well?" Mrs. Swanker Watson demanded. "Who? Who are you here with?"

"With—"

"Our dad."

What else could we have said?

And then Swanker Watson landed us in it. He turned to his mum, Mrs. Swanker Watson, and he said: "Their dad's the captain, you know."

Well, you've never seen a person's behavior change so quickly. Suddenly, instead of being all haughty and disdainful, Mrs. Swanker Watson became as nice as pie—as nice as two pies, apple pies, with cream.

"Oh, your father's the captain! Well, how nice! Well, just fancy!"

She turned to Swanker and gave him a black look.

"I thought you said that these were just ordinary boys, Angus," she reprimanded him.

"Oh, we are," Clive said. "We're dead ordinary. Even though our dad's the captain of this great massive cruise liner with hundreds of people at his beck and call, we still just carry on like we're ordinary and we're happy to rub shoulders with anyone. That's why he sends us to ordinary school, you see, so as we won't get proud and stuck up and think we're special."

"Oh, absolutely," Mrs. Swanker Watson said. "Quite so. We have the same philosophy. And what's more, it saves on school fees."

Now, while Mrs. Swanker Watson was doing all this talking, Mr. Swanker Watson was just standing there not saying a word and holding the baby—Baby Swanker Watson—in his arms. They also had a nanny with them—Nanny Swanker Watson—and she was trying to control Swanker Watson's sister—Brat Swanker Watson—who was trying to climb up the deck rail and fall into the sea.

I got the sort of feeling that even though Mr. Swanker Watson was a captain of industry, he wasn't a captain of family. When it came to home life, Mrs. Swanker Watson seemed to be in charge.

"Well I'm so delighted that Angus is making such good friends with the right sort of boys," Mrs. Swanker Watson said. "I expect that being the captain's children, you'll be in first-class cabins, like us."

"Em, not exactly," I said. "But we do have our own special private quarters."

"Of course," she said. "You would have."

"Yes," I said. "The only thing is that while we're on board, Dad likes to pretend that he doesn't know us."

"Oh?" Mrs. Swanker Watson said. "And why is that?"

"Various reasons," I told her. "He doesn't like people to think there's favoritism going on for one thing, and it also interferes with his job to an extent. And then there's always the risk of kidnapping."

"Oh yes. I see. Yes."

"Because if two kids like us got napped and held to ransom, we would be worth a lot of money."

"Quite."

"So basically, we pretend that we don't know each other. If we happen to see him on deck, we might say, Hello, Dad out of the corners of our mouths. But the arrangement is that all he does back is to pretend to look surprised, as if he doesn't know who we are and has never seen us before."

"Oh, how clever," Mrs. Swanker said.

"So we'd appreciate it," I said, "if you wouldn't go telling anyone that us and the captain are related, as it would only lead to jealousy and bad feeling on board, and we wouldn't want to be responsible for any mutinies, or for the crew turning ugly. Though to be quite honest with you, some of them are pretty ugly already. Have you seen the one with the shaved head?"

"No. But you can rely on our discretion," Mrs. Swanker Watson said.

And then, as luck would have it, the captain came along.

He was on a sort of grand tour of the boat. He went around once a day, waving and smiling at everyone, and saying hello, and trying to make sure that they were enjoying themselves and that they didn't have any complaints.

"Oh, here's your father now," Mrs. Swanker Watson said to us. "Oh yes," she exclaimed, as he got nearer, accompanied by a couple of ship's offi-cers, "I can see the family resemblance. You're both the spitting image of him."

"But he's got a beard, dear," Mr. Swanker Watson pointed out.

"I know that, dear," Mrs. Swanker Watson said (rather sharply too, I thought). "But if you have the imagination to picture these two boys with thick bushy beards and big moustaches, then you would be able to tell straightaway that they are the very images of their father."

"Ah, yes, right—if you say so, dear. Yes."

I looked at Clive and tried to imagine him with a beard. I then realized something that I had never thought of before—all people with beards look as if they're related. They all look as if they're members of the Beard family.

The captain and the ship's officers were only a few meters away now. They moved along the deck, nodding and smiling and saying hello to all the passengers, making sure they didn't miss anyone. They were all so friendly to everybody, you half suspected they were selling something.

They came to the Swanker Watsons and said hello, and then they came to us.

"Hello, Dad," Clive said, bold as brass.

The captain gave him a look.

"I'm sorry?" he said.

"Oh, sorry. I beg your pardon," Clive said. "What I meant to say was Hello, Captain."

And then he gave the captain a great big enormous wink as he said it. Just like they were both conspirators. It was such a big wink, it was practically the size of an eye patch.

The captain seemed a bit flustered.

"Yes, quite so," he said. "And are you boys enjoying yourselves?"

"Definitely," Clive said. "We'd particularly like to compliment you on the service. Especially on one of your stewards. The Senior Steward, in first class. We're very impressed with him and think he's one of the best stewards you've got."

"Really? Well, thank you for that information. If you'll excuse me now, I must press on."

"Right you are, Daddyo—that is, I mean— *Captain*."

And Clive winked at him again.

And then the captain was gone on his way along the deck.

When he had gone, Mrs. Swanker Watson looked at us and said, "He's so discreet, isn't he? So calm and in control. Such a figure of authority. You boys must be so proud of your father."

"We are," I said. "We are."

And that was true.

"You must come and dine with us tonight," Mrs. Swanker Watson said. "It'll be company for Angus. He hasn't had a chance to make many friends since we moved down from Aberdeen."

"Oh," Clive said. "I didn't know he was an Aberdeen Angus."

"Anyway," Mrs. Swanker said, "we'll reserve a table in the first-class dining room. For tonight?"

I could feel myself panicking.

"Yes, that would be nice, only—"

"We've nothing to wear," Clive said. "We forgot to bring our formal clothes."

"Oh, not to worry. As long as you look reasonably presentable, no one will mind. I don't think they're expecting children to wear dinner jackets and cummerbunds."

(Clive didn't know what a cummerbund was. I had to explain to him later that it was a bit like a tuba, only you played it with a spoon.)

"Yes, you must come and have dinner with us," Mrs. Swanker Watson insisted. "I won't take no for an answer. Eight o'clock it is then. And that's settled. Well, come along dear, shall we go to the pool? What about you, Angus? Would you like to stay with your friends?"

We hoped he'd say no, but he didn't. Swanker Watson voted to stay with us—his mates—the captain's kids.

It wasn't as bad as we thought it might be

though, and we spent the rest of the morning down by the pool and playing games on deck.

We had a go at this game called "quoits" which involved throwing a rubber ring around, a bit like a sort of heavy Frisbee with a hole in it, only Clive threw it so hard he chucked it over the side. He was normally quite an ace at Frisbee, so I felt he was doing it deliberately.

Then we had a few games of tennis, only Clive kept knocking the balls over the side. The man in charge of the rackets seemed to think that Clive was doing that deliberately too, and he warned him that if he knocked any more tennis balls over into the sea, he'd have to go and fetch them.

We went and had a swim in the pool then. The water was quite warm really and they gave you a towel. Then we lay in the sun and just idled the time away and we said to each other that this is the life. And it was really, for a while. I mean, you wouldn't have wanted to do it forever, but it was nice just then.

It seemed funny to have a swimming pool on a boat. Because there was the water, with the boat sitting in it, and there was the boat, and there was the water in the boat, and us lying next to it.

After sunbathing for a while, Clive and me went off to get some lunch and Swanker went to join the other Swankers and we promised to see him later.

After some more sunbathing to let our food go down, me and Clive investigated the Bosun's Club and we signed up for a couple of activities. They had archery and they had football and treasure hunts around the boat and quizzes and all sorts of things.

I was quite good at archery but Clive accidentally fired all his arrows over the side and so they made him use one with a bit of string tied to it. One end of the bit of string was attached to the arrow and the other bit was tied to Clive's leg so that he couldn't lose it—the arrow that is, not his leg. But he ended up losing the bit of string and then tried to fire the arrow up so it would fall down inside the funnel. But Big Billy Bosun, who was in charge of the club, said that was how people lost their eyeballs and he took Clive's bow away and gave him a piece of paper to do origami with instead. Clive spent ages doing origami and he designed this new thing himself which he said was called "Crumpled Ball of Paper," but it just looked like a crumpled ball of paper to me.

Of course, all the while that we were enjoying ourselves, there was this sort of lurking shadow, which at any moment could cross the sun.

The fear of discovery.

That's the trouble with being a stowaway. No matter what you do, no matter where you are, even in your happiest moments, always, in the back of your mind is the fear of being unmasked as an impostor.

In some ways it's like being a bank robber on the run. Here you are, in a new place, with a new identity, but you're always worried that somebody

will give the game away, or you'll suddenly be recognized.

Two things frightened us the most. The first
was that Dad would see us. The second thing—and
this was when we were most at danger—was that we
would be caught going to or from our cabin down in
rat class.

The rest of the time we were okay really. There
are so many people on board a big cruise liner that
even if they do notice you, they all think that you
are with somebody else.

Some of the crew thought that we were Mrs.
Dominics's grandsons. Others probably thought
that we were with the Swanker Watsons. And the
Swanker Watsons thought that we were with the
captain. But I really don't think that anybody suspected for a moment that we were stowaways. The
only person to give us shifty looks from time to time
was Lumpy, the steward with the bald, lumpy head.

This is the thing about stowing away. You are
most at risk when getting on or getting off the boat.
The bit in between is just a matter of keeping your
head down and getting on with things.

But, yes, there was Dad.

Clive and me felt more and more guilty as
time went by.

"What if Dad sees us, Clive?"

"Why should he? He's in first class all the
time."

"But say he did? It wouldn't get him into
bother, would it? Us having sneaked on board?"

"No, of course not—would it?"

And we did wonder if maybe we shouldn't have stayed at home. Because we didn't want to get our dad into trouble. That was the last thing we would ever have wanted to do.

But it was too late for thoughts of staying at home. We were there now. We just had to see the voyage through, all the way back to where we had started from, and then—we would just have to see.

A couple of times Dad walked right past us when we were at the pool. He didn't even see us. I suppose we'd got slight suntans by then, and we had our sunglasses on, and he just didn't recognize us at all.

He was too busy anyway, saying hello to people, and making sure they weren't running out of anything.

He was nice to everyone and most people were nice right back. But some people up in first class were quite rude sometimes. We heard one man getting all upset with Dad and going on saying, "There's no ice in this drink! I asked for ice! Are you deaf?"

Clive wanted to go over and kick the man up the backside, but I didn't think that was a good idea. Dad just stayed as polite as ever though, and he just calmly apologized and said the barman must have made a mistake and he took the drink away and brought the man another one.

And he didn't even thank Dad for it.

How could people be so rude? And so rich too?

You needed a lot of money to travel in first class, and there this man was, with all this money, and he was rude to our dad.

Why does having a lot of money entitle you to be rude to people?

I don't think it does.

And yet there was old Mrs. Dominics too, all dripping with jewelry and expensive watches. She must have been one of the richest people on the whole ship, and yet she was the nicest, politest, kindest person you would have wished to meet.

I thought that was strange really, the way that being rich makes some people think that they can be rude and ill-mannered and a bit of a bully, and yet other people have loads of money and are ever so kind.

Maybe it isn't the money and being rich at all. Maybe it's just the people.

About an hour after the incident with the drink, Clive wandered over to where the rude man was lying on his sun lounger and he accidentally tipped half a bucket of iced water over him.

The man wasn't very happy about it, but as Clive said, accidents do happen.

Later in the afternoon, we met up with Swanker Watson again and we had a game of hide and seek. But the boat was so big and there were so many places to hide that I had to give up looking for Clive, and he turned up an hour later, by which time me and Swanker were back lounging at the pool.

"Are you going on the trip on Tuesday?" Swanker asked.

Clive and me looked blank.

"Trip? What trip?"

"We're docking then," Swanker said. "It's our first port of call. We're going on the trip to see the ruins. Are you coming?"

"Eh, we might," I said. "We'll see tomorrow—it depends . . ."

"They're great ruins, apparently," Swanker said. "Hundreds of years old. We're going to see them."

"Right."

"You ought to sign up soon if you want to go. Well, I'd better go back to the cabin now," Swanker said. "See you at eight."

Eight.

Oh yes.

Eight o'clock in the first-class restaurant and dinner with the Swankers.

When Swanker had gone, I looked at Clive.

"What are we going to do?" I said. "If we don't go, it'll look suspicious. If we do go, we might run into Dad."

But Clive didn't seem worried at all.

"No we won't," he said. "Dad's a steward, not a waiter. He won't be working in the restaurant. He doesn't take the food to the tables. He works on deck and takes things to and from people's cabins and what have you. And anyway—look."

He pointed.

There was Dad, we could see him clearly on the first-class deck. He was talking to another steward, as if he was handing things over to him now.

We had tried to figure out Dad's working hours several times to see if we could avoid his work shifts. But his working day seemed completely irregular. He appeared to get hardly any sleep and to be working all the time.

But now it seemed as if he was going off duty.

"We'll be all right, see," Clive said. "He looks like he's going off duty. He'll probably be asleep for the next eight hours and won't be anywhere near first class at all."

"Okay," I said. "I suppose. Come on then. Give him a few minutes then we'd better sneak down to rat class and change into our best clothes. I just hope Mrs. Swanker Watson keeps it a secret about us being the captain's children, that's all. Or we're going to be in deep trouble. Deep, deep trouble. Deep-fried trouble, and no mistake."

But Clive didn't seem that bothered at the prospect of deep-fried trouble. I sometimes had the feeling that Clive was rather fond of trouble, and that deep-fried trouble was his favorite.

NINE

DINNER

TO BE QUITE HONEST, when it came to Clive's best trousers and to Clive's worst trousers, there was not a lot to choose between them.

Clive seemed to have the knack of turning everything into the same shade of dirt. You know how it is with the jam-jar of water that you use for cleaning your paintbrushes, and how sooner or later it always goes to a muddy brown or gray color? Well Clive's trousers were like that.

Even if you had given Clive a pair of bright purple trousers with pink cuffs and orange stripes down the side, they would still have ended up a muddy brown color.

Because of this, Dad had decided to buy Clive things that were muddy brown to start with. That way they would still look new, no matter how muddy and brown he got them.

We hadn't brought a lot of clothes with us for the trip, just the few that we could carry in our backpacks. We had realized that we might need something smart, however, and so had packed a good pair of trousers each and a shirt.

I had also brought enough pants to have a fresh pair every day. But Clive had only brought two pairs. He had said that he would wear one and wash one, and then when the washed ones were dry, he would change them around. That way he would always have a clean pair on and would have another pair in the wash.

But it didn't work out like that. He just wore the same pants all the time.

When I said he ought to change his pants, he said he couldn't as he had nowhere to wash them. So I said why didn't he wear the clean pair then, but he said he was keeping them for an emergency.

In the end I persuaded him to put on his clean pair and to wash the other pair in a sink in one of the bathrooms on the promenade deck. He then wanted to know how he was going to get them dry, so I told him to wave them over the side, only they fell off his finger and dropped into the sea. Some poor shark probably got its head stuck in them, and swam around like that until it died.

So then I had to give him a pair of my pants to make up for it, which left me a pair short. Also, the next time Clive washed his pants, he refused to try and dry them on deck as it was too risky. So he brought them back down to our cabin in rat class and he found a bit of string for a washing line and he tied it across the cabin and hung his pants on it.

The only trouble was that I was wakened during the night by Clive's pants dripping on my head. I don't know if you have ever been woken up by a pair of wet pants when you are fast asleep, but it isn't very nice. Also I didn't think it very fair that Clive's pants should be dripping on my head, when by rights, if they were going to drip on anyone's head, they should have been dripping on his.

So I made Clive swap beds around so that he was under the wet pants, to see how he liked it. The only trouble was that by then all the dripping had stopped, so he never got woken up at all.

But anyway, that was just an illustration of the kind of trouble that I had with Clive and his pants. I also had some difficulty with Clive and his socks, but I shan't go into details.

So anyway, we got changed and did our best to smarten up for dinner in the first-class restaurant with the Swanker Watsons. We didn't have a mirror in our cabin and so had to rely on each other for criticisms. Clive told me that I looked all right, but I didn't trust him, and when we got up to the bathroom I went and had a look at myself in the mirror, which was just as well, as I had a big black sooty mark on my nose which made me look like a teddy bear.

But before we went up, I gave Clive a bit of a lecture.

"We're going to have to be on our best behavior tonight, Clive," I said. "We could easily give the game away otherwise, and then not only will we be in trouble, Dad will be too. And you don't want Dad to be in trouble, do you?"

"No," Clive said.

And I think he meant it.

"Okay," I said. "Come on. And remember to cut your potatoes with your knife. No bashing them with your spoon like you usually do and pretending that they are boiled eggs and trying to cut the tops off. We've had that joke once too often, Clive, and it isn't funny any more."

"They won't have seen it," Clive said.

"And they won't want to see it either. Now come on."

Clive looked around our makeshift cabin in rat class. It did look a bit depressing, I have to admit.

"I peered into the window of one of the big cabins earlier on," Clive said. "And they've got televisions and comfy sofas and everything in there."

"I know, Clive," I said. "But we'll just have to make the best of it."

Then he had a bright idea.

"I know," he said. "Maybe we could ask for an upgrade."

I almost strangled him with his wet pants then and there.

"Clive! How can we go to the Cruise Director's office and ask for an upgrade when we're flipping stowaways! We shouldn't even be here!"

"I suppose," he said. "But it seems a shame, if they've got an empty cabin, that they can't give it to us."

We headed for the door. But as we did, I heard a voice. I stopped. It wasn't Clive's voice. It was someone else's, and it seemed to be coming—

Clive had heard it too.

"What's that?" he said.

"Shh! Listen."

The sound was coming down the ventilation tube. There were two voices. One of them I was sure I had heard before, only I couldn't put a face to it. The other was new to me.

"Well, she seems absolutely loaded to me," one of the voices said—the one I hadn't heard before. "Have you seen her? She's dripping with the stuff. That necklace alone must be worth fifty thousand, and as for the bracelets—"

"Yeah," the other voice said. "And she's not the only one. Have you seen the others? The amount of stuff these passengers have got with them—gold watches, jewelry, cash, you name it. You wonder why they didn't leave their valuables at home."

"Probably afraid," the other voice said, "that if they left it all at home, it might get pinched."

And then the two of them sort of cackled, as if it was the funniest joke ever. And then their voices faded, as they must have walked away from wherever the ventilation pipe came out up on deck.

Clive scratched his ear.

"What was that about?"

"Search me," I said. "I don't suppose there's any way of knowing where on deck this ventilation pipe comes out?"

"Shouldn't think so," Clive said. "There're millions of pipes."

"Oh well, come on. Let's go, or we'll be late for dinner. And remember Clive—best behavior."

"Of course," Clive said. "As if there could be anything else."

WE GOT TO THE first-class dining-room at eight o'clock exactly. The headwaiter was at the door, standing at a desk with a book on it with people's names in. He spoke with a bit of a French accent. But I don't really think he was French at all. Because that last time I'd heard him speak, he had been talking to another waiter as we passed them in a corridor, and he sounded like he came from Liverpool.

"Good evening, messieurs," he said. "*Bon soir.*"

"*Bon soir* to you, *aussi,*" I said. (We had done a bit of French at school.)

"Why are you saying *Bon soir*, Aussie?" Clive whispered. "He's French, not Australian."

I gave him a look to shut him up.

"You 'ave a reservation?" the headwaiter asked.

"We 'ave," Clive confirmed. "We are 'aving le din-dins avec les Swanker Watsons."

"He means the Watson family," I said hurriedly. "I think I can see them in the corner."

"Of course. This way."

He led us over to a nice table in the corner of the first-class dining room, right next to the window, with a lovely view of the boat and the surrounding sea.

Mrs. Swanker Watson welcomed us as we sat next to Swanker Watson and his sister. Baby Swanker wasn't there and neither was Nanny Swanker.

Mr. Swanker Watson was there, but he didn't say very much. All he seemed interested in was a bottle of wine that he had in front of him. All drinks on the cruise were free, and he seemed to be making the most of it.

"Well boys," Mrs. Swanker Watson said. "Have you enjoyed your day?"

"Very much, thank you," I said, *"Très bon!"*

"Spiffing," Clive agreed.

"Good," she said.

And then it came. I'd been suspicious all along as to why Mrs. Swanker Watson had invited us to join them for dinner. Most normal people didn't want Clive anywhere near them at dinnertime. Clive and dinnertime always seemed to end up in expensive visits to the dry cleaners.

"I wonder if I might ask you boys a favor," she said.

"Certainly," Clive said. "What is it?"

"Well now," Mrs. Swanker Watson said, "as you know, it's a great honor when on a cruise to be invited to dine with the captain at the captain's table."

"Ah," I said. "It is indeed, I'm sure."

"Well, of course you know that," she said. "I hardly need to tell you. Being—" then she lowered her voice, "—the captain's boys."

"Quite so," I agreed. "Isn't that right, Clive?"

"Quite so," he agreed too.

"Now I know that you're traveling incognito on this trip—"

"Beg pardon?" Clive said.

"Mrs. Watson means that no one knows who we really are," I said.

"No. And let's hope it stays that way," Clive said.

"However," Mrs. Swanker Watson said, "it would be so wonderful if you could have a quiet little word in private with your father, the captain, and possibly suggest that he might like to invite us to dine with him one night? Would you mind most awfully doing that? I know that you and Angus are such good friends at school and that you all fit in so well together with the ordinary boys."

"No trouble, Mrs. Watson," I said. "We'll do what we can. We can't promise anything of course, as he may already have made up his dinner dates for the trip. But we'll speak to him on the quiet and see what we can do."

"Thank you boys," she said. "Ah, here is the drinks waiter with our drinks. Have a look at the menu too, and see what you might like to order. Oh, and look—" and her voice dropped to a whisper, "here's your father too."

Clive and me practically ran out of the dining room.

For a moment we thought she meant Dad. Our dad. Real Dad.

She only meant the captain.

He was all dressed up in his best uniform, and very smart he looked. He was going from table to table, having a little chat with everyone as he made his way to the all-important and greatly sought after captain's table, where his guests for the evening would soon be joining him, along with a couple of his officers.

He got nearer to our table. Mrs. Swanker Watson took a mirror from her handbag and had a quick look at her appearance. Mr. Swanker Watson waved to the drinks waiter for another bottle of wine. Clive and me and Swanker Watson and his sister just sat there, looking at all the cutlery and wishing that we'd gone to Burger King instead.

"Enjoying the cruise?"

He was at our table. I saw Clive studying his beard. He was obviously trying to see if anything was living in it.

Mrs. Swanker Watson gave him a big smile. It was such a huge one, it looked as if she'd had extra teeth put in, just to be able to do it.

"We're enjoying ourselves enormously thank you, Captain."

"Good," he said. "Very glad to hear it. Well, if you'll excuse me—"

He made as if to go on to the next table, but

Mrs. Swanker Watson hadn't finished yet.

"If I may say—" she said. "If I may say—" And she got very conspiratorial. So much so that I think she even winked at the captain, just like Clive had done. He was probably starting to get a complex, wondering why all these people were winking at him. "If I may say so, I would just like to mention what remarkably fine children you have."

The captain looked blank. Then surprised. Then completely astonished.

"You—you know them?" he said.

Mrs. Swanker Watson gave him another wink, then smiled and put her finger to her lips.

"We do," she said. "But Mum's the word."

The captain looked a bit puzzled.

"Ah. Right. Well—"

"Such good-looking children too," Mrs. Swanker Watson continued.

"Especially the younger one," Clive said. But I got him under the table.

The captain looked more baffled than ever.

"Yes, well—very nice of you to—to say so."

"But don't worry," Mrs. Swanker whispered. "Your secret's safe with us."

The captain blushed bright red.

"S-secret?" he said. "Oh?"

Then he seemed in a sudden hurry to get away.

"If you'll excuse me then," he said. "I see my guests arriving."

And he was off.

"Such a nice man," Mrs. Swanker Watson said.

"Such a smart uniform. Such huge responsibilities he has too. Imagine being in charge of the running of a great ship like this. It's almost like being the mayor of a city. Only not only is he in charge of the city, he has to steer it and park it as well."

"Where's my other bottle of wine?" Mr. Swanker Watson demanded. "And what about some food?"

"I think I see a waiter now," Mrs. Swanker Watson said, "coming to take our order."

And that was when I saw him. I saw his reflection in the window. And Clive saw it too. It took me a moment to recognize him. Because he wasn't in his usual steward's uniform. He was dressed in waiter's clothes.

I suppose somebody must have gone sick, and he had been called on to take over for him for the evening.

Yes, the waiter heading for our table was the one reason why we were on that trip, and yet he was also the one person we didn't want to see.

No, let me put that another way. We did want to see him. We wanted to see him all the time. That's why we were there.

We just didn't want him seeing us. At least not just then.

That's right.

You've got it.

It was Dad.

TEN

NARROW ESCAPES

HE HADN'T SEEN us yet. We still had a chance. If only we could somehow just slip out of the restaurant, without Dad seeing us, and without Mrs. Swanker Watson suspecting anything.

"Excuse me—waiter!"

Someone called him over to another table.

"There seems to have been some confusion in the kitchen. I asked for my steak well done—this looks almost rare to me."

"I'm terribly sorry, sir. I'll take it back for you. I won't be a moment."

Dad picked the offending plate up and headed in the direction of the kitchen.

We had a minute. Maybe two.

I looked at Clive. Clive looked at me. We couldn't just get up and leave. Mrs. Swanker Watson would have thought that extremely odd. So what were we going to do? How *were* we going to get out of there?

"Ahhhhh!"

I looked.

It was Clive.

He'd vanished.

I could hear him though.

"Ah! Oooh! Ah! Eeee! Oooh! Ah!"

Mrs. Swanker Watson peeled the tablecloth back and peered under the table.

"Is your brother all right?" she said. "He seems to have slid under the table and to be writhing around for some reason."

"Don't worry," I said, catching on straightaway to what Clive was up to, "it's nothing serious. It's just one of his fits."

"Fits?" Mrs. Swanker said, sounding very concerned. "He has fits?"

"Ooo! Eee! Ah! Ooo!" Clive said, clutching at where he thought his heart was, only it was one of his kidneys instead.

"Yes," I said. "Just now and again. It's a disease he picked up in the tropics. It's called—it's called—Fits Disease."

I ducked under the table, got Clive by the armpits, and pulled him to his feet. He was rolling his eyeballs around, which is a trick he can do. He can make the peering-out bits disappear completely so that all you can see is ping-pong balls.

"Shall I call for the ship's doctor?" Mrs. Swanker

said. "I'm sure he'll come immediately—when he finds out who it is," she added in a whisper.

"No, it's all right," I said. "Thank you all the same, but he'll be fine. I know how to deal with it. A lie-down in a darkened room, a glass of cold water, and a bit of raw liver is the only thing. Sometimes a little additional homework can help too. But as we're on our holidays, we haven't got any of that. Don't worry, Mrs. Watson, he'll soon be all right. Thank you for inviting us to dinner. I hope we haven't spoiled your evening."

"No, not at all," she said. "I just hope he recovers as soon as possible."

"He'll be right as rain by tomorrow," I promised. "Right as rain. And that little matter we were talking about earlier—about dinner at the captain's table," I whispered. "You leave it with me."

"Thank you. Well—good night."

"Good night. Good night, Swanker," I said to Swanker. "See you at the pool tomorrow."

And I dragged Clive off out of the restaurant.

I realized, as we went, that the whole first-class restaurant had fallen silent, and that everyone in it was watching as I walked out backward, holding Clive under the armpits, and pulling him along with me while he rolled his eyeballs and groaned. They were probably worried that he had got food poisoning, and that they might be next.

We had to go past the captain's table too.

I felt I ought to say something, because Mrs. Swanker was watching, and if I didn't say anything at all to our "dad" it would have looked suspicious.

"He's all right," I said to the captain as I dragged Clive past his table. "It's just one of his fits. He'll be all right in the morning."

The captain looked at us, with a vaguely sort of disquieted look, as if he thought something fishy was going on, but he couldn't quite put his finger on what sort of fish it was.

"'Night," I said.

And we were out.

I dragged Clive out of sight along the corridor.

"Okay, Clive. You can walk now."

He made no effort to support his own weight.

"Drag me a bit farther, go on."

"No. My arms are tired."

"Drag me as far as the deck."

"I'm warning you, Clive. I'll let go of you."

"Drag me as far as the door then."

I dropped him on to the carpet.

"Ow! What was that for?"

"I warned you. Now come on."

He got up and we made our way to the little café on the promenade deck to get something to eat. It was open all day and all night and served drinks and snacks. We had some chips each and a chocolate bar. We didn't feel like facing another of the restaurants that night.

"That was a close escape, Clive," I said.

"Yes," he agreed. "It was."

Too close, I thought. It seemed to me to be only a matter of time before we got caught. How much longer before we did run into Dad? How much longer before Mrs. Swanker Watson stopped believing that we were the sons of the captain, traveling (as she had put it) incognito?

What exactly was the penalty for stowing away on the high seas? What exactly did being clapped in irons involve? Did it hurt? Did they clap children in irons, or only adults?

I wanted to share my anxieties with Clive, but what was the point in worrying him?

It was odd really, no matter how bad the situation, Clive always seemed happy in his own little world. It was his privilege, I suppose, for being five minutes younger. But I was the eldest, which meant that I got all the worrying and looking after to do. Clive was blissfully ignorant, really—with the emphasis on ignorant.

I wished that I was the youngest sometimes.

I really did.

AFTER WE'D FINISHED our chips and chocolate, we had a stroll around the deck and looked at the stars. You never got tired of that, never. The stars over the sea were so much brighter than at home. There were no city lights to detract from their sparkle. It was warmer too now, a beautiful balmy night.

Some people, who I guessed must have been on their honeymoons (as a lot of people go on cruises for their honeymoons) were standing at the rail holding hands and just looking at the moon and the sea and the stars.

I felt that it would have been nice to stand at the rail and hold someone's hand. Like your mum's hand maybe, if you had a mum, only we didn't.

The only hand I had to hold was Clive's hand. And I didn't want to hold that. Not considering where he puts it.

So we just stood there and didn't hold hands and looked at the stars. And I sort of sneaked a look at Clive and I thought that, well, maybe he wasn't so bad after all, and he was my brother, and if I didn't have him, who would I have? Well, just then, I wouldn't have had anybody. Not even a gerbil. I'd have been lonely and all on my own. So I thought of telling Clive that he wasn't so bad, but I couldn't think of any words that wouldn't sound all soft and smarmy. So I kicked him up the backside instead. And he said, "Ouch! What did you do that for?"

But I think he knew really, in his heart of hearts.

"I wonder," Clive said, "where Mum is. Do you think she's up there watching over us? Looking down on us from the stars?"

"Yes," I said. "I'm sure she is."

I didn't think she was really, but I thought that if Clive wanted to believe it, why should I spoil it for him?

"Looks like it's going to be a lovely night, Clive," I said.

"Yes," he said. "I suppose so."

Well, it was, and it wasn't. And before it was out, we ran into more problems. In the shape of Lumpy, the nasty-looking steward.

We were on our way back to our cabin in rat class. We'd brushed our teeth and cleaned our faces and Clive had promised to wash his pants in the morning.

We'd negotiated most of the tricky bits, and were now way down inside the ship, at the point where the corridors crossed and where the sign was that read "No Admittance Beyond This Point. Crew Only."

We hesitated, listening out for voices and foot-steps. It seemed all right.

"Okay, Clive. It's all clear."

But just as we were about to go into the Storage and Services area, a voice yelled from behind us.

"Oi! You two! Where do you think you're going?!"

It was Lumpy, the steward with the bald head. It looked like he shaved it too, every morning with an electric razor. He didn't just have a lumpy head either, he had lumpy everything. He had a lumpy chin, a lumpy nose, and his arms and legs were big muscly lumps. He also had a hole in his ear for an earring. He looked as though he should have been a wrestler. One of the ones who fights dirty and who everybody boos.

"Well? Where do you think you're going?"

"Eh—"

"Well?"

"Well—we thought we saw a rat," Clive said.

"A rat?"

"Yes. And we were following it."

"Listen to me, you two," Lumpy said. "I don't know about seeing rats, but I know about smelling them. And I think I do smell one—get me? I think I do smell a rat. And you two are up to something. I'm not sure what, but if I find out what it is—"

"We're not up to anything," I said. "We were just exploring."

"Well go and explore somewhere else," Lumpy said. "This is crew only down here. So stay out of it."

So Clive and I had no choice but to turn around and head back up for the deck.

"Just a minute," Lumpy said. "I know your gran, don't I? The one all dripping with jewelry and necklaces."

We didn't say anything. Answer no questions, tell no lies. Let him suppose what he wanted.

"Yeah," Lumpy said. "Well, you just be careful, that's all. You just be careful."

And he turned and went on into Crew Only.

It was a funny thing, but what he had said about Mrs. Dominics "dripping with jewelry" reminded me of something else. I'd heard that phrase somewhere before. Only I couldn't quite remember where. I couldn't quite place it.

For the time being I put it out of my mind.

"What now?" Clive said.

"Back up on deck," I told him. "We can't risk sneaking down to rat class tonight. Not with Lumpy about."

"But where are we going to sleep?"

"We'll find somewhere. Come on."

We went back up on to the deck. It was late by then, almost midnight, but the ship was still alive with music and dancing and everything you could think of.

There was a big casino on board where you could win or lose a fortune. We weren't allowed in as we were too young, but we looked in through the window, and we could see Mrs. Dominics in there, sitting at the roulette table, with a great big pile of gambling chips in front of her, which must have been worth thousands.

We watched her for a while as she bet on the numbers and the turning wheel. Sometimes she would win a small fortune, other times she would lose one. But it didn't seem to make much difference to her, one way or the other. It was as if the plastic chips were just that—plastic—and had no real value at all.

It was as if it really was just a game.

But other people were betting and gambling as if their lives and fortunes depended on it. There was one man, with a dark moustache, who was sitting at a card table, and somehow he never lost a hand, and the pile of gambling chips in front of him just went on getting bigger and bigger.

"Looks to me like he's cheating," Clive said.

If he was, I couldn't see how he was doing it. But maybe he was. Maybe he was some kind of professional gambler, who rode the cruiseliners, winning a fortune every trip.

We left the casino and went up to the next deck, following the sound of music and singing.

Believe it or not, the ship was so big there was a full-sized theater on board, and this was where the music was coming from.

We pushed the door open and went inside and found two empty seats at the back. Up on stage a lady was singing a song while behind her a long row of dancers were kicking their legs in the air.

I couldn't quite understand what the song was about but the audience seemed to be enjoying it. After the song a magician came on and did conjuring tricks. Then a man came on and told jokes, but Clive reckoned that they weren't very good and that he knew better ones, and so we left to do some more late-night exploring.

As well as a theater, there was also a cinema on board. We went to see what was playing, but you had to be eighteen and we couldn't get in, so we went on to do some more wandering.

The first-class restaurant was closed up now, and Dad must have finally gone to bed to get some well-earned rest.

We went and sat by the swimming pool. Nobody was swimming now, it was too late and the pool was closed, but it was nice to sit there anyway.

"Are you enjoying the trip, Clive?" I asked.

"Better than staying at home," he said.

And that was true enough.

Mrs. Dominics came by. You could hear her jewelry rattling a mile off.

"Hello, boys."

"Hello, Mrs. Dominics. Were you lucky tonight?"

"Lucky?"

"We saw you in the casino."

"Oh, yes. Yes, I was lucky, thank you. But I'd rather be young again."

She gave us a big wrinkly old smile. I'd never thought of that, that we had something Mrs. Dominics might have wanted.

"Only money can't buy that, can it boys? Not love or being young. They're the two things that money can't buy. But shall I let you into a secret? Well, I had those things as well once—love and youth. So I've had a good life really, haven't I? And I can't complain. And I won't either. Good night."

And off she went, back to her first-class cabin.

She wasn't a bad old soul really.

CLIVE YAWNED a big yawn. You could practically see all the way down to his intestines. Mind you, Clive looks like a plate of intestines even with his mouth closed.

"I'm tired."

"Me too."

"We can't stay up on deck all night."

"No. Someone will see us. And it might get cold later, and a bit damp if we stay out."

"Where'll we sleep?"

I looked around. There had to be somewhere. Then I saw it.

"Come on, Clive. Quick. Before anyone comes. I've seen a place where we can spend the night."

"Where?"

"Come on!"

And I headed off across the deck, and led the way to a lifeboat.

It only took a moment. The lifeboats hung in rows along the sides of the ship. There were ten of them on either side. That may not sound like many, but they were big, and they could hold a lot of people. Each lifeboat was contained within a small gantry, and we had to shin up the gantry to get to the one we had chosen.

All of the lifeboats were also covered in orange tarpaulins, which were there to keep the boat dry inside and to shield you from the sun and the sea and the elements, should you have to take to sea in it for real.

We pried the tarpaulin up until there was enough space for us to wriggle through, then in we went. Clive first, and then me.

"It's dark in here," he said.

"Let your eyes get used to it."

"Smells a bit too."

"That's just the tarpaulin."

"Not very comfortable."

"Hang on. Let me find a flashlight."

I knew there had to be a flashlight somewhere. Lifeboats were well supplied and were supposed to be stocked with things for all contingencies.

I opened up a chest and peered inside. I couldn't

see much, but I felt around and found one. I turned it on.

"Let's have a go," Clive said.

"Keep it pointed downward," I told him. "We don't want anyone knowing we're here."

Clive had a look around the chest.

"Look," he said. "First-aid box. Oh, and look at this—rations!"

"Get off, Clive," I said. "Don't you start eating the emergency rations. What if there's a real emergency, and we have to abandon ship, and we get into this lifeboat and set sail, only to find we've got nothing to eat because buzzard-face here has wolfed all the rations? Well, we'll have to eat something else instead. And it'll probably be you."

"I wasn't going to eat them," he claimed. "I was only looking. And who are you calling buzzard-face?"

"Come on. Let's get to sleep."

"It's not very comfortable."

"Then make it comfortable. Come on."

We opened up a couple of pouches and found some shiny survival blankets. They weren't all that soft, but they were nice and warm, and we got a couple of life jackets to use as pillows, and then we lay down on the floor between the benches, and we tried to get to sleep.

"It's a bit hard this floor," Clive said.

And it was too. We found a tarpaulin in the chest and we used that as a mattress. It softened the floor up quite nicely and we were able to get to sleep.

It was quite nice there, inside the lifeboat. You could feel it swaying a little with the motion of the ship. It didn't make you feel sick though. It was more of a calm, reassuring sort of swaying. It was almost like being a baby in a cradle again.

Rock a bye baby
In the lifeboat
When the bough breaks
The boat
Will float

I hummed. And that was the last thing I remember until a shaft of light coming in through a crack between the tarpaulin and the boat woke me up.

I prodded Clive.

"Clive!"

"What?"

"We have to get up."

He looked at his watch.

"It's only half-past seven."

"I know. But we need to get out before anyone's around. We can't be seen getting out of the lifeboat, can we? Come on. Let's go and grab a lounger by the pool. You can finish off sleeping there."

"Oh, all right. I suppose."

We quickly folded everything up and put it back where we had found it.

Then we listened.

"Hear anything?"

Yes. Footsteps. Somebody on an early-morning

jog around the deck. Somebody none too fit either, by the sound of it

Flap, flap, flap. Puff, puff, puff. Flap, flap, flap—but farther away now. Puff, puff, puff. Gone.

"Okay, Clive. Sounds all clear. Let's go."

And then it happened.

Even now when I look back on it, it gives me the willies. It gives me the willies to the power of ten. It gives me such horrible, awful willies, when I think what might have happened. It gives me the kind of willies that make you sit up in bed in the middle of the night, with the sweat pouring off your forehead and trickling down the back of your neck, and your pajamas sticking to you as if you've just been through the car wash, and your heart is thudding in your chest.

And then your heart isn't even in your chest. It's moved up into your mouth. And you want to scream, "No, no, no!" But you can't. You just lie there in terror, waiting for the worst to happen, with your heart stuck in your throat.

Clive got out of the wrong side of the lifeboat.

Not the side we had come in on, which was the gantry side. He must still have been half-asleep, sleepy and confused.

Clive stepped out of the lifeboat on the side that was hanging over the sea.

"Come on then," he said. "Let's get going."

And before I could stop him, before I even realized, he was gone.

Silence.

Nothing.

No Clive.

Just the sound of the sea, the sound of the great engines of the boat, subdued, coasting, not really exerting themselves, but mighty just the same.

He had gone.

Clive had gone.

Vaulted out of the wrong side of the lifeboat.

Dropped like a stone. Down, before he could even scream, down into the silence of the vast empty sea.

One hundred meters beneath us.

I swear, I chewed on my heart. There it was, right there in my mouth, as I slowly realized what he had done. For a moment I was frozen with horror. Things flashed through my mind. Clive. Me. When we were small. Faint memories of Mum. Dad. All of us. Dad now. Me having to tell him. About stowing away. About us. About everything. About Clive.

Lost and gone in the great silence of the sea.

I had to do something. Never mind about us being discovered now. I had to do something. Pull the emergency handle. Throw the life preserver over. Launch the boat. Something, somebody, please.

With great ships like this—it could take a mile or two miles for them to stop. They didn't have brakes, not like cars. All you could do was cut the engines and let the sea slow you down. And then the ship would have to maneuver around and set off back to look for him, and by that time . . .

The sharks? The cold? The panic? The terror?

I mean, Clive could swim; we could both swim. But swimming in a nice warm, shark-free swimming pool with a lifeguard on duty was one thing. Swimming all alone in a vast empty sea was another.

Always assuming that he had survived the fall.

One hundred meters into water?

Hadn't I read somewhere that water could be like concrete? I mean, I'd done a belly flop from the low diving board into the swimming pool. That was no more than two meters. And that had hurt something major.

What if Clive had belly flopped? A one-hundred-meter belly flop into the sea? Into the vastness of the ocean. And it was vast, so infinitely, indescribably vast. You don't know how big the sea is until you see it.

It's the biggest thing in the world.

I stuck my head out and looked down at the water.

Nothing. No one. He had already gone.

Soundlessly, silently gone. And he hadn't even said good-bye. And I hadn't even held his hand when I'd had the chance and told him that he wasn't so bad after all really.

I hadn't even called his name.

"Clive," I whispered. "Clive—"

And it was almost as though I could hear a small, quiet, faraway voice, so tiny that it was almost inaudible, calling back to me somewhere, from a distant recess of my mind.

And then I saw something.

Fingers.

And something else.

A face. White. Absolutely and utterly white with terror.

It was Clive. Holding on by one hand to the side of the lifeboat, with the sea far beneath him, and the strength ebbing from his hand, and his fingers visibly slipping away.

"Help," he said.

He didn't shout it. It was almost like an apology, a "sorry to bother you" kind of sound. Or maybe a farewell. A small, nearly silent good-bye.

"Help."

I grabbed him. I got him around the wrist with both my hands, just as his fingers lost their grip.

"It's all right, Clive, I've got you. I've got you."

He felt heavy. Ever so heavy. I pulled, but I couldn't move him. All I could do was hold on. I felt his weight sapping my strength. I started to cry. My nose began to run. I was going to lose him. I was going to have to let go of him or I was going to go too. The tears ran down my face. What could I do? What sort of a choice was that? To let your brother die or to die with him? What sort of a choice was that to have to make?

At my age.

"Clive, Clive, Clive . . ."

I just didn't have the strength anymore. I didn't. I just didn't.

ALEX SHEARER

So I said a prayer. I didn't know who I was praying to, because I'm not a very religious person, but I just prayed anyway.

"Please," I said. "Please help. Don't let Clive die. Please, please help!"

And someone helped me. Someone, somewhere gave me their strength. And I pulled and pulled as hard as I could and then there Clive was, back safely in the boat, and there I was too. We were sprawled on the floor, just crying and laughing and not really knowing what we were doing, and for some reason I was patting Clive on the head, almost as if to make sure that it really was him and he really was alive.

We just lay there for a while, getting our breath and recovering. And then Clive turned to me and he said,

"Thanks."

And I said, "That's all right, Clive."

Then Clive said, "We'd maybe better get out and on to the deck then, before people start arriving and somebody sees us."

"Yes," I said. "Good idea." And we both climbed out—over the right side, this time.

And I found I could hardly walk. My legs were shaking so much that all I could do was stand there for a while, waiting for the time to pass and for my strength to return.

Clive didn't seem able to move either.

"You know," he said, "that was a bit of a narrow escape back there."

"Yes," I said. "It was."

Clive did a most uncharacteristic thing then. He put his arm around my shoulder.

"Thanks," he said.

"That's all right," I told him. "You'd have done the same for me."

"I would," Clive said. "Honest, I would."

And we never mentioned it again. We never have, from that day to this. And I don't think we ever will. But I know that if I'm ever in big trouble like that, that Clive owes me one. And I'm sure he won't let me down. Well, I'm pretty sure.

· ELEVEN ·

ROUGH WEATHER

WE WERE STILL wearing our best clothes from the night before, so the first chance we got, we sneaked back down to rat class to change. We got down without running into Lumpy, changed, grabbed our swimming stuff, and went back up on deck.

Swanker Watson was sitting by the pool with his mum, Mrs. Swanker Watson.

"How is your brother?" she asked me. "Is he all right now? Has he got over his fit?"

"He's fine now," I said. "Thank you very much. You just never know when he's going to have another one."

We went off for a walk with Swanker Watson to see what was going on. There were a lot of people doing bends and stretches up on the promenade deck. Most of them were about sixty-five and had very big trousers. They were copying the actions of a woman in a leotard. It was the daily aerobics class. Clive said he was going to join it, but I managed to drag him away and we went on to the Bosun's Club to see what they were up to.

When the people running the Bosun's Club— Big Billy Bosun and Matey Matilda—saw Clive coming, they said sorry, but they were all full up for the morning and to come back in the afternoon. Or possibly even next week.

So we went and had a walk around the deck, and then we went and had a walk around the deck the other way.

If you're wondering why we hadn't run into Dad by now, well, you have to remember what a big ship the *Mona Lisa* was. It had fifteen different decks and it carried two and a half thousand passengers. And then there was the crew on top of that. Now you think that if you're at a big school, with say a thousand pupils in it, you could easily go a week or two and not see a particular person, if they weren't in your class.

Well, we weren't in Dad's class. He was in first class and we were in rat class, and we just never seemed to meet.

I was lying on a lounger thinking about this, with a long cool drink in my hand, when something happened to get me worried.

Drinks on board the ship were free, and unlimited; you could have as many as you wanted, you only had to ask.

ALeX SHeArer

So although I was lounging there with a long, cool drink in my hand, Clive, who was lounging next to me, had gone one better—he had a long, cool drink in either hand. He also had a long, cool drink by his foot, and another one by his other foot. Then he had a long, cool drink by his head, and another long, cool drink waiting for him on a little lounger table.

So, all in all, Clive was doing quite well for long, cool drinks.

Anyway, there we were, when suddenly this man in a white T-shirt, with the words Official Photographer on it, appeared in front of us holding a camera.

"Smile, lads," he said.

And before we could run for it, he took our photo.

"They'll be on display at the kiosk by this afternoon," he said. "Tell your mum and dad to go and see them. If they like them, they'll be able to buy a couple of copies."

And before we could stop him, he was gone.

"Oh no!" Clive said. "If he puts them up on display in the kiosk—"

"Dad might see them."

"What can we do?"

"We'll have to stop him—or something."

We spent a worried few hours then, waiting for our photos to appear in the official Cruise Photographer's Kiosk, down by the information desk.

Clive was so worried, he could hardly eat any lunch. He must only have had two or three starters from the buffet table, just one main course, and I doubt that he ate more than five puddings—if that.

We kept walking to and fro along the deck, passing the kiosk and looking casual. There were always people milling around, looking to see if their own photographs had been taken and whether they liked them enough to buy a copy as a souvenir.

Most people had cameras of their own, but they still liked to come and see if their photographs were up on display. Maybe the simple fact is that most people can't get enough of looking at themselves.

We were walking past, acting casual, for about the tenth time (in fact, I was getting concerned that all this acting casual was starting to look suspicious) when we saw our photographs go up in the window, along with some others, freshly taken that morning.

"There they are," Clive said. "What do we do?"

I didn't know. We didn't have a Cruise Card with which to go in and buy them, so we just had to somehow hide them from sight.

"There! That'll do it."

Clive spotted an events notice stuck to the information office window with Blu-tac. He peeled it off, brought it over, and stuck it onto the kiosk window, so that it covered our photographs inside.

The notice stayed there for the rest of the day, and the following morning, when we looked again, both the notice and our photographs had gone. Phew.

The Cruise Photographer was taking new ones all the time, so none of them stayed in the window for long. If you didn't buy them that day, they were replaced by new ones. In the morning there were always photos on display from the night before, of people dancing in the ballroom, or clinking champagne glasses together in the nightclub.

We had been at sea quite a few days by now, and maybe our legs were getting a bit hungry for a taste of dry land. The boat was due to dock in thirty-six hours at its first port of call, and people were putting their names down on to a list for a trip to see the ruins.

"Do you have any idea where we are, Clive?" I asked him.

"Yes," he said. "We're at sea."

"I mean where at sea."

"No," he said. "But it's hot."

"Well," I said, "we happen to be only a short distance away from Africa—Egypt in particular. We stop there for a day, and if we put our names down, we can go and see the pyramids as well. Do you fancy the pyramids, Clive?"

"I don't mind a few pyramids," Clive said. "That is, I can't say I'm all that big on pyramids, I mean, it's not as if I collect them or anything. But I've nothing against them as such. And to come all this way and not see the pyramids, when they're right on your doorstep, so to speak, would seem like a bit of a waste. So I don't mind seeing them. All right. Will there be camels as well?"

"Probably," I said. "You usually get the two

together as far as I know. I think it's due to the lumps and being pointed at the top. Camels have lumps which are pointed at the top and pyramids are lumps pointed at the top, and that's probably why they like to hang around together."

So we were going to put our names down on the list for the trip to see the pyramids when Swanker Watson reappeared.

"Are you going to see the pyramids when we dock?" he said.

"May as well," we said.

"Us too."

So we stood aside and let Swanker put the names of his family down for the pyramids, then when he had gone, we added our names to *his* list. Because you had to put your cabin number down next to your name, and we didn't really have one, and without one we probably couldn't have gone.

Mrs. Dominics happened by then, on her way to the swimming pool. She didn't swim anymore, but she liked to lounge.

"Afternoon boys," she said. "I see we're in for a little rough weather later."

It was the first we'd heard about it.

"Better batten down the hatches," she said (whatever that meant) and then she went off, with all her jewelry clanking.

Sure enough there was a warning later over the loudspeaker, when the captain said that there might be a little rough weather later on that evening and he advised passengers to keep to their cabins after eleven o'clock and not to go on deck.

Clive and me went off then and found a spot on the sundeck, near where the funnel started, where we had a good view of the first-class area, and where we could keep an eye on Dad.

He was to and fro all afternoon, bringing people drinks and snacks and fetching them towels and cushions and magazines. And somehow, he never seemed in a rush and he always looked cheerful, and he always had a good word for everyone.

One lady in particular kept getting him to bring her drinks all the time—even when she already had a drink that she hadn't yet finished. She'd make out that she needed a bit more ice, or that she'd lost her straw.

Clive and me had our suspicions about her.

"You know all those ladies who want to get engaged to Dad, Clive?" I said. "The ones who drag him off for a walk, and then stop outside the jewelers to look at all the rings?"

"I know the sort," Clive said. "You mean the kind who yawn a lot when it's time to go home and pretend they can't find their car keys?"

"Yes."

"What about them?"

"Well, she looks like one of those."

"Yeah," Clive said. "You're right. She's up to no good, if you ask me. Let's walk past her deck chair, casual-like, and drop a dead seagull into her drink. Have you got a dead seagull on you?"

"No," I said. "I haven't."

*

THAT EVENING WE decided to avoid the Swanker Watsons and to eat from the buffet in the Promenade Restaurant. Mrs. Dominics was in there on her own and she waved to us and asked if we would like to share her table.

We thanked her very much and said we would. We liked Mrs. Dominics, but it was also good for us to be seen with a grown-up, so as to allay suspicions.

"Are you going on the trip to inspect the camels, Mrs. Dominics?" Clive said.

"No, dear," she said. "It'll be too hot and too tiring and too much of a climb for me. And besides, I've already seen the camels and the pyramids, many times."

"Oh, have you?" Clive said. "I expect you must have been there when they were building them."

Mrs. Dominics burst out laughing.

"I'm not quite that old, dear," she said.

And all her jewelry jangled.

Then, "You know," she said, "you two remind me of someone. Do you know that?"

"Us?" I said. "W-who could that be?"

"Oh, someone," she said. "Just someone."

And, you know, just for a moment there, I felt that she knew. She knew that we were stowaways, and that Dad was our dad, and that we'd come there to be with him and to keep an eye on him. She knew. I just felt she knew. But I also felt that she would never tell anyone. That she just thought it was all rather amusing.

ALEX SHEARER

And then I thought no, I must have been mistaken. She didn't know or suspect anything at all. It was just me, getting paranoid and nervous. Because it can be quite a mental strain being a stowaway. You are always either looking over your shoulder or waiting for a hand to fall on it, which can be quite nerve-wracking, and eventually wear you down.

In some ways it's a bit like being a criminal on the run. It's a bit like being a fugitive from justice, and you're hiding up among all these people who don't even know that you've done anything, or that you're a wanted man.

"Have you ever met any pirates in your travels, Mrs. Dominics?" Clive said.

"No, dear," she said. "I'm glad to say I haven't."

"Do they still exist?" I said.

"Oh, I believe they do," she said. "Especially in the Far East and the China Seas. But I don't think they'd ever trouble a great ship like this. I can't see a little pirate boat stopping a huge cruiseliner. They wouldn't have a hope. They could run the Jolly Roger up the flagpole and shout and threaten and bluster as much as they liked. But this ship would just keep going and totally ignore them. They'd be no more of a danger to us than a little dog, barking at a car and running after it."

"No," Clive said, "I suppose not."

And he sounded a bit disappointed. Anyone would have thought that he wanted to run into pirates.

After dinner we said good night to Mrs. Dominics and we sneaked to the bathroom where we brushed our teeth (we kept our toothbrushes and toothpaste hidden behind a pipe there now, so we didn't have to carry them around) and Clive washed his pants so that he would have a clean pair for the morning, and then we did some more sneaking, back down to our cabin in rat class.

As we got ready for bed, we heard the whispering again, coming down the ventilation pipe. It was the same two voices as before.

"So when's it to be?" said one.

"Day after we embark again."

"Sure?"

"Positive."

"They know our position?"

"Give or take. They know the route and what speed we travel at. Shouldn't be any problem."

"Right."

Then there were footsteps as they walked away.

"What was that about, Clive?" I said.

I don't know why I asked him. I knew he didn't know. He just shrugged.

"Search me," he said.

And he hung his pants up to dry.

We got into our beds and said good night.

And that was when the storm started.

Now, if you imagine the shape of a boat, and if you picture it rocking from side to side, you'll know that the people at the top of the boat will be doing more rocking than the people at the bottom—as they have farther to go.

Down in rat class, things were bad enough for us, but what they were like for people up at the top in first class, I couldn't imagine.

The storm began slowly and gradually, with just a little swaying from side to side. It was almost a restful kind of motion, a bit like a lullaby, putting you to sleep.

I realized something was up though when my bed started to slide around the room.

Crash!

It bashed into Clive's bed and woke him up.

"Oi!" he said. "What are you doing?"

But then we were swaying back the other way.

Crash!

Clive's bed bashed into my bed, and my bed bashed into the wall.

Then we were back the other way.

My bed bashed into Clive's bed and his bed bashed into the wall.

Crash!

"Help!" Clive shouted. "Abandon bed!"

But there was nowhere else to go to. Bed was the safest place to be.

"Let's go up on deck!" Clive wailed. "It's got to be better up there than here."

"I shouldn't think so. It's probably a whole lot worse. They probably aren't letting people go up on deck anyway, in case they get blown overboard."

Then the ship started to pitch as well as to roll. It didn't just sway from side to side; it swayed from back to front as well.

Crash!

We pitched into a pile of spare beds.

Crash!

We rolled back again.

Crash!

The first pile of spare beds collapsed, and that sort of jammed us in a bit so that we didn't roll about too much.

"You know," Clive said, "this reminds me of that death ride—the one at Alton Towers."

"The one you were sick on?" I said.

"Yes," he said. "That one."

I pulled my duvet over my head.

It was a long night. A long, long night.

The ship pitched and rolled and swayed and rose and plummeted like a cork in the sea.

It may have been a great big massive cork, weighing tons and tons and tons, but as far as the sea and the storm were concerned, it could as well have been a paper boat, or nothing but a twig, being carried along by a torrent. It doesn't seem to matter what people build or make, how big or impressive it is, the power of nature is always greater, and it looks at the best you can throw at it, and just laughs.

But believe it or not, we fell asleep. There we were, snug down in rat class, wedged in by all the other beds, and we didn't pass too bad a night at all. I did have the odd dream or so, in which I dreamed I was on a rocking horse, going up and down and round and round, but it wasn't unpleasant.

And when I next opened my eyes, it was

morning. Not that I knew that from the light, of course—our cabin had no porthole. But I put Clive's flashlight on and looked at my watch. It was eight-thirty. The storm had stopped and the boat was sailing smoothly again.

I shook Clive awake.

"Come on, Clive," I said. "Let's go up on deck, see what the storm has done."

He rubbed his eyes and looked at me in the dim light.

"Let's have breakfast first," he said. "I'm starving hungry."

But what was new about that?

IT WAS CREEPILY quiet in the restaurant that morning. There was only me and Clive and a couple of other passengers, and one or two waiters and waitresses, and a great mountain of breakfast, which nobody seemed to be eating.

"Dig in!" Clive said, spooning out the cereal and grabbing the chocolate croissants. "Where is everybody? They're surely not letting all this grub go to waste, are they?"

But they were.

"They're probably all still in their cabins, I should imagine, Clive," I said. "Feeling a bit ill."

He looked surprised.

"Why?" he said. "It wasn't that bad—pass the marmalade."

"Not for us it wasn't," I told him. "It might have been a bit different up here."

After breakfast we went for a stroll around the decks. We could see a coastline in the far distance, and it was really quite hot now—you needed your sunhat on and your sunglasses.

The sky was cloudless (the storm must have cleared it), and the sun beat down on the deck.

A lot of rather pale and delicate-looking people were sitting on loungers. They seemed rather frail and shaky, as if they'd been up all night, being ill.

As we strolled around the deck, we came upon a familiar face. It was Mrs. Swanker Watson. She was leaning on the deck rail and looking down at the sea as though she was thinking of ending it all very soon.

"It's Mrs. Swanker Watson," Clive said. "She looks a bit unhappy. Let's go and have a word and try to cheer her up."

Over we went.

"'Morning, Mrs. Watson," Clive said. "Bit of a rough night last night."

"Ohhh," Mrs. Swanker Watson groaned, and I noticed then that she was holding a big, brown paper bag for some reason.

"Did you sleep all right?" Clive asked, trying to make polite conversation.

But all she said was "Ohhh" again, and she sort of slumped forward and gripped the deck rail with the hand that wasn't holding the bag.

"Feeling a bit queasy, are you?" Clive asked. "What you probably need is a spot of breakfast. That would soon sort you out."

"Gaaaaa—" Mrs. Swanker sort of gurgled, and her eyes sort of rolled around a bit, as if she couldn't quite get them into focus.

"There's nothing like a spot of breakfast to line the stomach," Clive went on. "And there's plenty in the restaurant. Loads. No one seems to be touching it for some reason—apart from me. No, for my money, you can't beat a nice bit of greasy bacon in the mornings, a nice juicy bit, with a decent wodge of fat on it, all sort of lying there on the plate, shimmering in its own grease. And there's scrambled eggs too, if you don't fancy the fried ones. Nice and runny as well, they are, just the way I like them. Some people don't care for runny scrambled eggs, I know, but personally I can't get enough of them. How about you, Mrs. Watson? Do you like your eggs to be runny? Or do you prefer them to be a bit on the chewy side—"

He was interrupted by Mrs. Swanker Watson, who made this most peculiar noise, and then she did something that I don't really want to tell you about, as it's not the sort of thing that ladies normally do—especially when they're staying in the first-class cabins.

But she definitely did it, and it went all down the side of the boat.

I quietly led Clive away then, as I felt that Mrs. Swanker Watson might prefer to be alone with her emotions for a while. I also had a feeling that if I had allowed Clive to go on telling her about what she could have for breakfast, that he might be all down the side of the boat as well.

So we just quietly tiptoed away and got over to the Bosun's Club, and as we were first there, Matey Matilda, the lady in charge, couldn't say she was full up for the day. So we got our names down and had a nice time doing all the activities and playing with the other children on board.

There were quite a few children there with their parents, but none of them were like us. None of them were stowaways, and none of them knew that that was what we were.

It made you feel quite good sometimes, to be a stowaway, quite different and special.

The rest of the time though, it was just terrifying.

· TWELVE ·

⚓

PORT OF CALL

THE NEXT DAY we came into land. Everybody lined the decks, all wanting a good view of the harbor as we sailed toward Egypt.

By now, Clive and me were so suntanned and our hair had got so bleached in the sun, that I don't think Dad would have recognized us even if he'd walked right past us.

It was dead exciting too, coming in to tie up in another country. We'd never really been to a faraway country before, not one as far away as this anyway. We'd been to the Isle of Wight once, but that is only really fifteen minutes on the ferry, and is not strictly speaking what you would call "abroad." Nor is it what you would call "exotic." And if they do have any pyramids on the Isle of Wight, then all I can say is that I must have missed them.

It was dead hot in Egypt, but instead of walking around in T-shirt and shorts, most people wore long robes to keep the heat off—though by the look of them you would have thought that they would have made you even hotter.

As we were waiting for the gangplank to be lowered, Clive happened to see Mrs. Swanker Watson. She was looking a lot better by now and seemed to have recovered from the storm.

However, when Clive mentioned that the deck seemed hot enough to fry eggs on, she hurried away and said she would see us later, or maybe not as the case may be, but she had important things to attend to just then and was rather busy.

We mingled with the crowd who were waiting to get off the boat, and we reached our hands out and got a boarding card each, so that we could get back on after the trip.

Air-conditioned coaches were waiting for us and Clive and me got seats at the back, and off we went.

We drove though heat and dust and crowds; past bazaars and market stalls, and then out into the desert. Here we saw people leading camels, loaded up with packages and parcels. Some of the camels carried people—sometimes two people, or women with babies.

Clive said he wanted to buy a camel, but I told him he didn't have the money for one thing, and for another they'd never let him take it back on the boat as it wouldn't have a boarding pass.

ALEX SHEARER

Clive said camels didn't need boarding passes. But I said that even if they didn't, it still wouldn't make any difference, as no one was going to let you bring a camel onto a big cruise liner, and anyway, where would it sleep?

So he said that it could sleep with us, but I said no way was I sharing a room with a camel. I said it was smelly enough sharing a room with Clive, without having a camel making pongs in there as well. And anyway, how could we ever get a camel down to rat class? He said we could if we were careful, but I didn't think so. And anyway, what about a bed for it? He said it could have my bed. So I said there was no way a camel was going to have my bed. If it was going to have anyone's bed, it was going to be Clive's. So he said, where would he sleep then? So I said he could share with the camel. But on second thoughts, I said that if the camel was at all fussy— which it probably would be—it wouldn't want to share a bed with Clive and would be offended at the very suggestion.

Clive said that he was never going to go on any more cruises with me ever again now in that case, and I said good. Clive then brought up all that old business about how I had pushed in and how he should have been born first and that by rights he should be the eldest.

Well, I told him that if he thought being the eldest was such a prize, he ought to try it some time, and then he'd know what it was all about and he wouldn't be so smug then.

And by that time we were at the pyramids.

We got out and followed the guide and everyone into blistering heat. There were loads of people everywhere wanting to sell us postcards and souvenirs, and they pestered you to buy some.

They say that the people in Egypt are very good at haggling and at striking a bargain. Well, they hadn't met Clive. The fact that we didn't have any money didn't stop Clive from trying to haggle with this man who wanted to sell us some postcards and a little souvenir pyramid to take home.

After about twenty minutes, the man turned and walked away, but Clive wanted to go on haggling and wouldn't leave him alone.

In the end the man gave Clive a free postcard and a little pyramid just to get Clive to go away and leave him alone to get on with his business.

I don't think that there are many postcard and souvenir-sellers in Egypt who have been out-pestered by a tourist before, but that one was. And to give Clive his due, he said I could have the post-card, so I wouldn't need to go home empty-handed.

To be honest, although the pyramids were all very beautiful and most impressive, it was so hot that all we really wanted to do was to get back on to the air-conditioned coach and get back to the ship and lounge by the swimming pool with six or seven long, cool drinks apiece.

It was a long journey to and from the boat and by the time we got back to the dockside, the day was cooling down a little and the sun was low in the sky.

We were last off the bus and there was a big crowd of people waiting to get back on board the ship.

As it had cooled down a bit, Clive and me decided to go for a little wander and to let everyone else get on board first.

We set out for a stroll around the docks then. It was fascinating to see all the sights and to watch the cargoes being loaded and unloaded. There was a smell in the air of spices and oil and you didn't know what—strange, different, exotic smells. There were boats and people there from all around the world. There were sailors and dock workers calling to each other in what seemed like a hundred different languages. There were white people and black people and brown people and all shades in between.

We shouldn't really have been there, as docks are dangerous places, but there was no one to stop or to challenge us, and we kept out of the way of the cranes and the fork-lift trucks and the other machinery.

We must have wandered around for ages, looking at the ships, taking in the sights and smells, hearing the toot of the ships' whistles and the great blare of their horns as they came in to tie up or set off out to sea.

Finally I looked at my watch. Two hours or more had gone by since we'd returned in the coach.

"Come on, Clive," I said. "Let's go back now and get on board. Everyone else should be on by now."

"Okay then," he said. "I suppose. I'm getting a bit hungry anyway, and they should be serving dinner soon."

And there was the echo of a foghorn as some great ship left the harbor and headed out to sea.

"Come on then. Let's go."

We retraced our steps, walking back the way we had come. The sun was low on the horizon now, like a great blood-red orange.

"Look at that!"

We stopped a while to look at it. We'd never seen the sun like that before. It looked as if it filled half the sky.

"You do have your boarding card, don't you, Clive?" I said, as we made our way back toward the ship. It would be just like him to have lost it.

"Of course I have," he said, patting his pocket to make sure. "Have you got yours? Huh?"

I did. I knew I did. But I checked anyway. Yup, there it was.

"Okay, here we are then. Should be just here."

We turned a corner by a warehouse.

And that was when it happened. One of the worst things that had ever happened to me in my entire life.

That was when we realized.

Our ship wasn't there.

It had gone.

· THIRTEEN ·

TROUBLE

JUST FOR A MOMENT, I thought of chucking myself into the docks. Then I thought of chucking Clive into the docks. Then I thought it might be best if we both jumped into the docks together, and that would be the end of our worries.

Gone.

The ship had gone. Those blasts on the siren we had heard, it must have been the last call to go on board, a warning that the *Mona Lisa* was to depart at any minute.

Gone.

Suddenly even the heat of the evening seemed icy cold.

"How much money have you got on you, Clive?" I asked.

He rummaged in his pockets.

"Fifteen pence," he said.

"Got any Egyptian money?"

"I've got a postcard and a little pyramid," he said. "They might be worth something."

We looked around the docks. They seemed vast and unfriendly and forbidding.

"Maybe I could sell them," Clive suggested, "and the proceeds would pay for a hotel room and a flight home."

But I doubted it.

"Do you speak any Egyptian, Clive?" I said— though I knew the answer in advance.

"Not a lot," he admitted. "Just a few words— like pyramid, Sphinx, and camel. And fez. And yashmak. And Porta Potti."

"We're in trouble, Clive," I said.

"Yes," he said. And he sat down on top of a capstan and buried his head in his hands. "I think I'm going to cry," he said.

I sat down on the capstan beside him.

"I think I might join you," I said.

Things had never looked so bad.

"Do you think they'll realize we're not on board and come back for us?" Clive asked hopefully.

"No," I said. "I don't. How will they realize that we're not on board when they never knew we were on board in the first place?"

"Mrs. Swanker Watson might miss us," Clive said.

"After you telling her all about greasy bacon and scrambled eggs I think all she wanted to do was avoid us. If she doesn't see us again, she'll probably look on it as a great relief."

"How about Mrs. Dominics?"

"Maybe. But by the time she starts to wonder—well, the ship could be miles away."

"Knots away."

"Whatever."

"Who else might miss us?"

"Nobody."

"Swanker?"

"Might do. But then he might just think that we were only going as far as Egypt and forgot to mention it. That's all some people do. They do one leg of the cruise then get off and go somewhere else, or catch a plane home."

"That's what we'll have to do then," Clive said. "We'll have to catch a plane home."

I started to get a bit exasperated then.

"How, exactly, Clive?" I said. "How do we catch a plane home? Here we are, in a foreign country, miles from home. We don't have any money, we don't speak the language, something terrible could happen to us at any moment. We might be kidnapped, or abducted for the slave trade, and put to work mucking out camels and never see home again. And no one will know where we are. And when Dad gets home we won't be there. And he'll never know what's happened to us, and he'll go frantic and blame himself and we'll be all over the front pages of the newspapers."

"That'll be good," Clive said. "We'll be famous."

"No, it won't be good," I said. "It won't be good at all. It'll be horrible."

"We'll still be famous though," he insisted.

"Clive," I said, "what use is it to be famous as a disappeared person? If you're going to be famous, you want to be famous for doing something good. Or for having something lucky happen to you—like winning the lottery. It's not much fun being famous because you've disappeared, is it? It's no good being known as Clive the Disappearing Camel Boy, is it?"

"I wouldn't mind," Clive said. "It would be a way to get back at some of them at school. They'd be sorry then that they hadn't been nicer to me when they realized that I was Clive of Egypt, the Camel Boy."

"Clive," I said, "don't you understand, the fact is that probably nobody will ever hear of us again."

He looked thoughtful for a time, then said,

"Well, look on the bright side, maybe a rich Egyptian might adopt us. And instead of Clive the Camel Boy, I could be Clive the Mercedes Benz Boy. Or Clive the Ferrari Boy."

"Clive," I said, "the way things are going, you'll be lucky to be even Clive the Skateboard Boy."

"Well anyway," he said, "that aside, if we can get an airplane home before the ship gets back, then Dad'll be none the wiser and he'll never even know that we've been away. And then we won't get into trouble."

"Clive," I said, "we have no money, no credit cards, and we don't speak a word of Egyptian. How, exactly, do we catch a plane home? Eh?"

"I've got a plan," he said.

"Being?" I said.

"It's worked before," Clive said, "and it can work again."

"So what is it?"

"It's simple."

"Well?"

"We go to the airport—"

"And?"

"And we find a plane that's flying to Britain—"

"And?"

"And when we've found one—"

"Yes?"

"We stow away."

To be perfectly honest, I did think that I might kill Clive around about then. And had things not been otherwise, had I not glimpsed something out of the corner of my eye, I might well have done so. Even at this moment, Clive might be lying in a morgue somewhere in Egypt, just lying there on a cold slab or in the deep freeze, with a little cardboard tag attached to his big toe with string, and on it would be written (in Egyptian), "Unknown Boy. Fished From Docks With Head Wounds."

I froze. Froze and thawed both together. It was like one of those moments when you see disaster coming, like when you think you've lost something, something that cost a lot of money, and you're going to get into big trouble for losing it, and then it suddenly turns up.

"Clive," I said. "Our ship—"

"Yes?" he said.

"Which berth number did you say it was in?"

"Seven," he said.

"Clive," I said. "Look around the corner. To berth nine."

He looked.

There, just above the cranes and the warehouses, you could see the funnel of the *Mona Lisa*, a thin plume of smoke rising from it.

"Oh," he said. "That looks like our boat."

"You idiot, Clive!" I said. "You nearly killed me. You nearly gave me a heart attack. You're doing me in with all this worry. It's awful having to be the eldest all the time and to have to look after a twerp like you!"

"Well, if you're so clever, why didn't you remember which berth it was?" he said.

"Stop dragging things in that have nothing to do with it," I told him. "And come on."

We hurried on to berth nine, and there was our boat. A few other stragglers were making their leisurely way up the gangplank.

We got out our boarding cards and showed them to the sailor in charge.

"Cut it a bit close there, boys," he said.

"When are we leaving?"

"Half an hour," he said. "Where are your parents?"

"Just coming," we said.

A small crowd of people were approaching the

ship behind us. They'd do for parents, as long as he didn't inquire too closely.

We got on board and went straight to the bar.

"Cokes," Clive said. "Large ones. And put a shot of ice cream in that."

We knocked them back and started to feel a bit better.

"Clive," I said, "have you ever thought what's going to happen when we get back home? How are we going to go on fooling Dad into thinking that we've been at Gran's while he's been away? I mean, our suntans alone are going to make him suspicious."

"I don't know," Clive said. "Best not to think about it if you ask me. Something'll turn up."

Of course, that was Clive all over—something'll turn up. The story of his life. But on this occasion, he was right. Only what turned up wasn't necessarily better than what didn't turn up.

In many ways it was a whole lot worse.

WE HAD A BUFFET dinner with Mrs. Dominics that night, and Clive asked her if she was going to the casino later. She said she was. She also said that there was a man who went in and gambled there every night. She said he had four friends with him, and that was all they ever did. They never went swimming, they never went for walks around the deck, all they ever did was sit in the casino and gamble, morning, noon, night and into the small hours.

The man always wore dark glasses too, even when he was inside. And whenever it looked like his drink was running out, one of his friends would wave the steward over and order a refill for him immediately.

Mrs. Dominics said that they didn't seem like your normal cruise passengers at all. They looked like they had booked themselves on to the wrong holiday, and that they should really have gone to Las Vegas instead.

We'd seen them and knew who she meant. We'd also noticed that Lumpy, the steward with the shaved, lumpy head, was always fawning over them. Clive reckoned that he was after Big Tips, and he probably thought that if he kept the drinks and snacks coming that these gamblers would remember him when they had a big win on the roulette table and give him a few pounds for his trouble.

Anyway, after our long and eventful day, Clive and me managed to sneak down to our cabin in rat class without incident. We had a good long sleep and awoke the next morning feeling much refreshed.

In many ways, things had gone pretty well for us. We'd had a few narrow escapes and close shaves, but we hadn't actually been caught yet. We'd had some good meals and seen some great sights and we'd enjoyed first-class facilities (apart from the cabin, of course) and really had no complaints.

But sometimes the cards are just stacked up against you, and that is how they come from the pack. Luck seems to play a part in everything, be it good luck or bad. On the whole we'd had good luck so far, but then it started to change.

Sometimes it seems as if someone has turned a tap on. First there are little drops of bad luck, dripping out from this big leaky tap in the sky—almost as a warning to you not to get too confident. Then the hand of fate reaches out and turns the tap on full blast.

And before you know it, you're soaked.

IT STARTED WITH Mrs. Swanker Watson.

Clive and me were resting by the pool. We had long cool drinks with umbrellas in them. Not big umbrellas, mind. Just little, decorative sorts of umbrellas, the kind that come stuck into an orange slice, or a pineapple cube.

We were lounging behind our sunglasses, soaking up the heat and reading a couple of books we had got from the ship's library.

I was reading a sci-fi book and Clive was reading *The Story of Bluebeard,* the pirate. Clive had got into pirates in a big way—he had taken to going around with his Swiss army knife between his teeth, pretending it was a cutlass.

Anyway, instead of pretending not to see us, as she had been doing ever since that morning when Clive had gone on about the greasy bacon, she headed straight for us, all smiles and glee.

"Oh, there you are!" she said. "I must thank you. We got our invitation this morning."

Clive and me looked blank. Well, Clive looks permanently blank anyway, especially when he's wearing his sunglasses, but on this occasion, he looked extra blank with bells on.

"Beg pardon?" he said.

Mrs. Swanker Watson looked around as if to make sure that she wasn't being overheard, lowered her voice and said, "Your dear papa!"

"Who?" Clive said.

"Your dear papa," Mrs. Swanker said again.

"No," Clive said. "Not us. We haven't got one."

"Your father—" Mrs. Swanker said.

"Oh, yes—"

"The captain—"

I got them again—the cold chills of horror and fear. The dreads. The dreads that came with them. There it was once more in my stomach, that feeling that disaster was imminent and unavoidable.

"The c-captain—?" I said. "Oh yes, Clive, our dad—the captain!"

"How could I forget," Clive said. "As if I could ever forget dear old Dad—the captain."

"Well, you two boys obviously have quite an influence with him," Mrs. Swanker Watson said.

"We do? That is—yes, we do, obviously, us being so closely related and all."

"And I don't know what you said to him, but our invitation came this morning. Delivered to our cabin. By the steward. Your father has invited us to dine with him at the captain's table—tonight!"

I looked at Clive. For a moment there, he didn't have his suntan anymore. Then slowly it came back.

"Tonight?"

"Tonight. Mr. Watson and I are invited to dine with the captain. I'm sure I owe it to you boys. So thank you both very much. I'm so pleased that Angus is going to a good school with nice boys like you in it for his classmates."

"Er, one thing, Mrs. Watson—if—that is when you have dinner with the captain—that is, dear old Dad tonight—you won't mention us, will you?"

She gave me a funny look.

"Why ever not, dear?" she said.

"Well, it's like I said," I said. "He doesn't want people to know that we're on board—"

"For fear of kidnapping, jealousy and favoritism," Clive explained.

"Oh yes," Mrs. Swanker Watson said blithely. "In public I wouldn't dream of mentioning it. But over a quiet dinner—a little *tête-à-tête*—in confidence—I'm sure he'll be only too delighted to hear what wonderfully behaved boys he has."

And she went.

I looked at Clive. Clive looked at me.

"We're done for," he said. "Why on earth—why on sea, rather—did the captain ever invite the Swanker Watsons to join him for dinner?"

There was no answer to questions like that. Maybe he just felt he had to. Maybe it was part of his duties. Maybe he just liked suffering.

"Whose bright idea was it, Clive," I said, "to tell Mrs. Swanker Watson that we were the captain's children, eh? Just exactly whose bright idea was that? Answer me that one then, Clive. You just answer me that!"

"It was your idea, wasn't it?" he said.

I couldn't remember if it was or it wasn't, so I let it pass.

"The point is, what do we do? Dinner's in eight hours. Eight hours, Clive. That's all we've got left. Eight hours and the clock's running. And then they're going to find out the truth. And then—"

"The brig."

"The brig!"

"Clapped in irons. With the cat-o'-ten-tails."

"Nine tails, Clive. Not ten! Cat-o'-nine-tails— whatever that is."

"What are we going to do?"

There was only one thing to do. We somehow had to stop the Swanker Watsons from having dinner with the captain. Or otherwise I could almost hear the following conversation (or something along these lines) taking place:

MRS. SWANKER WATSON: Oh, by the way, Captain. I must compliment you on your two children. Such nicely behaved boys. And such fine table manners too.

CAPTAIN CONNERTON: *(after giving Mrs. Swanker strange and puzzled looks)* My children, Mrs. Watson? You say you know my children?

MRS. SWANKER WATSON: Oh yes. Very well.

MR. SWANKER WATSON: *(glassy-eyed)* Waiter—more wine, please. A big bottle.

CAPTAIN CONNERTON: And can I ask how you come to know my children, Mrs. Watson?

MRS. SWANKER WATSON: They go to the same school as our son, Angus, who was born in Aberdeen. Indeed, they are in the same class. They sit together and are the best of chums by all accounts.

CAPTAIN CONNERTON: *(chewing his beard in bewilderment and confusion)* The best of chums, you say, Mrs. Watson?

MRS. SWANKER WATSON: Oh yes.

MR. SWANKER WATSON: Waiter—hurry up with that wine.

CAPTAIN CONNERTON: But this is most strange, Mrs. Watson, because neither of my children go to school.

MRS. SWANKER WATSON: *(perplexed)* I beg your pardon? Your two boys *don't* go to school?

CAPTAIN CONNERTON: Indeed no. Not any longer. In fact my eldest boy is a doctor and my younger boy is at university.

MRS. SWANKER WATSON: University! Then—

CAPTAIN CONNERTON: And moreover, Mrs. Watson, I also have to tell you that both of my boys are girls!

MRS. SWANKER WATSON: *(shrieks)* Girls!? Then who—how—where—what—why?

CAPTAIN CONNERTON: Steward! The first-aid box. Smelling salts for Mrs. Watson.

MR. SWANKER WATSON: Where's my wine got to!

(The smelling salts are brought. Mrs. Swanker Watson makes a partial recovery, enough for her to say—)

MRS. SWANKER WATSON: But, if those two boys are not your children, Captain—which they assured me they were—what are they doing on this boat . . . on their own?

(*The captain goes ghostly pale. He summons the First Officer, Mr. Pensley.*)

CAPTAIN CONNERTON: Mr. Pensley, take some men and arm them heavily. I fear we have desperate boys on board—two of them—stowaways!

FIRST OFFICER PENSLEY: Aye, aye, Captain. On the double.

(*He goes to collect the men and to seize the fugitives. They are taken away in chains and put in the brig.*)

I LOOKED AT Clive, all mysterious behind his sunglasses.

"Well?" I said.

"We have to stop her having dinner with him."

"It won't be easy," I said. "She's got her heart set on it. In fact, I think it was the only reason she came on this cruise in the first place. I don't see how we're going to stop Mrs. Swanker from having dinner with the captain. I really don't."

"We'll have to poison her," Clive said.

I was so worried and desperate, I was prepared to consider it.

"How?"

"Dunno. Somehow. We don't have to kill her, just make her ill for a bit. Perhaps I could go and tell her a bit more about runny eggs and greasy bacon?"

"No, Clive," I said. "We're going to need a bit

more than runny eggs this time. Not even runny ostrich eggs would put her off dinner at the captain's table."

"Then maybe we could poison the captain."

"That's mutiny," I pointed out. "They can lock you up for that."

"Then maybe we could create some kind of emergency, so that the captain would have to be on the bridge and couldn't keep his dinner appointment."

"Like what?"

"Dunno. Something."

We were stumped.

We lay by the pool like condemned men, like those people in America who are going to get the electric chair in the evening, unless there is a last-minute reprieve. We considered all the possibilities—poisoning Mrs. Swanker Watson, pushing her overboard, locking her in the bathroom, locking her in her cabin, getting dressed up and pretending to be her, but none of our solutions seemed feasible. Or they did, but they weren't very humane.

And all the while the ship sailed on, over a beautiful, calm, blue sea. And now and again we got a glimpse of Dad, moving around on the other deck, bringing people drinks and collecting their glasses.

And somehow, just then, I understood. I understood why it was so difficult for Dad to leave all this behind, to leave the sea. Despite the storms and the rough weather and the times you feel queasy and are ill over the side, there is still something about the sea that must call you back to it, again and again.

"When I grow up, Clive," I said, "I'm going to be a sailor, like Dad."

"Me too," Clive said. "Me too."

And, you know something, I was glad that we had stowed away. No matter what might happen to us now. I was glad. Because we had seen new places and wonderful things. And especially because we understood, now, why Dad found it so hard to tear himself away. We understood why he was always putting off leaving the sea and saying, "Just one more trip, boys. This will be the last one. I mean it this time."

I felt that if Dad had to give up the sea he would never be happy again. He would be like a wild bird, put into a cage. And every time we went past the docks, he would look at the great ships, with a kind of longing, and he would wish that he was on board one of them, and sailing away.

But he wouldn't be able to go, because of us.

"Clive," I said, "if we ever get out of this, let's agree never to complain again about being left at Gran's while Dad goes to sea. Okay?"

"Okay," Clive said. "Okay."

And I knew then that even though he was five minutes younger than I was and nowhere near as mature, that he understood too.

I think in some ways we had inherited the sea. Some people say, "You have your father's eyes," or "You've got your mother's nose," but we had the sea.

ALEX SHEARER

We had the sea in our veins, and every time our hearts beat, the tide rose and fell, rose and fell, and boats were bobbing at anchor.

I bet if a doctor had put a stethoscope to our chests, he wouldn't have heard hearts beating at all, he'd have heard the lap of the waves, and the sigh of the sand and the shingle, and the seagulls squawking in the distant sky and the faraway cry of the whales.

Something inside us had changed, I felt. Things were somehow different now. I guess that's what happens to you when you make a journey— a real journey, that is. A journey both inside and out.

"THE CONDEMNED MEN *ate a hearty meal."*

That's what they say, don't they? About people who are about to get the chop? That they ate a hearty meal before they went.

Well, I don't know how they do, because I certainly couldn't.

How can you eat a hearty meal with the fear and dread of discovery hanging over you? Let alone the fear and dread of the electric chair.

It was different for Clive, of course; he's about as sensitive as a concrete post. Clive could eat hearty meals in any situation. You could tie him to a bomb and set the detonator for it to go off in five minutes, and Clive would still eat a hearty meal before he went. He'd probably eat the bomb as well.

Well, we knew we were doomed and there was

nothing we could do about it now. So we went down to our cabin in rat class to change for dinner one last time.

"We may as well eat a hearty meal," Clive said, "before Mrs. Swanker Watson spills the beans."

I was in no mood for hearty meals at all, and even the mention of spilled beans was making me feel a bit queasy.

As we were getting changed, we heard more whispering coming down the ventilation pipe. There was the half-familiar voice again, and then other, unknown voices.

"Tonight it is then."

"Everything ready?"

"Have they made contact yet?"

"Don't worry about it. Just make sure you're prepared."

And then the voices faded away.

"You know," I said to Clive, "who that sounded like?"

"Lumpy," he said. "It was Lumpy's voice."

"I wonder what he's up to?"

"He's probably stealing silver forks from the restaurant," Clive said. "He probably takes them home and melts them down for jewelry."

But I didn't think it was all that likely.

We looked around our cabin in rat class, the way condemned men look around their prison cells for one last time, knowing that they will never return.

"What'll I do with my pants?" Clive said—

eyeing his pants up, which were drying on the makeshift line.

"Leave them," I said. "Your pants are the least of our worries. We've got bigger fish to fry than your pants."

"I'm going to say good-bye to everything," Clive said. And he did. "Good-bye rat-class cabin, good-bye all the beds, good-bye pants, good-bye cruise . . ."

He went on like that for ages. When he started to say good-bye to the rivets, I felt I had to stop him.

"Come on, Clive. Let's go."

He took one last look around.

"You know," he said, "this has been the biggest and the best adventure of my whole life. I'll probably never have another adventure like this as long as I live. I'll grow up and have to get a job and get to be old and boring and responsible. I'm glad I was a stowaway. I'm not saying it's right. But I'm still glad just the same."

"Me too, Clive. Me too."

And we closed the door on our cabin in rat class, and we went on up for our hearty meal.

Clive stuffed himself, but I hardly ate anything.

"Not feeling well, dear?" Mrs. Dominics asked.

I felt that maybe we ought to tell her the truth. But in other ways, I felt she knew it. And either way, she'd find out soon enough.

"Just not much of an appetite somehow," I said.

The captain went by, on his way to the main restaurant, to the captain's table and his invited guests.

Soon then, soon. Soon they'd all start talking around the dinner table. Mrs. Swanker Watson would mention his "two sons" and then we were done for.

I waited. I chewed. Nothing.

Clive went and got a pudding. Still I waited, for the hand on the shoulder, for the First Officer to come and clap us in irons. Still nothing.

Clive went and got another pudding. The suspense was getting to me. I couldn't hold out much longer.

"I think I'll go and turn myself in to the authorities, Clive," I said. "Just to get it over with."

"No hurry," he said. "Early days yet. Time for another pudding."

He went and got a third one.

On the ship sped, around the clock went, still nothing. Mrs. Dominics finished eating and went to the casino. Still nothing.

We went up on deck.

"Will they find us here?" Clive asked.

"They'll find us," I said. "Don't worry."

Nothing.

We went down to the theater to watch the cabaret.

Nothing.

We came out.

"What's showing in the ship's cinema?" Clive said. "Anything we can see?"

And then, incredibly, the captain walked by, his dinner over. He gave us a nod and went on his way.

Mrs. Swanker hadn't mentioned us! We'd got away with it. We'd got away with it again.

And then who should we see but Swanker Watson, coming along the corridor with a drink in his hand.

"Hello, Swanker."

"Hi. Hello, Clive."

"I thought your mum and dad were eating with the captain tonight—our—er—*dad* the captain, that is?"

"That's right," Swanker said. "They were supposed to, only when Mum was getting ready to go to dinner, she sat down on the bed in the cabin, and the whole bed collapsed."

"Collapsed?!"

"Yes. On her foot. She had to get the doctor. She says she's going to sue."

"Oh my, my," I said. "What a disappointment."

"She's so annoyed about it, she says she wouldn't eat with the captain now if he paid her."

"Oh dear. Well, I hope her foot gets better soon, Swanker."

"Thanks. I'll see you then. I'd best get back."

And off he went.

Clive and me practically danced for joy, all the way down to rat class.

We had charmed lives. We really did.

Somebody up there was looking after us, they really were.

We thought.

For a moment.

But we thought wrong.

Because when we got down to our cabin in rat class, and when we opened the door, and when we went inside . . .

. . . somebody else was in there.

Looking for a new bed.

For Mrs. Swanker Watson's cabin.

And can you guess who that someone was?

You're right.

It was our dad.

Fourteen

MORE TROUBLE

TO BE PERFECTLY HONEST, I think that Dad was a bit surprised to see us. Well, maybe more than a bit, quite a lot really. It was one of those difficult and awkward moments when nobody really knows what to say. It was a bit like opening the door to a bathroom stall and finding somebody in there, a complete stranger, perched on the seat with their trousers around their ankles. You look at them, and they look at you. It's maybe a vicar, or somebody like that. Or a policeman. Or a headteacher. You both feel shocked and embarrassed. Neither of you really knows what to say. You slowly start to edge toward the door, to be off and away.

Dad just stood there looking at us, as if we were two big boy-sized tomatoes, or something unusual like that. His mouth was opening and closing, as if a few words were about to come out—or there again, maybe not.

Meantime, my mind was racing, and so was Clive's. You could practically see it. You could almost see his brain behind his eyeballs, whizzing round and round, like one of those slot machines in the casino, trying desperately to come up with a winning line—three oranges, or three strawberries, or something like that.

"Hi, er—Dad," he finally said. "Fancy seeing you here."

Oddly enough, although I hadn't mentioned anything to my feet about edging toward the door, that was exactly what they seemed to be doing. And so were Clive's. And there we were, Dad standing there with his mouth opening and closing, and me and Clive with the magic feet, sort of heading toward the corridor.

Dad regained the power of speech.

"What the ****** ****** ******** are you doing here?" he said.

In case you don't know what the star-shaped things are in the last sentence, they are called asterisks. You usually use them when you are writing things down as a substitute for swearing. Now, I shan't go into the exact details of what Dad said, as I don't think it is suitable for younger and more impressionable children. But maybe you can guess. I have to say on Dad's behalf that he never usually swore at all. The only other time we had heard him swearing was when Clive accidentally hit him on the knee with the garden spade.

I suppose that seeing us there in the cabin in rat class must have come as quite a shock. Dad is always saying that we should try to put ourselves in someone else's shoes before we go making judgments, and that is what I did.

From Dad's point of view, we were safely tucked up in bed, back at home, around at Gran's. We were hundreds and hundreds of miles away, and had been, for days and days. How could we possibly be on the boat? So to him, we must have seemed like ghosts suddenly appearing out of nowhere. What were we doing there? How had we got there? How on earth . . . ?

And hence the swearing.

Clive's feet meanwhile (and mine as well) were still shuffling casually along, making their way toward the door. I'm not altogether sure just what Clive's feet had in mind after that. Once they got to the door, I don't know if his feet really knew what to do. I suspect that once there, they intended to make a run for it. It is also my theory that the rest of his body was going to follow his feet, and the chances were that both of them would then disappear. It is also my theory that my feet intended to follow his.

But they didn't get the chance. Dad reached out and closed the cabin door. Then he stared at us with both eyeballs, which somehow seemed a lot larger than usual, and he repeated what he had just said.

"What the ****** ****** ******** are you doing here?"

Only there might have been a few more asterisks this time.

"What—? How—? How did you—? Why have—? What—? But—?"

He still seemed as upset as ever, but I was pleased to see that the asterisks had stopped.

He sat down heavily on one of the beds.

"Well? Well? **Well!**"

Clive looked at me, as if it was my job to explain.

"He's the eldest," he said.

"Only by five minutes!" I reminded him.

"I don't care who does the explaining—just do it! Well?"

"Well, Dad—"

"Well?"

"Well—"

"Well? Well then? Come on. Out with it. What are you doing here? How did you get on this boat?"

"Well, I suppose we sort of—"

"Yes? Well? Sort of what?"

"Well, sort of—"

"Yes?"

"Sort of stowed—"

"Stowed? What do you mean, stowed?"

"Well, like—away."

"Away?"

"Yes—away."

"Both of you?"

"Yes."

"Stowed?"

"Yes."

"Away?"

"Yes."

"And whose idea was this?"

"It was his."

"No it wasn't, it was his."

"Well, whose was it then?"

"His!"

"One at a time!"

"His."

"His."

"Right. I see. It was both your ideas then?"

"Sort of."

"Sort of? What do you mean, sort of? Was it or wasn't it?"

"I suppose."

"Suppose what?"

"It was both our ideas—sort of."

"Right. I see. Right."

"You're not angry with us are you, Dad?"

"Angry? Angry? Angry!!! Clive, I can't begin to tell you! I can't even start to put it into words! I cannot even start to describe it! I'm on the verge here, you know that? You know that? One little thing, that's all it needs! One little thing to topple me, and I'll be right over the edge. You understand that, Clive? I mean, you know you see in the paper, about these parents, who lock their kids in cupboards, and make them eat dog food? And you say, '*How could anyone treat a child, their own child, like that?*' Well, I'm starting to understand why, Clive. I'm starting to understand. And you know when people who have committed murder stand up in court and say, '*I don't remember anything about. it, your Honor. I just suddenly saw red, and that was the last thing I recall.*' Well I'm starting to understand them too, Clive. Does that answer your question?"

"Ah, good. Thanks, Dad. So you're not angry then?"

"I'm livid, Clive! I'm livid. I'm furious beyond putting into words!"

"Ah, good. As long as you're not angry."

Dad sat quietly on the bed for a while. He closed his eyes and seemed to be counting to ten. When he got to ten, he started from one again. This time, he counted to fifty. Then he opened his eyes again.

We were still there. We hadn't gone away.

I'm not sure if he was pleased about that or not.

"Okay," he said. "Now I know this is maybe going to seem like a stupid question, but perhaps you could tell me one thing. Just one thing. It's only a one-word question, but I'd appreciate if you would give me an answer to it. And the question is this—*why?*"

"Why?"

"Yes, why? That's all I want to know. Why? Because do you know what you have done? Do you

ALEX SHEARER

have the slightest notion, the slightest inkling of what you have done?"

"How do you mean, Dad?"

"Look at it this way, Clive. Here I am—a Senior Steward, on an expensive cruiseliner. I look after the first-class passengers, make sure they're happy, that they're enjoying themselves, and having a good time. I now discover that my two sons have stowed away on board the ship I work on. They have been here, eating and drinking and sunbathing too, by the look of it, at the company's expense. Who's going to be held responsible for this, Clive? I am. And what do you think they're going to do when they find out, Clive?"

"What, Dad?"

"They're going to fire me, Clive. I'm going to lose my job!"

We hadn't thought of that. It was funny but we'd never once stopped to think about it from Dad's point of view. We'd always thought about what might happen to us if we got discovered, not what might happen to him.

"Do you understand what you've done now? Do you finally see the seriousness of it? Not only have you taken chances and risks I hate to even think about, you have also both lost me my job."

I looked at Clive. His lower lip was starting to tremble. He sat on the bed next to Dad, and so did I.

"Sorry, Dad," Clive said. "We didn't think."

"No," Dad said. "You didn't think. You never do, do you, either of you, you never do think!

Because if you did think, if you had just stopped for one second to think, of all the trouble and all the repercussions, you wouldn't be here, would you? And we wouldn't all be in this mess. What am I supposed to do now? What do I say? So will you please just answer one question for me: why?"

"Please don't be angry, Dad," Clive said. "I mean, it's not that bad—worse things happen at sea."

"In case you haven't noticed, Clive, we are at sea!" Dad snapped.

There was a long silence. Clive was next to Dad on one side, I was on the other. I didn't know how to put it really. I didn't know quite what to say. I opened my mouth to try and explain. But Clive was there ahead of me.

"We did it, Dad," Clive said, "because—we wanted to be with you."

Dad stared at him.

"What?"

"We—we wanted to be with you. We get tired of you going away, and being left with Gran. We just wanted to go with you, that was all."

Dad didn't say anything for a while. There was another long, horrible silence. I thought that maybe he might start with the asterisks again, but he didn't. He just sat there staring into something long ago and far away. And then he looked at Clive, and then he looked at me, and he put his arm out and put it around Clive's shoulders, and he put his other arm around mine.

And we just sat there, on the bed, with our arms around each other, all staring at the rivets, at the long ago and far away. And nobody said anything for a long, long time. And then finally Clive did say something. He said the one thing that we all were thinking.

"I wish Mum was here," he said.

And Dad just held us a bit tighter and said, "Me too, Clive, me too."

And nobody said anything then. Not for ages.

Then there was a sort of shaking. It was Dad. I was afraid to look at him, because I was afraid that he was crying. And if he was crying, I didn't know what I was going to do.

But he wasn't. He was laughing. And he started to laugh more and more. And then he looked at us both, and he laughed some more still. Then he started to laugh and splutter all at once, and he had to get his hankie out to blow his nose.

"I don't believe it," he said. "I mean, how did you do it? How did you get on board?"

"We just walked on," I said. "With a crowd of passengers."

"But what about all the security? It's supposed to be impossible to get on this boat without a ticket."

"Maybe it is if you're grown-up, Dad," I said. "But when you're our age, somehow different rules seem to apply. People just don't seem to suspect you somehow. They always think you're with someone else."

"And how long have you been in this cabin?"

"Since the beginning."

"And what did you do when we got to Egypt?"

"We went and had a look at the pyramids," Clive said. "And I got a postcard. And a little pyramid to take home—see?"

And he showed Dad his little pyramid.

And for some reason, Dad thought this was immensely funny. I don't know why. And he just sat there, almost hysterical with laughter, laughing and laughing until the tears were streaming from his eyes, holding up Clive's souvenir and saying,

"He got a pyramid! He got a little pyramid!" over and over again.

"And a postcard," Clive reminded him. "Only I'm giving it to him."

"And a postcard!" Dad hooted. And the postcard seemed even funnier than the pyramid. And then the pyramid would seem funnier than the postcard. And it went on like this for quite a while, until we thought we might have to get some cold water to throw over him, or possibly wave Clive's pants in front of his face.

Eventually he calmed down, but he went on muttering as he wiped the laughter tears from his eyes. "Oh dear, oh dear," he said. "Oh dear, oh dear." And he went on chuckling and blowing his nose in his handkerchief as if he might even blow a hole in it.

I decided that telling him about how we thought we had missed the boat wouldn't be a very good idea. Not now that Dad finally seemed to have got back to normal.

He looked around the cabin at all the stored and stacked-up beds, and seemed to remember why he was there.

"I came to get a bed," he said. "For Mrs. Watson—her bed collapsed—"

And then he was off laughing again. And this time, me and Clive were laughing too. Why it was so funny, I really don't know. I mean, it wasn't funny that Mrs. Swanker Watson had gone and hurt her foot when her bed had collapsed. It was just that *her bed had collapsed!*

And we'd all be away again. And we laughed so long and so loud and so inexplicably, that I'm sure I heard a fish outside, banging on the hull, telling us to be quiet and to shut up.

And eventually, as laughs always do in the end, they unwound and ran down, and finally they were over.

"Oh my," Dad said. "Oh my. I haven't laughed so much in years. My ribs ache."

And he passed his packet of tissues around so we could all have one to dry our eyes with and wipe our noses.

Then we were sensible again.

"Well then, boys," Dad said. "What do we do?"

"Er, I suppose—"

"What, Clive?"

"I suppose—we couldn't just carry on as we have been?"

"What do you mean?"

"Well, if we've got away with it this long,

Dad—and nobody knows that we shouldn't really be here apart from you—and if you didn't mention it to anyone—and you could bring us breakfast on a tray in the mornings and . . ."

Dad stared at Clive. He looked a bit shocked.

"Not mention it to anyone?"

"No, Dad. We could just carry on as we have been—sunbathing during the day, sneaking down here at night. No one need ever know. And then, when we got back home in the ship, you could help us sneak off, and no one need be any the wiser."

For a second, he almost seemed tempted. He almost seemed inclined to go along with it. But then he shook his head.

"I'd like to say yes, Clive, but I can't. I can't in good conscience leave the two of you down here, stowing away—I mean, if you were someone else's children, I wouldn't leave them to stow away. There can't be one set of rules for you and a different set for everybody else."

"But Dad—"

"I'm sorry. I've got to go and report this. I've no choice. And I guess I'd better offer my resignation too, while I'm at it. It's the only way. I can't leave you down here. For one thing, though you may not realize it, ships are dangerous places. Especially down here in the working area. If you'd gone and wandered into the engine room or—"

"We wouldn't do anything stupid like that, Dad," I protested.

But he gave me a look as if to say, "Wouldn't

you?" or maybe, "Haven't you already?"

"Okay," he said. "Come on. Let's go up. Let's find the captain and make a clean breast of it, and tell him the truth."

"Do we have to Dad?" Clive said. "It's not that I'm against telling the truth, it's just—is it always necessary, that's what I ask myself. I'm sure the truth is all well and good—but is it always necessary?"

"I'm afraid it is, Clive. It is this time."

Dad stood up.

"Come on," he said. "Let's go."

We stood up beside him. He looked dead smart in his uniform. I hoped that he wouldn't have to lose his job, not because of us.

"Dad," I said, "we won't mind you going to sea anymore. And we won't follow you. We'll be quite happy to stay at Grandma's, won't we, Clive?"

"Yeah," Clive said. "Yeah."

"We'll see," Dad said. "We'll see. Maybe I left you on your own too long. It's just that when you really love something—it's hard to give it up."

"You love your job, don't you, Dad?"

"Yes, I do—but I love you two more. So come on."

We gathered our stuff up.

"What'll happen to us, Dad? Will they clap us in irons and lock us in the brig?"

"No. I shouldn't think so. They might send you home from the next port of call though. Put you on a plane—at my expense."

"Oh."

Not only were we going to lose Dad his job, we were going to cost him a fortune as well, probably all the money he'd make on the trip.

"Never mind. What's done is done. We just have to move on."

"I'll just pack my spare pants," Clive said. "You never know when you'll need them."

"The funny thing is," Dad said, "that although I didn't know you were on the boat, I kept thinking I was seeing you. I kept imagining that I was getting little glimpses of you, flitting in and out. I kept seeing children who looked a bit like you, in baseball hats and sunglasses, up on deck, or lounging around the pool. It all falls into place now. It all makes sense."

"I'm ready," Clive said. "Warts and pants and all."

"Okay."

"What about Mrs. Watson's bed?"

"It'll just have to wait. I'll sort it out later. Okay then. Let's go."

Dad held his hands out and we took one each. We weren't proud of what we had done, but we weren't ashamed either. And now it was time to face the music. But at least we were together.

Clive and me took a last look around our cabin in rat class. I was sad to leave. It was hot and cramped and full of beds and it didn't smell all that lovely, but it had been home to us for a while, and we were fond of it just the same.

"Do you want your clothesline, Clive?" I said.

"No," he said. "I'll leave it. Somebody else might want it one day."

And we were ready to go and turn ourselves in, and to face whatever fate awaits stowaways.

"At least you won't have to walk the plank," Dad smiled. "Not like in the old days."

"Was that what they made you do?" Clive said. "If they caught you stowing away?"

"They did if they were pirates," Dad told him.

"But there aren't any pirates anymore, are there, Dad?" Clive said.

Only before Dad could get a word out, somebody else answered that question for him. And the answer to Clive's question as to whether or not there were still pirates in the world, at large upon the high seas—turned out to be yes.

There were.

And they were armed to the teeth, and extremely dangerous.

And what's more, they were on board our ship.

FIFTEEN

FINGERS CROSSED

"GOOD EVENING, LADIES and gentlemen, this is your captain speaking."

There wasn't a loudspeaker in our cabin down in rat class, but we could hear the tinny echo of the captain's voice coming from a speaker out in the gangway. We were just about to step out of the door when his voice came over the public address system.

"What's he saying, Dad?"

"Shhh! Listen!"

We listened. The captain didn't sound too good. His voice sounded a bit tense and throaty, as if he suddenly had a rather difficult emergency to deal with.

"Ah hem. Yes. This is your captain speaking, ladies and gentlemen, and I regret to tell you that we have a somewhat difficult situation on our hands."

We stood stock still, craning to hear, wondering what he would say next.

"You don't think it's an iceberg do you?" Clive whispered. (He seemed a bit obsessed with icebergs. We should never have rented that *Titanic* DVD.)

"In the tropics?" Dad said.

"It might have got lost."

"Shh!"

The loudspeaker crackled. Another voice, somewhere in the background growled, "Get on with it, we haven't got all night."

And then the captain spoke again.

"Yes, I'm rather afraid, ladies and gentlemen—though I don't want anyone to panic, there's no necessity for that. If we all keep our heads and stay calm, there's no reason for anyone to get hurt. But the fact is that our ship has been taken over, in what I can only describe as an act of piracy—"

"Never mind all that," the voice in the background said gruffly. "Just tell them what they have to do."

"—an act of unbridled piracy on the high seas. I have to inform you that right at this moment, as I stand on the bridge, I am in fact looking down the barrel of what appears to be a loaded gun."

I gulped. I looked at Clive. He looked at me. We both looked at Dad. He held up his hand for quiet.

We listened—nothing. I wondered what Dad was hearing.

"Hear it?" he whispered.

ALEX SHEARER

"What?"

"We're not moving. The engines have stopped."

And sure enough they had. While we were sitting on the bed having a fit of the laughs, the engines had been cut. We were just bobbing on the waves now, drifting in the ocean.

And then there was a clank. Right next to us, right next door. Metal against metal. Just outside. Outside upon the sea.

"What is it, Dad?"

He looked at us, worried, concerned.

"It's another boat," he said.

The loudspeaker crackled again.

"—yes, a loaded gun. The bridge here has been taken over by armed men and I have been instructed to cut the engines. I would request all passengers to go to their cabins immediately, for their own safety, if they are not already there. Please do as requested, and do not offer any resistance, under any circumstances. The men who have taken the ship over are all armed. They say they are ready and willing to use their weapons if necessary. And I believe them."

There was that low, growling voice in the background again.

"Good. And you better had believe it," the voice said.

"Please return to your cabins now. Anyone remaining on deck or in any of the public areas will be placing their own lives, and the lives of others, in considerable danger."

There was silence then. Just the crackling of the loudspeaker. Then the growling voice.

"Tell them what to do."

The captain spoke again.

"Once you have returned to your cabins, please take all the valuables you might have with you—watches, jewelry, cash, anything of that nature—and place them into a bag or an overnight case. I would strongly advise you not to withhold anything, or attempt to hide or conceal anything in your cabins or about your person."

"Very strongly advise," the growling voice said. "Very strongly indeed."

The captain spoke again.

"All cabin staff and crew members, other than those on watch and those required to remain on duty for the safe maintenance of the ship, are ordered to go to their cabins at once, and to remain below deck until further notice. This order is effective immediately. For the reassurance of passengers, I believe that if the orders of these—gentlemen—are complied with, no harm will come to anyone, and we will be allowed to go on our way within the next hour or two. Thank you for your cooperation. I apologize for this situation having arisen, but regret that it is beyond our control."

There was a click, and the loudspeaker went dead.

We all just stood there. Clive and me looked at Dad, wondering what to do. There was that dull clank again, from the other side of the hull, as if a boat was out there, its fenders rocking against the ship.

"Where did they come from, Dad? How did they get on board? They couldn't have climbed up the side, could they? It's hundreds of meters."

Dad shook his head.

"No. They didn't climb up the side. I rather suspect that they were like you two—"

"Eh?"

"They've been aboard all the time, and nobody knew it."

"You mean—the pirates—they're passengers?"

"Yes. You think about it," Dad said. "What better way to do it. You buy your ticket, you come on board, you look like anyone else on their holidays. You let some time go by, you wait until the ship is way out at sea, far from the major shipping lanes, and then you get your gun out of your luggage—"

"But how are they going to get away?"

The dull thud again. The ship on the other side of the hull, bobbing in the water. Dad nodded toward the sound.

"That's how they're going to get away. They've got accomplices. It must all have been arranged in advance. Where they were going to do it, when—"

"How would they find the ship?"

"Easy. The pirates on board would have given them the coordinates."

"How?"

"You can buy a global positioning receiver for

a hundred pounds. Then all you need is a mobile phone with a satellite link—you ring them up and tell them where to meet."

I had an idea.

"Wait though, Dad," I said. "There must be lots of passengers on the boats with mobile phones—"

"I'm sure there are," Dad said. "But most of them won't work here. We're too far from land. And even if somebody's got one with a satellite link, and even if they can get through to somebody and ask for help, well, I'm rather afraid that by the time anyone gets here, the pirates will have gone. Long gone."

"Long Gone Silver," Clive said.

"What?"

"Nothing, just thinking out loud. You know, in *Treasure Island*—Long John Silver, the pirate? Well, that was in the old days. He'd be Long Gone Silver now. You know, you'd never catch him."

Dad and me shared a look. Sometimes Clive was a bit inappropriate—almost as if his mind was wandering along corridors that no minds have wandered down before. He's a bit first-feet-on-the-new-carpets sometimes is Clive.

"Never mind Long Gone Silver," Dad said. "These blokes will be long gone *with* the silver—and with the jewelry, and with everything else. And there are some pretty wealthy passengers on board this ship too."

I thought of Mrs. Dominics, all dripping with

jewelry. She must have been worth a good half a million for her right arm alone. When you added up her neck, her left arm, and the brooch on her cardigan, she must have been worth about two million—and that was just for lying by the pool. When she got dressed up for dinner and put her best jewelry on, she was probably worth more than the ship.

And then I thought of somebody else. I thought of the men in the tinted glasses, who spent all their time in the casino, gambling on the roulette wheel and playing cards—the men who didn't like the sunlight too much. And I thought yes, maybe. Maybe they were the ones. Maybe they'd just been sitting there, biding their time, waiting for their moment. Waiting, and watching, and remembering who was rich, and who had lots of jewelry, keeping their eyes open behind their tinted glasses, watching, and waiting, and not missing a thing.

And then I thought of Lumpy, the steward, and how friendly he had been toward the men in the tinted glasses, how anxious to please. Almost as if he was with them, as if he was one of them, in a way. And maybe he was too. Because that would be useful, wouldn't it? To have someone on board who was a member of the crew, someone who would know their way around, below deck, as well as above it.

Lumpy would have known the way to the captain's bridge. And Lumpy would have been allowed onto the bridge—possibly bringing the captain his late-night cocoa. A passenger wouldn't have been allowed onto the bridge, except by request and prior arrangement, or by invitation only. But who would have suspected Lumpy, with his cocoa on a tray? (Because sailors are very fond of their cocoa, even when the weather's hot. And they always try to have some cocoa, at least once a day.)

And there Lumpy would be with his tray of cocoa, all smiles and plates of biscuits, and, "There you are, Captain! That'll keep you going." But the next thing the captain knew, it wouldn't just be Lumpy there, it would be men in tinted glasses too. And instead of looking down into a mug of hot, steaming cocoa with chocolate sprinkles on top and cream, he would be looking down the barrel of a loaded gun.

Yes, that was how it all seemed to me.

And then I thought of something else still. I thought of all the other passengers, the ones like Mrs. Swanker Watson, and Mr. Swanker Watson, who maybe weren't as rich as Mrs. Dominics, but who weren't exactly hard up for cash. And by the time you added all their valuables to Mrs. Dominics's valuables, you soon had an awful lot of valuables.

And then, as you went on down from first class with windows to standard class with windows, to standard class with no windows, to economy class with no windows (as well as no doors and probably no beds either) you would collect more and more money and jewelry and cash and silver watches and Swiss-made timepieces that cost a thousand pounds each.

By the time you multiplied all that by the two and a half thousand passengers on board, and you added in the money in the ship's safe and in the on-board shops and boutiques, and you threw in the crew's money and valuables for good measure, well, you probably had yourself a few million pounds' worth.

Not a bad little haul for a night's work. And on top of it, you got a nice cruise into the bargain, which, admittedly you had to pay for in advance, but as you probably paid for that with stolen money in the first place, the whole thing cost you absolutely nothing.

Not bad, really. Not a bad little bit of piracy at all.

"Listen!"

We listened. But there was nothing to hear. That was what was so eerie. None of the usual noises, the throb of the engine, the sounds of movement and conversation and occasional laughter, filtering down through the ventilation shaft.

The sea must have been flat and calm out there; the ship hardly rolled. Just a little maybe, and when it did, we heard the dull sound of the other boat, its fenders scraping gently against the side, nestling close to our hull, clinging to the great ship like a tiny lamb to its mother.

"What do we do, Dad?"

"Just listen."

Silence. The great ship was still. It was like the mystery of the *Marie Celeste*—the old boat that had been found empty and abandoned, with half-eaten meals on the galley table, and no sign of anyone anywhere.

All disappeared, maybe—into Davy Jones's Locker.

Only who was Davy Jones? And where was his locker? And why did he have one? And what did he keep in it?

"Shhh!"

Dad held his finger to his lips. We didn't dare move. We just stood there, listening. I thought I heard a rat scurrying, somewhere deep down under the metalwork, but it was probably my imagination.

I thought of the shipbuilders, who had made this great ship. I thought of the sound of hammers and steel, the flash of welding guns, the heat, the clamor, the resounding clang as the rivets were hammered home. I thought of the great boat being launched, sliding from its dry dock into the water, the bottle of champagne smashing against its prow, the cheers, the cries, the celebration, and now—

Silence.

"Shh! Listen."

We listened.

Voices now. The same ones as before, the gravelly ones. Lumpy's too. We'd been right about him. He was in on it; he was with them. The voices came from far away, way up on deck, floors and floors above us. But for all that they were far away, it was as though the men were standing right next to us. Their voices came down the ventilation shaft, sounding clear as bells on a silent night.

Only if we could hear them—perhaps they might hear us.

So, "'Shhh!" Silence. Nice and quiet now. We stood, me and Dad and Clive, not saying anything, just conversing with our eyes.

"Okay," the low, growling voice rumbled. "Let's get this done as quickly as we can. Start with first class, get the pricey stuff first. Bag it up and leave it on deck. Then down to the bottom, and work our way back up. We work in twos. One cabin at a time. One stands guard, one gets the valuables. And make sure they give you everything. Search the cabins, if you have to, but don't take too long. If you feel they're hiding anything, or holding anything back, well . . ."

"Well what?" came another voice. Not Growly or Lumpy now, but it definitely sounded like a dark-tinted glasses kind of voice. The kind of voice which had spent most of the cruise up in the casino, calling for "another card" and "another drink" and "another handful of chips for the roulette table."

"If we think they're holding anything back?" prompted the casino voice.

"Persuade them. Make a few examples. Crack a few heads. Get me?"

"Right."

"Right. Okay. Let's do it. When you've finished each deck, carry the bags and what have you up to the next deck. Then do that level, then on up again."

"Then what?"

"Get everything up on deck, then down to the boat, and we're away."

"How long have we got?"

"As long as it takes."

"It's going to take hours, to do the whole ship."

"Okay. We'd better get started then. And keep your eyes and your ears open. There's a good chance that one of these bright sparks on board will have a phone that can get a signal, even out here. We have to assume that the cavalry's on the way. So one of us had better stay here, as lookout. If you hear three shots, or three blasts from the boat's whistle, it means another ship's been sighted—the Navy, or the Coast Guard, whatever. Either way, three blasts and it's time to go. So get up here as quickly as you can."

"Right."

"Okay. Let's do it. Go!"

Footsteps retreating. They were gone.

Dad looked at us.

"Any idea who they are?"

We told him all about Lumpy, and the men in the casino with the tinted glasses, who spent the whole cruise gambling and staying out of the sun.

"Lumpy? Who do you mean?"

"The steward. With the shaved head. You know, he's all head and shoulders and no neck. Muscly looking, like his jacket's too small. And his arms look like if he wasn't careful they might drag along the ground."

Dad nodded.

"I know who you mean. He just signed on for this trip. I'd not seen him before. Doesn't say much either, at least not to the rest of us. How many of the other men were there?"

"Four or five. That we saw."

"Yes, there might be others, of course. Maybe the gamblers weren't the only ones in on it."

"How can just a few men hijack a whole ship, Dad?"

"Very easily. It doesn't take much. Just a couple of small things—like guns."

"But if there's only six of them—add up the passengers and crew, there's thousands. Couldn't we—?"

"But who's going to be the first? Who's going to risk the bullet? Fear incapacitates people. And anyway, they've been clever—"

"What do you mean?"

"The rest of the passengers don't know how many of them there are. The captain probably doesn't know how many of them there are. There might be dozens. How would they know? And everyone's in their cabins. They don't have to face a great mob of people, just one or two at a time."

"What are we going to do?"

"Well, I can tell you two what you're going to do, you're going to stay right here until all this is over and they're on their way."

"But Dad—"

"But nothing."

"What if they find us?"

"They won't come down here. At least I shouldn't think so. Why should they? There aren't any passenger cabins down here. No passengers—no valuables. I shouldn't think it's likely that they'll want to take a few beds with them."

I suddenly thought of Mrs. Swanker Watson, and Mr. Swanker Watson, and Swanker Watson himself, and his sister, Sister Swanker Watson, and the baby, Small Nappy Swanker Watson, and the nanny too. I thought of poor Mrs. Swanker, sitting on her collapsed bed with her bad foot, and the pirates banging on the cabin door, and searching around, making sure that she had put all her valuables and trinkets into the bag, and hadn't kept anything back, or hidden anything. Not even the pearl necklace which she had worn when we had all had dinner.

We were better off in rat class in some ways. At least the pirates wouldn't come looking for us.

"We just wait here then?"

"Yes. You wait here. And don't move until I come back. Not unless you hear their boat go."

"How'll we know?"

"You'll hear it through the hull. You'll hear its engine start, and the sound of it moving away. Then you'll know it's safe to go up on deck."

Yes, safe if you were a proper passenger, maybe, I thought. Not so safe if you were a stowaway. Because even when the pirates had gone, we were still in deep, deep trouble. I looked at Dad and wondered how he could even contemplate turning me and Clive in, and handing us over to the captain. But then I thought maybe he did have no choice, now that he had found us out. He had to do what was right; he had to do what was best and safest. And maybe it had only ever been a matter of time anyway, before somebody had found us out.

"Just stay here and you'll be all right."

"But the pirates, Dad, they're going to steal everything—"

Then he said something that shocked me a bit.

"That doesn't matter," he said.

"What? It doesn't matter? That there's pirates on board and—"

"I mean it's not the most important thing. The most important thing is that nobody gets hurt or injured. Possessions can be replaced, but not people."

And we all knew that was true. You can always get another watch. But you can't get a replacement for someone you love.

"Okay. You stay here then, all right?"

"But what about us stowing away, Dad—"

"We'll deal with that later."

"But, Dad, what are you going to do? Aren't you going to stay with us?"

"Don't worry. You'll be okay." Dad looked at us. He was serious and solemn.

"I'm part of the ship," he said. "I'm a member of the crew. It's my duty to try and do something. I can't just let pirates hold a gun to the captain's head and take the ship over. I'm honor-bound to do something, boys," he said. "I don't have any choice."

And it was just like in the movies, really, the desperate and heroic bit, when the man with the hat goes back on his own to fend off the enemy and to wrestle with lions and tigers while everyone else escapes. Only you don't ever think of your own dad being like that. You think of your dad as he is every day, doing the cooking, or washing up, or helping Clive with his homework, or watering the plants. Or you think of him in his uniform, bringing people their drinks on the sundeck, and always having a smile on his face and a cheerful word for everyone, even the old ladies. You don't ever think really that your own old dad might be the man with the hat.

"But Dad, it might be dangerous, you might get shot!"

"Don't worry, Clive, I'll be careful."

"But what are you going to do? You can't hope to stop them. Not when they've got guns."

"No. I'm going to try to get to the radio room."

"But Dad, won't it take hours for a ship to get here?"

"Maybe, yes. But you never know. There might be another boat quite near. There might be an aircraft carrier, anything. If I can just get a Mayday out. A plane or a helicopter could be here within an hour. And even if the pirates make a getaway, someone might still be able to intercept them. If I can just broadcast a message out."

"But Dad, won't they have thought of that? Won't they have put a guard by the radio room, to stop anyone even trying? They might even have smashed the radio up."

But he'd plainly already weighed this possibility up.

"Maybe," he nodded. "But I still have to try. So you stay here, remember? Stay here and don't you move until the pirates have gone. Now, I'm trusting you. Do I have your word?"

"Yes, Dad. I suppose so."

"Clive?"

"Yes, Dad. But you will be careful, won't you?"

"Don't worry. I'll be careful. I'll see you in a little while."

And then he gave us both a hug, and he said, "Close the door behind me, and keep it closed."

And he was gone.

Gone. To be the man with the hat who does the rescues.

Me and Clive sat on our beds and looked at each other.

"He's gone," Clive said.

"Yes," I nodded.

"He's gone off to be brave," Clive said.

"Yes," I said, "that's right."

"I hope he'll be okay," Clive said.

"Me too," I said.

"I hope the pirates don't hurt him," Clive said.

"Me too," I said.

"Because it's bad enough not having a mum," Clive said, "Not to have a dad too, that would be horrible."

"It would," I said. "It would."

"I'm proud of Dad going off to be brave," Clive said.

"Me too," I said. "So am I."

"Only it doesn't seem very fair that he has to be brave on his own. Not when there's other people here, who could try to be brave with him. It doesn't seem right to me, with all these people on the ship, that Dad has to be the one doing all the being brave."

"That's right," I said. "It doesn't seem fair at all. Only we gave him our words, didn't we, Clive, that we'd stay here in the cabin."

"That's right," Clive said. "Only, thing was, I maybe had my fingers crossed behind my back when I said that."

"Is that so, Clive?" I said. "Is that a fact?"

"Yes," he said. "It is."

"Well, that's quite a coincidence then, Clive," I said.

"How's that then?" Clive said. "Why's that a coincidence?"

"Well, it just so happens, Clive," I said, "that I had my fingers crossed behind my back too."

"Is that right?" Clive said.

"Yes," I said. "It is."

"In that case," Clive said, "maybe we don't have to stay in the cabin."

"No," I said. "Maybe we don't."

"Maybe we ought to try and help Dad out with the being brave and the rescues then."

"Yes," I said. "Maybe we should."

"Perhaps we should just give him a minute to get going then," Clive said, "and then when the coast is clear, we can go after him."

"That's not a bad idea, Clive," I said. "Not a bad idea at all. I didn't used to think all that much of your ideas, but lately they seem to have been improving."

"Good," Clive said. "It's a deal then."

"It's a deal."

So we sat there a minute to give Dad a chance to get going, and then we tiptoed quietly to the cabin door, opened it gently, peered out to make sure the coast was clear, and then crept out into the corridor.

We stood there a moment, listening for sounds of movement. There was nothing. Even the rats in the bilges (if there were any rats, and I'm sure there must have been, though we never saw any) were as quiet as mice.

We tiptoed on, quiet as mice in our own way too. We came to the first set of steps and went on up.

To see what we could do, about these pirates, and to help Dad out with the being brave.

SIXTEEN

TO THE BRIDGE

WE MOVED ON UP through the deck levels. It was quiet as the tomb, quiet as a great floating coffin, adrift on the sea.

"Fifteen men on a dead man's chest! Yo ho ho and a bottle of—"

"Shh, Clive. Be quiet!"

"—rum!"

It was like coming up from a deep, dark mine, into the sunshine and light. Only it was starlight now. We peered out of one of the small portholes. There were the stars, like a million pimples.

"The sky's got more spots than you have," Clive said.

"Belt up," I told him. "This isn't the time for personal remarks."

"Look!"

There was the boat, the one belonging to the pirates' accomplices, ready to take them and all their stolen goods on board, and to whisk them away into the remoteness of the sea. Then they'd find a quiet port somewhere, where nobody asked any questions, or if they did, nobody answered them, and they'd put in to harbor and divide the spoils. Or maybe they would head for a small, unknown island, with clear blue seas, a coral reef, and sand-flies, and divide some of the treasure out there, and bury the rest under a palm tree, and draw a little map with an X on it to mark the spot.

Maybe.

We could see the figures of men in the starlight, moving about the deck of the boat. It wasn't a large ship, about the size of a tug. The cruiseliner dwarfed it—a minnow alongside a whale.

One of the men looked straight at us, right at our porthole.

"Duck!"

We ducked, then gradually lifted our heads to peer out again. He was still there, still looking in our direction.

"He can't see us."

"No."

"He looks pretty tough."

He did too. A long scar ran down along the left side of his face, from his ear, all down his neck, and down into his shirt. He looked half-European, half-African. He was chewing something in his mouth. He spat a squirt of saliva overboard into the water.

ALEX SHEARER

"Disgusting."

"Come on."

On we went, up to another level, up again. We came to the atrium—a huge public space in the center of the ship. There was even a little waterfall in it, which tinkled as the water fell. But other than that, silence. Nobody. Nothing.

"Come on."

We walked through the theater; it was empty, silent. The doors swung shut behind us. We walked across the aisle, pushed the doors open on the other side. Through the library then. Quiet and deserted too. Some books lay open upon the reading table; someone had turned the corner of a magazine down, to mark their place.

Silence. Eerie silence. Up to the next deck. We walked through the empty casino. The ball lay still in a groove in the roulette wheel. Number 28. Lucky for somebody. Maybe.

Perhaps.

"Where's the radio room?"

"Look at the map."

There were little maps of the ship posted everywhere. We looked at one and found the radio room marked, it was up by the bridge—the control room, from which the ship was steered and all the navigation done.

"Come on."

We walked through the restaurant. Uneaten food lay on plates. Steam was rising from a big tureen. Crumpled napkins lay on tablecloths. A bottle of wine had been upset and red drops fell to the carpet, looking like spots of blood. I righted the bottle and tried to sponge the stain out with a napkin.

"What are you doing?"

I didn't know, really, I just felt I couldn't leave the wine to drip there, all over the beautiful carpet. But I couldn't soak the stain out. It looked like the scene of a murder, after the body had been taken away.

"Come on."

We went up to the next level. Here were lines of cabins, stretching away along the corridor. It looked like a hall of mirrors, going on to infinity.

"Look."

"Get out of sight!"

We hid behind the bulkhead. Far at the end of the corridor, one of the pirates stood, holding what must have been a gun in his hand. He was next to an open cabin door. Coming from inside was the sound of voices.

"That everything?"

"Yes!"

"It had better be!"

"I swear!"

"If you're holding out on us—you'll get this across your head—"

"No, honestly, that's everything. Just this pearl necklace, maybe, and that's all."

"Good. That's better. All right. Now shut up, and shut your door, and stay in here. Got it?"

"Right."

A second pirate emerged from the cabin. For a second we saw a frightened woman's face, then the cabin door closed and she was gone from view.

"Well?"

"Not bad. A few grands' worth. Let's do the next."

They banged on the door of the next cabin along.

"Open up!"

Nothing.

"Open it up or I'll shoot the lock open!"

The door opened. Another frightened face peered out.

"Yes?"

The pirate pointed to a bag that was sitting in the corridor by the cabin door.

"Is it all in here?"

"Yes."

"Certain?"

"Yes."

"Let's have a look around inside, just to be sure—shall we?"

The second pirate pushed his way inside. The first one remained where he was, keeping a lookout, glancing up and down the corridor, his gun at the ready in his hand.

Outside of almost every cabin door was a small backpack, case, or overnight bag, plainly containing the cash and valuables of the people inside. As they moved along, and once they were satisfied that nothing had been hidden or held back, the pirates took the smaller bags and dumped their contents into a large canvas one that they dragged along with them from cabin to cabin. It grew heavier and heavier as they went.

"I hope we're going to be able to carry this lot up the stairs."

"Don't you worry, we'll manage. Wherever there's a lot of valuables, somehow you can always manage to lift it."

They both cackled, one of them laughed with a deep, low growl. It sounded like someone driving a car over thick, scrunchy gravel.

"Come on, Clive," I whispered. "Let's move, before they see us."

A click. They both spun round. Their guns were in their hands. I glared at Clive. What had he done to make the noise?

But it wasn't him, and it wasn't us they were looking at. There were only the tips of our noses to see anyway, peering around the bulkhead at the far end of the corridor. I didn't think they would see us—especially not with their tinted glasses on.

It was one of the cabin doors, slowly opening. The pirates stood, their guns pointing, watching as a hand came out, holding a bag. It put the bag down on the floor outside the cabin, then it disappeared back in, and closed the door behind it.

The pirates laughed. I think they'd been frightened for a moment, but didn't want to show it to each other, and the laughter was a kind of disguise.

"Come on, Clive. Let's get to the radio room. Dad might be needing our help."

"Okay."

"Wait till they're looking the other way, then dash across the corridor to the next staircase."

"Okay."

"Okay."

The second pirate banged on another cabin door.

"Who is it?" a woman's voice called.

It seemed like a funny question, really—*Who is it?* How was the pirate supposed to answer? What was he supposed to say? Something like, *"Oh, it's the pirates, actually. Sorry to bother you. Hope we're not disturbing you and that we haven't caught you at an inconvenient moment. The thing is, we just want to make sure that we're robbing you properly, if that's okay. We just want to make sure that you've put all your valuables into the bag out here. Because if you haven't, we're going to crack your head open with the butt of one of these pistols. Is that all right?"*

But all the pirate actually said was, "Open up!"

"Go!" I hissed at Clive.

They both had their backs to him. He ran across the corridor. He made it to the staircase. He waved at me to come.

"You now!" he mouthed.

I couldn't. One of the pirates had gone into the open cabin, the other was half facing my way. I waited. Clive was waving frantically at me to get a move on. But I couldn't. Not with one of them looking our way. I had to wait.

The other pirate came out of the cabin. They moved on to the next.

He wouldn't turn away now. He didn't turn away at all. He kept facing in our direction, and they were getting nearer and nearer, moving from cabin to cabin, dragging their bag of loot behind them.

Clive was driving me nuts. He was out of their sight, by the staircase, making more and more frantic, beckoning gestures, and doing tapping at an invisible watch signs, as if we had to get a move on. As if I didn't know that. So I tried to make equally frantic "I can't risk it" movements, and to give him "Hang on a moment" looks. But he just replied with more "Get your finger out!" motions, which irritated me more than ever.

So it was Clive's fault really. He should have left me alone. I was getting pressured, it was coming at me from all sides. There was stupid Clive safely across the corridor, with his big hurry-up pantomime, winding me up. And there were the two pirates, going from cabin to cabin, scooping up their loot, emptying small bags into big bags, and getting nearer and nearer. And always looking in my direction. I'd ducked back, but I could still see them through a part of the bulkhead that was a sort of ornamental metalwork with a plant growing up it. (A real plant too, not a plastic one.)

I had to act. If I ran and they saw me, I had a chance. We might still get away from them, outrun them, and be able to hide. They maybe wouldn't want to leave their big bag of loot anyway. Not just to come after little old us.

But if I left it any longer, in the hope that they might look the other way—only they didn't look the other way—then I'd have left it too late. We'd never be able to outrun them then. And if they didn't get both of us, they'd certainly get me. And I didn't want to be got. Not by two pirates with guns in their hands, who probably split people's heads open for breakfast, and then bashed their brains for lunch.

So I had to decide. Weigh up the risks, assess the chances, and do something before it was too late.

I made "Here I come then!" signals at Clive. "Here I come, be ready to run for it, and don't get in my way."

I didn't know if he understood. I hoped he did. There's never any real telling with Clive. You just have to hope for the best and to take your chances.

And that was what I did. I took a deep breath, said a small prayer, got on my mark, got ready, got steady—and ran.

"Oi!"

They saw me.

"What was that?"

I got to the staircase.

"Go, Clive! Go!"

We ran up the staircase, and up to the next deck. The doors to the cinema were straight in front of us. We pushed them open, ran inside, and hid behind some seats. We lay still on the floor, listening, waiting.

They came.

"Where'd they go?"

"Search me. In here maybe?"

"Have a look."

The door opened. A sliver of light ran like a spark across the floor. I could see Clive's eyes, big and wide and worried—the same as mine.

"Anything?"

"No."

I could see their feet. Big and flat in polished shoes, standing at ten to two.

"Think we should tell the boss?"

"I wouldn't worry about it. Come on, let's get back to the cabins. What're they going to do anyway? It was just a couple of kids, wasn't it?"

"Yeah, you're right. Nothing to bother about, like you say. It was only a couple of kids. Come on. Let's collect the rest of the stuff."

The door swung shut again. We stayed where we were for a minute or two, in case it had been a trick and they were waiting outside to see if we would appear once we thought they had gone.

Out we went, cautiously, quietly, opening the door a little bit at a time.

"It's all right," Clive said.

And it was. They had gone back down to the lower deck to finish robbing people in their cabins. They weren't bothered about us. We were just a couple of kids. They'd plainly offended Clive by saying that.

"They said," he told me, sounding highly

indignant, "that we were just a couple of kids."

"That's right," I agreed. "They did."

"The nerve!" Clive said.

"Yes," I said. "The nerve!"

Because it has always been my firm opinion that it is a mistake to underestimate people.

"Just a couple of kids, indeed!" Clive said. "We'll soon see about that."

And off we went, to see about it.

First we consulted one of the little maps of the ship again, to make sure that we knew where we were going, then off we went to get there.

We passed along by the first-class cabins, by the premium class and then the staterooms. It was all swank and luxury here: cabins with big picture windows and patio doors and en suite this and en suite that. Some of them didn't just have bedrooms, but sitting rooms too, with sofas, and big tall lampshades and chocolates on your pillow at night. They probably even had champagne coming out of the taps too. Well, the cold tap. And cocoa coming out of the hot one.

We saw inside one of them. There were the Swanker Watsons, sitting looking worried and grim faced. Mrs. Swanker Watson seemed to have an empty necklace case in front of her, and she was dabbing at her eyes with a tissue, and Mr. Swanker Watson was trying to console her.

Then we passed Mrs. Dominics's cabin. We saw her through a crack in the curtains, sitting there with the TV on, watching a film and eating peanuts, with a glass of whisky by her hand. All her jewelry had gone too, and she looked a bit smaller without it. But strangely she didn't seem the slightest bit bothered. Maybe she had plenty more jewelry at home, maybe she had just got too old to care, maybe it was all insured anyway. Or maybe, which I thought was more likely, she thought that life was more important than possessions. Just like Dad.

Dad!

What had happened? He'd be at the bridge by now, in the radio room, sending out a Mayday and an SOS, calling all ships in the vicinity and telling them there had been a hijack and that we had pirates on board. Unless the pirates had seen him first, of course. In which case . . .

But I didn't want to think about that.

"Watch out!"

I spotted two more of the pirates. They were dragging a couple of heavy suitcases up onto the deck. Clive and me hid under the shadow of one of the lifeboats.

The men dragged the cases to the port side (that's the left side when you're facing toward the front of the boat, in case you've forgotten). It was also the side where their boat was waiting for them, a long, long way down in the water.

The night was warm and humid. The men were perspiring heavily and one had a damp streak down the back of his shirt.

"Okay. Leave them there for now. Let's go and get the rest."

They left the cases by the rail and went back down into the ship.

"Let's go and look."

We scuttled quickly across the deck to where the suitcases stood. I tried to lift one of them. It weighed half a ton and must have been full to bursting with jewelry, expensive watches, purses, handbags, and wallets.

"How are they going to get it all off the ship?" Clive said.

We peeked over the side. There was the pirate boat, looking small and insignificant, clinging to the hull like a barnacle to a rock. It was a long way down. That hundred meters, which Clive had nearly fallen. How were they going to get everything down there? All the bags and cases of stolen jewels and cash? They couldn't just chuck them overboard and hope for the best, that they would land on the deck of the boat down below and not plop into the sea. And then, how would they get off the ship themselves?

"How are they going to do it?" Clive said.

I shrugged.

"I don't know. But they're going to do it somehow. They didn't come all this way and plot all this out and not have a plan for getting off the ship. Come on. Let's get to the bridge."

The bridge, of course, was out of bounds. The only passengers who went there had been invited by the captain. It was considered a big honor to get a look around the bridge. It was a bit like being on an airplane and getting a look inside the cockpit and watching the pilots fly the plane.

We passed a sign reading "No Public Admittance—Crew Only" and hurried along past rooms and cabins containing maps and charts. Someone's jacket was sitting on the back of a chair, there was gold braid around the sleeves, but the jacket's owner had gone.

"Look!"

Clive had stopped by a room with a heavy metal door with a spyhole in it.

"It's the brig!" he whispered. "The prison!"

It didn't say that. It just said "Detention Room." But he was right, it was the ship's jail, just the same, no matter what they called it.

"Come on, Clive!"

"I want to see inside!"

Typical of Clive that was, always wanting to do the most unnecessary things at the most inappropriate and inconvenient moments.

"Clive!"

"Just a look!"

Well, I thought to myself that it was probably only a question of time before Clive saw the inside of a prison, so why not sooner rather than later. In fact, I thought that it might even do him a bit of good to see inside a cell. It might bring him to his senses and help him see the error of his ways and make him knuckle down to his homework. It might even be his salvation.

We pushed the heavy metal door open and

looked in. It was grim. There was a shiny metal toilet in one corner, a small bed in the other, a table, a chair, and that was it.

"Take a good look, Clive," I said. "And remember what you see. Because unless you buck up, this is the sort of place you'll be going to when you leave school. It won't be five-star hotels for you, Clive. It won't even be university or the technical college. No, it'll be chokey for you, Clive, and this is just a taste."

"I'd rather be here than share a room with you," Clive said.

"Are you trying to tell me, Clive," I said, "that you would rather share a room with a toilet than share a room with me?"

"Yes!"

"Oh? And why is that, might I ask?"

"Because the toilet probably smells better," Clive said.

"Oh, really?" I said. "Is that a fact? In that case, Clive, how about I stick your head down the toilet then, so that you can find out?"

And I was just about to give Clive the benefit of this educational and life-enhancing experience, when I remembered where we were and what we were supposed to be doing.

"All right, Clive," I said. "I've changed my mind. This isn't the time or the place for personal quarrels. So I'll just let you off with a warning. But just be careful in future, that's all."

"Lucky for you you didn't try it, that's all,"

Clive said. "If you'd tried to stick my head down that toilet, I'd have shoved you out of the porthole—bum first. And seeing how big it is, you're bound to have got stuck."

Fortunately for Clive, I am above personal remarks and immune to criticism. Harsh words cannot hurt me. Anyway, I knew it wasn't true, as I have a very slim and elegant figure, and am not a fat bum like Clive, who usually looks as if he is sitting on a loaf of bread, even when he is standing up.

"Come on," I said. "The radio room. Let's try and find Dad."

The quarrel was instantly forgotten and we were back out in the corridor and heading for the bridge. A sudden wave of tiredness came over me, and all I wanted to do was sleep. I looked at my watch. It was past three in the morning. I yawned, and that seemed to wake me up a bit. It wasn't any time to go nodding off. It was time to be alert.

We came to the bridge. We ducked down low and crawled to the door and then gradually raised our heads to look inside.

Lumpy was in there, along with one of the men in the tinted glasses. He looked different now. He wasn't in the steward's uniform anymore. He was wearing a lightweight suit and an expensive-looking watch (probably stolen) and lounging in the helmsman's chair with his feet up on the wheel.

"How much longer, boss?"

Lumpy looked at the expensive-looking, stolen-looking watch.

"No more than an hour. We don't want to cut it too fine."

I stared at Clive, shocked.

It was Lumpy who was the boss! With his shaved head and his hole in his ear for an earring. Lumpy was the brains. Lumpy was the mastermind. You'd never have thought it to look at him though. He just looked too ordinary.

Well, Dad wasn't in there. But neither was the captain, nor any of his officers. What had happened to them? I nudged Clive and nodded toward a cabin along from the bridge. There was a sign on the door, the one we had been looking for—Radio Room.

We scurried along, still keeping low, and got to the radio-room door. I looked inside. There was a man in there with his back to us, sitting in a chair, holding a gun. Next to him, tied to another chair and with a gag in his mouth was the captain. And next to him, tied to a third chair, and with a huge bruise on his forehead and a trickle of blood running down his face was—our dad.

I caught my breath. Dad. With blood all down his face and running on to the collar of his shirt. His white steward's jacket bloodstained too. How could they have done that? I bet it hadn't been a fair fight. It wouldn't have happened if it had been fair; Dad would have bashed them all. Or maybe that was what happened sometimes to people who were brave; maybe they just got hurt. All because you were being brave, it didn't mean you would win.

I nudged Clive to look inside the radio room,

and to be quick and careful about it. He did and then squatted back down. We crawled to a corner of the corridor where we could at least talk in whispers without being overheard.

"They've got Dad."

"I know. Did you see him?"

"Yes. Of course I saw him."

"He must have gone in to rescue the captain—"

"And radio for help."

"Only someone was waiting behind the door—"

"And hit him with the gun."

"We'll have to do something, Clive."

"You're right. We will, only—"

"Only what?"

"What?"

"What do you mean—what?"

"I mean what do we do?"

I thought it over for a moment. Then, "I've got a plan," I said. "It works like this. Now—do you remember the way to the brig?"

· seventeen ·

CLAPPED IN IRONS

WE WENT BACK to the door of the radio room. We didn't crawl on all fours this time, keeping low and out of sight. We just walked there, bold as brass, bold as the brass compass on the bridge.

The man with the gun still had his back to us, but Dad was looking straight in our direction.

We waved.

A look of surprise appeared on Dad's face, then one of absolute horror. He was making frantic eye signals to tell us to go away before we were seen by the man with the gun.

But that was just what we wanted.

The captain was the next to see us. He looked pretty horrified too. But whether that was from surprise, or whether it was because he didn't like the look of us, I didn't really know, nor did I have the time to find out.

Clive waved at the captain too, and then he gave him the thumbs-up, so as to let him know that his fate was in good hands.

The man with the gun must have seen the expression on the captain's face, and have wondered what he was staring at. He slowly turned, and there he was, standing staring right at us, with only a door and a panel of glass between us.

Clive gave him the thumbs-up as well. Then he went and put his thumbs in his ears and waggled all his fingers at once.

"What the—"

Then we were off. And he was right behind us. I heard him wrench the door open. I heard his footsteps on the floor. We ran back the way we had come, back toward the brig.

He lost his footing in the corridor, stumbled momentarily.

"You two! Come back here."

Then we split up. Clive pretended to stumble. I sprinted on ahead. I rounded the corner, came to the brig, yanked the door open and hid behind it.

Only just in time. Half a second later and Clive came pelting around the corner shouting, "Help! Help! There's a man after me!" And he ran straight into the brig.

Without thinking, the man ran straight in after him, just as I put my foot out. He tripped over it and went sprawling. There was a loud clunk as he bashed his head on the stainless-steel toilet.

Clive ran out, I ran out after him, we pulled

the door closed and slammed down the bolt.

"Ohhhhh!"

I peered in through the spyhole, and then Clive wanted a turn, and then it was my go again.

The pirate was lying nursing a big lump on his head. I tried to feel sorry for him, but considering the lump he had put on Dad's head (not to mention ruining his uniform, because bloodstains are very hard to get out), I felt that he had only got what he had deserved.

"We should have taken his gun with us," Clive said.

"Doesn't matter," I said. "As long as he's in there he's got no one to shoot—apart from himself, of course."

The pirate dragged himself to his feet and then went and sat on the bed. When his head had stopped spinning, he staggered over to the door and started to bang on it.

"Let me out," he said. "Let me out you brats! Or I'll ******* kill you!"

(It was the asterisks again. In fact, the pirates all seemed to speak fluent asterisks all the time. I shan't bother including them again. You'll just have to imagine that they're there.)

When we still didn't let him out, he gave up on the threats and tried to appeal to us with his better nature.

"Come on now, boys," he said. "There's good boys. I know you're not bad boys really. There's just been a misunderstanding, see. I'm not a pirate. I'm actually an undercover agent from Interpol, the international police. I've been infiltrating these pirates and pretending I was one of them. But all the while I had my eye on them and was gathering information. So you let me out now, and I'll go and arrest them."

"If you're from Interpol," I shouted through the door, "hold your ID card up to the spyhole."

The pirate patted his pockets and then said, "I don't have it on me. It was too dangerous to carry it about in case one of the pirates came across it."

"If you're not a pirate," I said, "then why have you got a skull and crossbones tattooed on your wrist?"

"Er—it's just a transfer," he said. "It washes off. I just have it there to look authentic."

"Wash it off then," I said. "And then I might believe you."

He glared at the spyhole. His eye went right up close to it. And then he started getting nasty again.

"Open this door or I'll blow you both to kingdom come!"

"You'll have to kingdom come and get us first!" Clive said.

And we left him then, ranting and raving and banging against the brig door, as we headed back toward the bridge.

"Let me out! There's a rat in here. And I hate rats!"

We hesitated by the corridor door, one of the fire-doors that divided it up.

"He's just trying to play on our sympathy,"

Clive said. "And anyway, if there is a rat in there, and he doesn't like it, he can lump it—or shoot it."

"You're right," I said. "Let's go."

The corridor fire-door swung shut behind us, and the shouts died away.

"Have you got your Swiss army knife on you, Clive?" I asked.

"Never travel anywhere without it," he told me.

Which, considering the circumstances, was just as well.

WE DIDN'T KNOW whether we should untie Dad or the captain first. Dad was always telling us that when it came to manners, it was guests first and family last. But then again, the captain didn't have a big lump on his head. He only had his beard to worry about, and whether he had anything living in there (apart from himself that is, of course). And besides, it wasn't as if he had been invited around for dinner.

"Let's go and let them out," I said. "Dad first."

"Okay."

We made our way back toward the radio room, but first, of course, we had to pass the bridge. We stopped and listened. We didn't want Lumpy walking out and barging straight into us. There was easily room for two in the brig, but we'd have trouble getting him in there.

He was talking to one of the men with the tinted glasses.

"That'll have to be it," he said.

"But they won't have finished," the other man said. He sounded a bit annoyed.

"Too bad," Lumpy told him. "They'll have collected enough."

Then it sounded as if he had gone up to the other man, and was talking to him from no more than a couple of centimeters away.

"You may want to spend the rest of your days rotting in a prison somewhere in Africa——" he said, "for hijacking, piracy and robbery on the high seas—but personally, I have other plans."

"Yes, boss," the man grunted.

"Like lying on a beach in the West Indies, with a long, cool drink, and five-star accommodation. Or possibly even going on a nice, long, luxurious, and expensive cruise."

"Right, boss," the man said, and then they both chuckled.

"Because up until now," Lumpy said, "I've never really been able to afford one. Had to work my passage, see. The only other way of doing it would have been to stow away. And you'd never be able to stow away on a ship like this. I can tell you that for nothing."

"Yes, boss," the man agreed. He had obviously decided that if he agreed with Lumpy, everything would run a whole lot smoother.

"So give the signal. If we stay much longer, we'll be pushing our luck. So let's get the stuff up to the deck and down into the boat and let's get out of here."

"Okay, boss."

"So do it."

Clive and I ducked down low and ran past the door toward the radio room. We pushed the door open and got inside.

"What the heck are you two doing here!" Dad said when we came in. "I told you to stay down in the cabin!"

They'd gagged the captain, but they hadn't got around to Dad. Maybe they thought the lump on the head would be enough to keep him quiet.

Clive got his Swiss army knife out and started sawing through the ropes.

"Stay in your cabin, I said, didn't I? Or it could be dangerous."

"Sorry, Dad!"

"How many times do I have to tell you that when I tell you to do something, you're supposed to do it."

"We got worried, Dad. Thought you might be in trouble."

"Well I wasn't. I just got a knock on the head and got tied to a chair. It was nothing I couldn't handle. But—"

"Yes?"

"Thanks anyway."

Dad massaged his arms, where the ropes had been cutting into his wrists. He tried to stand, but couldn't immediately.

"Pins and needles," he said.

"Shall I untie the captain?" Clive asked.

The captain's eyes were flashing like fireflies,

full of curiosity and unanswered questions, full of whats and whos and hows and whys and who the hells and all the sorts of complicated things that you don't want to deal with when you're busy.

"Of course you should untie him," Dad said. "Come on! Do it now. Quick. And I'll send a Mayday out on the radio . . ."

Clive raised his Swiss army knife and selected the biggest and sharpest blade. I noticed the captain was looking a bit nervous. But then, people often do look a bit nervous, whenever Clive and sharp implements are involved. Knowing Clive, he'd probably cut all the braid off the captain's cuffs in the process of hacking through the ropes.

"Don't worry, Captain," Clive said. "This is going to hurt me more than it'll hurt you."

Clive is full of reassuring sorts of stuff like that whenever people are in a tight corner. I decided that maybe *I* ought to cut the captain free, but Clive can be very possessive about his penknife.

But before either of us could do anything, there were three loud blasts on the ship's siren. Long, loud and clear. The signal for the pirates to get up on deck with all the loot and to make the getaway.

I looked at Clive. He looked at me.

"They're going to get away," he said.

"Yes," I said. "Unless someone stops them."

Dad was twiddling with the radio controls. He looked up.

"No you don't," he said. "Where do you two

think you're going? You stay right here now—you hear me! You stay right here!"

"We're only going to look, Dad," I said. "Just to see their faces. For purposes of identification. In case we're ever asked to pick them out in an ID parade."

"Yes, an ID parade for pirates," Clive said. "Perhaps you could untie the captain, Dad. I'd leave you the knife but we might need it. Bye."

I think Dad would have run after us if he could, but he couldn't—his legs were still too numb from where the ropes had cut his circulation off. He tried to stand, but almost fell, and grabbed at the desk for support. Before he could say or do any more, Clive and I went to the door of the radio room, checked that it was clear outside, and left.

Once outside we paused a moment, listening for sounds of voices from the bridge. Nothing. We waited a few seconds more, just to be on the safe side. All quiet. We moved on. As we did, we heard the captain's voice. Dad must have got the gag untied and was now probably doing the ropes.

"Who were *they*?" we heard the captain ask.

"Er—just a couple of kids," Dad said.

"But they called you Dad," the captain pointed out.

"Ah—yes—well—we maybe are—distantly related," Dad admitted.

"But, Steward," the captain said, "what are your two children doing on board my ship?"

"Now that," Dad said, "is a good question, sir. A very good question. Yes."

WE GOT OUT on to the deck. The night was really humid now, each breath tasted of salt water and our T-shirts stuck to our backs. We hid in the shadows of the great towering funnel and watched as other figures sprang from other shadows, bringing bags and satchels, dragging expensive suitcases full of expensive loot.

"What're they doing?"

"Shh. Watch."

As we watched, I remembered something. The map of the boat. I remembered that there was a loading bay, down at the water line. It was a hatch that opened out so that supplies could be taken into the boat without it docking. I wondered why the pirates hadn't headed down to the bottom of the boat instead of up to the top. But maybe it wasn't that simple. Maybe they couldn't open the lower hatch that easily. And also, the sea was swelling a little now, the waves were choppier and their whitecaps could be seen in the moonlight. Maybe it was too dangerous to open the hatch.

But they still had to get down to their boat. And how were they going to do it?

"Watch."

I did. They were all up on the deck now, all except the one we had locked in the brig.

"Hey, we're one short. Where's Paulo?"

"He should have heard the signal."

"Maybe he didn't."

"How could he not?"

"We'd better go look for him."

"Isn't the time!"

"We can't leave him."

"He knew the rules. Come on."

Lumpy picked up one of the suitcases, and then another. He walked across the deck with them as though they weighed nothing.

He took them to one of the lifeboats.

Clive nudged me in the ribs.

"The lifeboat! Look! The lifeboat. Our lifeboat!"

"I can see!"

It was the one we had spent the night in when we couldn't get back to our cabin. So that was how they were going to do it. They were simply going to load up the lifeboat, clamber on board, then winch themselves down to the water and to their own boat. And then make their getaway. Simple.

The others followed Lumpy, bringing more bags and cases. Lumpy climbed up and tore the tarpaulin from the lifeboat.

"Come on then. Get a move on."

They formed a human chain and passed the bags and cases from one to the other. The last in the line was Lumpy, who threw the luggage into the boat.

"Okay. Let's go."

"What about Paulo?"

"Too bad about Paulo. There might be a Navy gunboat on its way here right now. You want to wait and find out while we look for Paulo? Or maybe you'd like to stay behind and keep Paulo company? Huh?"

They all got on board.

"What can we do?" Clive said. "What can we do to stop them?"

"Nothing."

"There must be something."

"Just let them go. Remember what Dad said—it's only things."

And then someone appeared. I didn't recognize him at first. But then I did. He looked a bit mad, to be honest, wide-eyed and disheveled, with sticky-up hair going everywhere.

"Hey! You! I want you!"

It was Mr. Swanker Watson. He looked mad and he sounded drunk and he was holding an empty bottle in his hand, brandishing it by the neck, like a weapon.

"You!"

Lumpy looked up. He seemed worried at first, but then he began to laugh.

"You've got my wife's necklace," Mr. Swanker Watson shouted. "You've got my wife's necklace. You give it back. Or I'll break this bottle over your head."

He lurched and staggered toward the lifeboat. He hardly seemed to know where he was going or what he was doing. But despite that—or maybe even because of it—he was dangerous and unpredictable just the same.

ALEX SHEARER

And Lumpy wasn't laughing now. And he wasn't going to take any chances. He pulled the gun out from his pocket.

"You stay right there my friend," he said.

But Mr. Swanker Watson didn't. He just went on lurching and staggering across the deck, bent on getting Mrs. Swanker Watson's pearl necklace back at any price—even at the cost of murder or suicide.

"I'm warning you! I warn you!"

Lumpy wasn't even smiling anymore. His piggy eyes were hard and cold. Mr. Swanker Watson lurched on, like a drunken crab, like a big, pink, sunburned lobster with an empty whisky bottle in its pincer.

Lumpy raised the gun. I couldn't believe it. He wouldn't, would he? I mean, it was Mr. Swanker Watson. Swanker Watson's dad. I mean, I don't say Swanker Watson was our best mate or anything, but he was all right. It wasn't his fault he was a Swanker. They were all right really. It wasn't their fault they were rich. He wouldn't shoot Swanker's Dad would he? Not just like that? And leave him on the deck? In a pool of blood?

Would he?

And then I realized that he would. And all the stuff I had read about pirates and treasure and islands and all the rest came back to me. And I remembered that underneath all the fun and adventures was something I had forgotten. Something about the romance of pirates that we all forget.

They killed people.

And didn't think twice about it.

"Clive! Mr. Swanker Watson! He's going to shoot him!"

It was like watching a road accident start to happen, and there was nothing you could do to stop it.

There was poor old Mr. Swanker Watson, all full of anger and whisky, and maybe feeling he was a failure for not having protected Mrs. Swanker Watson and all the little Swankers against the nasty pirates.

And maybe Mrs. Swanker Watson had been giving him a bit of an earful about how he was only half a man and half a Swanker for not stopping them making off with her lovely pearl necklace. So Mr. Swanker had poured another glass of whisky and had got to drinking and to brooding as the pirates looted the ship.

Until finally he was full of whisky and misplaced courage, and was tired of Mrs. Swanker Watson bending his ear and said, "Right! That's it! I'll go and get your necklace for you, if that's what you want!"

And he had stormed out of the cabin in a fury, with Mrs. Swanker Watson pleading with him not to go now, and suddenly realizing that she didn't want the necklace at all anymore. And suddenly she remembered Mr. Swanker Watson as he had been when they had got married, and how she had loved him, and how they never had any pearl necklaces then or any first-class cabins. Maybe all they had had was rat class, like me and Clive. But it didn't matter. Because as me and Clive can tell you, you can be quite happy in rat class. And we never had any pearl necklaces at all. And we didn't feel the lack of them either.

But now Mr. Swanker Watson was off in a blind fury, all fired up and ready to show everyone what he was made of. He was going to get the pearl necklace back, and that would show them what was what. That would show them that there was more to Mr. Swanker Watson than a receding hairline and a pot belly and a broken-veined red nose.

And now he was going to die. For a stupid pearl necklace.

I didn't know what to do. I really didn't. Usually I'm never stuck for an idea. But I didn't know what to do. We stood in the shadows, me and Clive, frozen like statues, standing like stones, just watching this disaster about to happen, steaming down the track.

And it was all so stupid. Mr. Swanker Watson was going to be shot. And Swanker Watson wouldn't have a dad anymore. The same way we didn't have a mum. And everyone would be unhappy and cry and nothing would ever be the same again. And all for what? For a stupid necklace.

I suddenly felt so angry and helpless and full of this stupid rage, just like I had once after Mum had died, and I had felt so angry with the whole stupid world that I just wanted to kick it, all the way out into space, and never have to see it again, or any of the people on it. Ever. As long as I lived. Not even

Clive or Dad or anyone. Because there was only one person I did want to see, and I wouldn't ever see her anymore.

And it all makes you so stupid angry sometimes—you could stupid cry.

It's just all so stupid stupid.

"No!"

It was my voice. I saw his eyes flicker toward the shadows—Lumpy's eyes. Then they turned back toward Mr. Swanker Watson. He was still advancing, the bottle held high, ready to strike it down on to Lumpy's head. And Lumpy was going to shoot him first. Right in the center of his chest.

Bang, bang. Dead. Like in the movies. Only no getting up again afterward when the cameras stop rolling. Because in real life the cameras never do stop rolling. Real time just rolls on and on. You don't get the chance to play the same scene again. There's only ever the once.

But then there was a flash of silver. I saw it from the corner of my eye. It was Clive. He'd picked up a steward's drinks tray that had been left on one of the deck tables. I didn't know what he was doing. Didn't have a clue. I just had a horrible feeling that it was stupid Clive being stupid again.

But I was wrong.

I have to give him credit where credit is due. You see, Clive isn't really very good at much (not like I am) but he is good at Frisbee—even when it's not a proper Frisbee. Even when it's only a drinks tray. Even when it's only a flash of silver.

And then the flash of silver was spinning through the night. It winged across the deck, it whistled past Mr. Swanker Watson's ear, it flew like an arrow, like a gull in the moonlight, skimming over the ship, its silver wings glistening. And then—

"Ow!"

And the gun was gone. Falling, falling, down into the sea. And Lumpy was nursing his wrist and his face was contorted with pain. And Mr. Swanker Watson was still coming, on his way to deliver his bash with the bottle, his moment of triumph and justification. He raised it high. Lumpy covered his face with his good arm to protect himself, and then—

Mr. Swanker Watson just collapsed, like a deflated balloon, and he passed out cold on the deck.

Lumpy laughed. He was flexing the fingers on his injured hand, bringing the life back into them.

"Good shot, Clive," I said. "You got lucky there."

"Lucky nothing," he said. "It was pure skill and judgment all the way."

Lumpy prodded Mr. Swanker Watson with his shoe. But that was all he did. He turned to the rest of them.

"Come on. Let's go."

And he got into the lifeboat.

And they started the winch up, and began to lower themselves down to the sea.

We ran to the deck. Mr. Swanker Watson was

snoring gently. He still had hold of the whisky bottle and he seemed happy now, and content. Maybe he was dreaming, and in his dreams he had gotten the necklace back.

"Boys! There you are."

It was Dad. He was one deck below us, looking up.

"Boys! Leave them now. I've sent out a Mayday. There's a boat on the way. Let them go now. That's enough."

But it wasn't enough as far as we were concerned. All because there was a boat on the way, it didn't mean they'd catch them.

"Clive," I said. "Do you still have your Swiss army knife?"

"Never travel anywhere without it," Clive said.

We climbed up to the lifeboat gantry and looked down. The lifeboat was slowly descending. It was maybe a third of the way down.

"Give me your knife."

Clive handed it over.

"Mind your hands," he said.

It wasn't easy to cut the moving rope as it ran slowly through the pulley. You hacked at one piece, but you couldn't cut it deep enough before it ran on.

"Mind your fingers. Get them stuck in that pulley and you'll never see them again."

The knife wasn't going to work. I looked down at the deck. Some equipment was stowed by one of the emergency stations—a life perserver, some flares, and—

"Clive. Pass me that axe."

It's one of those things that you seldom get the opportunity to say to anyone.

Pass me that axe.

Clive passed it up.

"Mind your face," he said. "When the rope goes it'll snap like a whip."

"I'll be careful."

I swung the axe. Missed. Tried a second time. Missed again. The lifeboat was over halfway down now. Another minute and they'd have made it.

Third time lucky maybe.

Hit it, but it didn't cut. Fourth time then. Didn't cut. Fifth time. Cut it a bit. Sixth time, cut it a bit more. It began to unravel.

"It's going! Get out of the way!"

Clive was right. You could hear it. The sound had changed. The rope was breaking. I threw the axe away, leaped down to the deck and—

Droooooong!

A weird, ripcord nose, then the rope leaping into the sky like a snake about to strike, then silence.

We looked over the side. The lifeboat had stopped. The winch in the gantry had gripped the end of the broken rope, but the boat was no longer moving. It was no longer horizontal either. One side had dropped two or three meters lower than the other and the pirates were clinging to the seats and to the sides of the lifeboat to stop themselves from falling out.

They couldn't get back up, and unless they fancied a twenty-meter jump into shark-infested waters—with the chance that they might miss the water and land on the waiting boat instead—they couldn't get down either.

We looked over the side.

"That should hold them for a while," Clive said.

"Yes," I nodded. "Reckon it should."

"You know," Clive said, "I'm starving. Do you think it'll be time for breakfast soon?"

But I didn't answer. I got distracted. I saw this great huge red thing, like a massive blood-red orange. It suddenly appeared from nowhere, and it was so amazing, so beautiful, so magnificent, that all you could do was stare.

It was the sun.

On the far horizon.

Coming up.

For a new day.

⚓

EIGHTEEN

WALK THE PLANK

WELL, THE REST is history. (And maybe a bit of geography too.) Once everyone realized that the pirates had gone and were no longer patrolling the corridors with guns in their hands, they cautiously put their noses around their cabin doors and then headed for the deck to see what was going on.

Everyone was very interested in the lopsided lifeboat with the pirates in it and wondered how long it would be before they fell out. They were also quite interested in how long it would be before all the suitcases fell out—as their money and valuables were inside.

The pirate boat meanwhile, seeing that things had gone wrong, sailed off at full steam ahead, leaving the others behind. But the boat didn't get very far as several ships had received Dad's Mayday message, and among them was a Coast Guard patrol and a naval destroyer. They sent out speedboats with marines in them, and they caught up with the pirate boat in no time.

Lumpy, meanwhile, was hanging on to the lifeboat, ranting and raving about what he was going to do to "those stupid kids" if he was ever to "get my hands on them!"

Clive and me assumed he meant us, and we resolved that we wouldn't let him get his hands on us if we could possibly avoid it, as if he did, it would probably hurt.

The captain ordered some of the crew to throw a winch line over the side of the boat. The pirates tied it on to the lifeboat, but the captain refused to haul them back up until they'd thrown their guns into the water—which they finally did.

The lifeboat was then winched up again and the shaky-kneed pirates stumbled back on to dry land. (Well, dry cruiser deck, anyway.) They were then taken away and handed over to the Coast Guard, to be charged with piracy on the high seas. (And possibly piracy on the low seas as well, as it wasn't the first time they had done it.)

Lumpy started to moan and groan and pretend that he wasn't part of it at all. He said that he was nothing but a poor innocent steward who had been forced to do things at gunpoint by the wicked pirates. But we knew it wasn't like that, and said as much, and Clive got hold of another drinks tray and sort of brandished it threateningly about, so that

Lumpy knew that he would be in for more of the Frisbee treatment if he didn't behave himself. Dad made Clive put the tray down and told him to stop waving it about before he hurt someone—like himself.

There was a bad moment when the pirates came back on board though. As they did, the lifeboat rocked slightly and one of the cases fell off and went bouncing down, rolling down the hull, to land with a great splash in the sea.

Everyone rushed to the rail and watched, all wondering if their wallets and valuables and diamond rings and platinum watches were in that suitcase, or if they had been spared and the bad luck had happened to somebody else.

"It's all right," someone said. "It's floating. We can send out a boat."

But before the captain could even give the order for someone to go and get the case back, it suddenly sank. It went down in a blaze of bubbles and probably with a big gurgle, only we were too far away to hear it. And then the water closed over it, and I could imagine it sinking down and down to the very bottom of the ocean. I could see it spinning around in the inky black water, slowly turning, slowly falling, passing strange fish and curious creatures of the deep. And down it would have gone, miles and miles maybe, beyond the reach of anyone, to lie and to sleep forever on the bed of the sea. Then the sand would cover it, and all the things in it would never be seen again.

Unless one day some poor fisherman caught a fish, and it would be wearing a platinum watch, or have its head stuck in a diamond necklace. Or someone would go to cook their dinner and find a ruby ring around their fish finger.

Before the pirates were removed from the ship to be taken away by the Coast Guard, Clive and me felt that we ought to tell somebody about the one we had locked in the brig. I tried to have a quiet word with the captain.

"Excuse me, sir," I said.

"Not now, son," he said. "Later."

"It's important," I said.

"I'm sure it is, son," he answered. "Only we have a bit of a crisis on our hands at the moment, so if you wouldn't mind . . ."

That's the trouble with hanging around with Clive, nobody takes you seriously.

So anyway, on things went, and the pirates were put in handcuffs, and were about to be taken off the ship and still nobody would listen. And even when me and Clive tried to tell Dad about the pirate we had locked in the brig, he was too busy to listen too.

"In a minute boys," he said. "When all this is sorted out."

So in the end Clive just had to stand on a table and shout at the top of his voice.

"Will you all shut up a minute and listen," he screeched—as Clive is very good at screeching. "There's another pirate! You're missing one! Me and my brother locked him in the brig. But you'd better be careful about letting him out as he's got a gun!"

Well, you could have heard a pin drop. You could have heard a fish swim by. The whole deck went quiet, and all the commotion stopped. And everyone looked at us, the passengers, the crew, the captain, everyone.

"You—locked one of them—in the brig?"

"Yes, Dad. The one who bashed you on the head in the radio room."

"The one with the gun?" the captain said.

"Yes, sir. The one who tied you up."

And well, I don't like to blow my own trumpet or anything, but credit where it's due, and to be quite honest, several people looked pretty amazed when they heard that.

"Those two boys—" we heard people say.

"Locked up one of the pirates—"

"In the brig!"

"Well, I never!"

And then the captain seemed to remember that Dad had promised him an explanation of exactly what we were doing on board his ship. So he turned to him in front of everyone and said, "Steward, these two sons of yours seem like remarkable boys to me in many ways. But I have to confess that I don't exactly understand what they're doing here and how they come to be passengers on my ship."

Well, Dad looked at me, and I looked at him, and we both looked at Clive, and nobody seemed willing to say anything, but somebody had to say it, so I did.

"I'm afraid, sir," I said, "that we're stowaways."

The captain's beard seemed to suddenly go a sort of gray color, and then, just for a split second, I could have sworn it went quite white, and then all the color flowed back into it, and it was ginger again.

"Stowaways!"

"But our dad didn't know anything about it until a few hours ago. But quite honestly, sir, if we hadn't stowed away, nobody would have stopped the pirates. Because as well as the one in the brig, it was us who stopped the rest escaping, by cutting through the rope on the lifeboat."

"The rope? On the lifeboat?"

"Yes, sir. With Clive's Swiss army knife."

"I never travel anywhere without it," Clive said. And he took it out of his pocket to show it to the captain so that he could see the various attachments, but it didn't seem like the right time somehow.

"You cut the ropes with a penknife?"

"And a few swipes with the axe."

"A few swipes? With an axe?"

"And if it hadn't been for Clive, sir, they'd probably have shot Mr. Swanker Watson too."

"Mr. Swanker Watson?"

"At least that's what we call him. He was going after the pirates with a bottle, and Lumpy pulled a gun on him, and he would have shot him stone cold dead, only Clive did his Frisbee on him."

ALEX SHEARER

"Did his Frisbee on him? Did he now?"

"With a drinks tray."

"Is that a fact?"

"Yes. And if we hadn't cut the rope and locked the pirate in the brig and if Clive hadn't done his Frisbee with the tray, well, Mr. Swanker Watson might be dead by now and the pirates would have got away and everyone's valuables would have been lost forever—not just the one case that fell in the sea. So in a way, it was a good thing that we stowed away, wasn't it, sir? Don't you think?"

Well, there was a long, long silence then. And there was a lot of sucking of teeth, and of people giving each other meaningful looks. There was a lot of "on the one hand" and quite a bit of "but then on the other."

Finally the captain turned to Dad and said, "I think I'd better see you and your two sons in my cabin, Steward. For a word in private."

But Clive and me weren't too worried. We felt we had good grounds to be optimistic.

It was a bit of a tricky business getting the pirate we had locked in the brig to come out. The captain said that he wouldn't open the door until he handed his gun over; the pirate pointed out that he couldn't hand his gun over until someone opened the door.

Finally a compromise was reached. As someone watched through the spyhole, the pirate emptied all the bullets from his gun, then he fired it to prove that it was empty, then he went and dropped it into the stainless-steel toilet. Only then would they open the door and let him out. He was immediately carted off with the other pirates and taken on board the Coast Guard boat to be charged with piracy and hijacking.

Mr. Swanker Watson meanwhile, had been taken off to the sick bay, where he awoke with a bad headache and a big hangover.

People's valuables were returned to them then—which took a long time, as everything was all jumbled up in the bags and suitcases, and some people weren't entirely honest (they were as bad as the pirates really) and they said a certain piece of jewelry belonged to them when it didn't, and all sorts of arguments started.

But then people started saying, "Oh no, it's not mine after all. I must have made a mistake."

Finally it was all done, and the only people remaining on deck were those whose valuables had been in the one case that had gone to the bottom of the sea.

And among them was old Mrs. Dominics and Swanker's mum, Mrs. Swanker Watson.

"Oh well, never mind," Mrs. Dominics said. "It was all insured. They did have a lot of sentimental value, but they were still only things at the end of the day. At least we're all still alive."

And she went back to her cabin to start filling in her insurance forms.

I thought that Mrs. Swanker Watson might take it bad—the loss of her pearl necklace and everything. But she didn't. She just shrugged too. And she turned to Mr. Swanker Watson (who was back on his feet by then, even if he did look a bit green) and she said, "Never mind. It doesn't matter. There are plenty of pearls in the ocean—and now there are a few more. That was where they came from, and that is where they have returned."

And then she started to speak in a rather loud voice, as if she wanted everyone to hear.

"Of course, my husband George had a go at the pirates. Which is rather more than a lot of people did. My husband George and the two boys here and their father and the captain, at least they had a go. All very brave, I thought. And what do a few pearls matter when you have a brave husband like my George, who's willing to go off and be heroic when pirates steal the necklace of the woman he loves!"

Well, to be honest, I didn't think it was quite like that. It wasn't so much that Mr. Swanker Watson had been brave, it was more that he had been dead drunk. But I didn't say anything, because Mrs. Swanker looked so proud and happy and Mr. Swanker looked so cheered up that I didn't want to spoil it.

And they both went off together, holding each other's hands, which was something they maybe hadn't done in a long while.

Clive and me didn't go off hand in hand though. We never do that sort of thing. Clive has never forgiven me for being born five minutes before him and will go on resenting me for it until his dying day.

Dad came and got us and we went off to see the

captain. He had a book on his desk entitled *Marine Regulations.*

"I've just been looking up the penalty for stowaways," the captain said. "And I would be perfectly within my rights to put you off the ship at the next port. Alternatively, I could lock you in the brig until we get back to our port of origin, or failing that—"

And he gave us a very grave and serious look.

"I could make you walk the plank."

Clive gulped. It was a long way down from the deck to the water.

"B—but—I mean—you haven't got a plank, have you, sir?" he said hopefully.

The captain fixed Clive with a steely-eyed, bushy-bearded stare.

"We have plenty of planks, young man. Plenty of them. We have a whole cabin full of planks."

And then he just couldn't keep it up any longer. And neither could Dad. They both started laughing at poor old Clive believing that he was going to have to walk the plank and end up in the arms of an octopus.

"Sit down, boys," the captain said. "We need to have a little talk. But first, can I offer you a drink?"

Well, I shan't go into all the details, but the upshot was that the captain gave us a king-sized ticking off for stowing away on his ship and he read us the riot act from start to finish.

He told us how stupid it had been, how foolhardy, how dangerous. He listed all the nasty things that could have gone wrong and could have happened and he scared the wits out of us. Dad joined in then, and he agreed with everything the captain had said.

Then the captain wanted to know how we had actually managed to get away with it—how we had managed to sneak on board, where we had stowed away and how we had managed to remain undetected. So we told him our story and explained how easily we had sneaked on, and how we had got away with it just because we were kids, and no one pays them much attention and always thinks they are the responsibility of somebody else.

He wanted to see our cabin in rat class then, so we took him down and showed him.

Then we went back up to his cabin and he said that he was going to have to make out a major report for the shipping company, outlining all the weaknesses in its security. The simple fact was, he said, that our stowing away should never have happened.

Then he asked us why we did it. Was it just for the joy ride? he said. But we told him it wasn't, and explained about Dad and how we didn't have our mum now, and how we didn't want to be left behind anymore and only wanted to come along to be with him. And the captain just sort of nodded, and said, "Yes, yes . . ." and that he understood. And I don't know if he did or not, but he looked as if he might.

He then said that he couldn't approve of our

stowing away in any form, but he agreed that there were mitigating circumstances.

Me and Clive (especially Clive) didn't know what mitigating circumstances were. But it turned out that they were reasons for letting you off with a warning.

The captain said that we had done such sterling work in saving the ship from the pirates that he was going to recommend to the ship owners that we shouldn't be prosecuted for stowing away.

In fact, he was going to recommend that we should be rewarded. But as he couldn't guarantee we would be, he was going to give us a small reward himself, right now.

He was going to let us stay on board for the remainder of the cruise.

And he was going to upgrade us from rat class to a better cabin—first class, with a big picture window, and satellite TV.

I wondered where he had got an empty cabin from, but of course it had been one that two of the pirates with the tinted glasses had been staying in. Well, they wouldn't be needing it anymore. They'd be in jail class now, and for quite a long time to come.

So me and Clive got the best of service really, all the way home. It was first-class treatment all the way and dinner at the captain's table. We apologized to Mrs. Swanker Watson about pretending that we were related to the captain, but when we did wangle her a second invitation to dine with him, she forgave us. (And this time the bed didn't fall on her foot.)

We saw lots of interesting places and quite had the time of our lives really. Dad had to carry on working and sometimes he'd even bring us the odd drink as we sunbathed by the pool. But whenever he did, he always used to say things like, "Look at you two. I don't know!" and "You'd better not get too used to this!" and "Talk about luck—I don't know how you got away with it!"

But everyone else seemed to think we were the bee's knees. Although to be honest Clive has *always* thought he was the bee's knees. Personally, I don't really know what a bee's knees look like, but if they look anything like Clive, then I think I shall give up eating honey.

Anyway, after we had sailed all over the place, the ship finally had to head for home. The weather started to get cooler again and there wasn't so much sunbathing. People began to pack up their souvenirs and to unpack their old lives and routines.

Home was waiting and all the usual things. It's sad somehow when a journey ends. You sail back into harbor and you think—here we were just a few weeks ago, and we've been to so many places and done so many things, and had so many adventures, and now here we are, back, in the early morning of a cold gray drizzly day, and it's just like it always was.

On the last night, me and Clive and Dad went up on deck to watch the sun go down. We leaned on the rail and watched it go, big and gold and disappearing.

"Dad," I said, "we can tell now why you love the sea, and find it so hard to leave."

"Can you?"

"I think so."

"Yes. I maybe think so too. But this will be my last trip."

"No, Dad," Clive and me both said together. "You can't give the sea up, not because of us."

He gave us a smile. It was a sad smile, but a smile just the same.

"I think it might be best," he said. "I think maybe it's time. You'll be growing up soon, and your gran's not getting any younger. I can't expect her to look after you when—no. This will be my last trip."

"What'll you do, dad?"

"I don't know. I'll find something."

And then we noticed that someone had joined us. It was old Mrs. Dominics, come to watch the sun go down too, like she didn't have a lot of sundowns left, and couldn't afford to miss one—though she could afford about everything else.

"Hello, John."

"Hello, Mrs. Dominics," Dad said. "Lovely night."

"Yes. Hello boys."

"Hi."

"May I join you all?"

"Please."

She leaned against the rail too, and we all watched the sunset—which was so expensive

nobody could afford it, and yet it was free to everyone.

"I hope you'll forgive me, and not think me
nosy," she said. "But I couldn't help overhearing
what you said just now—about giving up the sea—
and what you might do instead . . ."

"Yes, Mrs. Dominics?"

"And I hope you won't think it impertinent,
but I wondered if I might make a small suggestion?"

We didn't think it was impertinent at all.

NINETEEN

A VISITOR

SO HERE WE ARE. Everyone's forgiven us, more or less, apart from the pirates. Gran forgave us too, for lying to her and for sneaking off. Dad was as good as his word, he gave up the sea to stay at home with us and to stop Clive and me (especially Clive) from getting into trouble.

Dad's not a steward anymore and he's not a sailor either, but he still keeps his hand in at carrying the trays, and he still keeps his eye on the sea.

He runs a restaurant now. He's in charge of the whole place. It's a proper restaurant too, in the good food guides, with rosettes and stars and all sorts. He's got a proper chef too, a real French one, who loses his temper in the kitchen and throws all the pans about. But he does cook some nice grub.

It's Mrs. Dominics who owns the restaurant.

She'd been planning on it for ages.

"You can't just stop and give up, dear," she said. "Not even at my time of life. You must always have new things on the go. Otherwise you're finished."

At least that's what she said. But I'm not so sure. In some ways I feel she just wanted to help Dad, because he'd always looked after her.

So Dad's the manager. He greets all the people and makes them feel at home and shows them the menu while they have a drink. He's soon got them smiling and laughing and at their ease. Dad's not the cook. That's not what he's best at. He's best at making people feel happy.

Mrs. Dominics comes in sometimes to see how the business is getting on and to sample the cooking. She always gets the best table. The one in the window, with the best view of the sea.

Because that's where the restaurant is, right there by the harbor. You can see the great ships go by, with the little tugboats towing them out so that they can begin their journeys to who knows where.

I always wonder, as I watch them go. I wonder about the people on board, and the places they will see, and the adventures they will have.

And whether there will be pirates.

Sometimes I see Clive and Dad looking out of the window too, at one of the oceanliners, as it heads out to sea. And I suspect I know what they're thinking. They're thinking that one day they're going to go again, on another trip, another voyage. Maybe not tomorrow, maybe not even this year, or the year after. But one day, yes, one day. One day, we'll be going again. And this time, we'll hopefully have tickets.

SO THAT'S IT. That's what happened. That was how Clive and me came to be stowaways and those were the adventures we had when we did. And there's no more to be said now really, apart from one thing. Which is very interesting. Or at least I think so.

You see, last week, we had a visitor. A lady it was. I didn't know her, and neither did Clive, nor Dad. But she asked if she could come in anyway, as she said she had been to a lot of trouble to track us down and had something important to say.

So Dad invited her into the sitting room.

It turned out that she was a midwife. And not only that, she was the midwife who had been there when me and Clive were born. She said that something had been preying on her mind ever since.

We all looked a bit puzzled and wondered what it could be.

She said that she thought there had been a mistake. She said that when Clive and me had been born, everything was all so fraught and confused that after we had been born she thought she had got us mixed up.

She had told Mum and Dad that it was me who had been born first. But afterward, when she went home, she realized that it wasn't. It was Clive.

And it had been preying on her mind ever since. She knew that it didn't really matter, that it wasn't that important. It was only five minutes. But now she was due to retire and she just wanted to set the record straight.

So she did, and we thanked her, and then she left.

Dad says he can't see that it matters and he's not going to change the birth certificate. But Clive's gone a bit quiet. Very quiet. Very quiet indeed. He's gone upstairs and locked himself in his room. I think it's suddenly hit him in a big way.

You see, Clive's the eldest now. Not me. I don't have to be sensible anymore. I'm the one who can be a nutcase. And he's got to be responsible for me. I can't tell you how it feels! It feels like the sun's come out. (And it hasn't, it's raining.) I can't believe it really. I feel like I've been carrying a big heavy backpack around and I finally got to put it down. I feel like I've been wearing too-tight shoes all my life and suddenly I can take them off. I feel—

I feel like I'm going to enjoy myself.

You know what I'm going to do? You know where I'm going to start? I'm going to buy myself a new Swiss army knife. And then I'm going to get a Frisbee.

DID I TELL YOU the name of our restaurant? It's called The Stowaway. It's down by the harbor. You can't miss it. Come and have a meal with us some time. It's the best food for miles. You might even meet Mrs. Dominics. Or our waitress, Julia, who Dad's got very friendly with. She looks a bit tired some evenings, like she might not be going home. And if you go at the weekend, sometimes we'll be there too, sitting in the back office, maybe getting on with our homework. You're bound to recognize us. My brother Clive's the serious-looking, sensible one—the one who looks old before his time and weighed down with responsibilities and cares.

And as for me—well I'm the youngest.

CONRAD SULZER REGIONAL LIBRARY
4455 N. LINCOLN AVE.
CHICAGO, ILLINOIS 60625